Also by William Maxwell

Also by William Maxwell

OVER BY THE RIVER
and Other Stories

OVER BY THE RIVER

and Other Stories

WILLIAM MAXWELL

NONPAREIL
BOOKS

DAVID R. GODINE · PUBLISHER · BOSTON

This is a *Nonpareil Book* published in 1984 by
DAVID R. GODINE, PUBLISHER, INC.
306 Dartmouth Street, Boston, Massachusetts 02116

Copyright © 1941, 1945, 1953, 1954, 1956, 1963,
1964, 1969, 1974, 1976, 1977, 1984 by William Maxwell
Jacket illustration copyright © 1984 by Brookie Maxwell
First published by Alfred A. Knopf, Inc.

Library of Congress Cataloging in Publication Data

Maxwell, William, 1908–
Over by the river, and other stories.

Contents: Over by the river.—The Trojan
women.—The pilgrimage.—The patterns of love.—
What every boy should know. [etc.]
I. Title.
PZ3.M45180v3 [PS3525.A9464]   813'.5'4   76-30608
ISBN 0-87923-541-1

This book has been printed on acid-free paper. The paper will
not yellow with age, the binding will not deteriorate,
and the pages will not fall out.

First printing

Printed in the United States of America

For Sylvia Townsend Warner

Contents

OVER BY THE RIVER
and Other Stories

Over By the River

The sun rose somewhere in the middle of Queens, the exact moment of its appearance shrouded in uncertainty because of a cloud bank. The lights on the bridges went off, and so did the red light in the lantern of the lighthouse at the north end of Welfare Island. Seagulls settled on the water. A newspaper truck went from building to building dropping off heavy bundles of, for the most part, bad news, which little boys carried inside on their shoulders. Doormen smoking a pipe and dressed for a walk in the country came to work after a long subway ride and disappeared into the service entrances. When they reappeared, by way of the front elevator, they had put on with their uniforms a false amiability and were prepared for eight solid hours to make conversation about the weather. With the morning sun on them, the apartment buildings far to the west, on Lexington Avenue, looked like an orange mesa. The pigeons made bubbling noises in their throats as they strutted on windowsills high above the street.

All night long, there had been plenty of time. Now suddenly there wasn't, and this touched off a chain explosion of alarm clocks, though in some instances the point was driven home without a sound: Time is interior to animals as well as exterior. A bare arm with a wristwatch on it emerged from under the covers and turned until the dial was toward the light from the windows.

"What time is it?"

"Ten after."

"It's always ten after," Iris Carrington said despairingly, and turned over in bed and shut her eyes against the light. Also against the clamor of her desk calendar: *Tuesday 11, L. 3:30 Dr. de Santillo . . . 5:30—7:30? . . . Wednesday 1:45, Mrs. McIntosh speaks on the changing status of women. 3:30 Dr. F. . . . Friday 11 C. Get Andrea . . . Saturday, call Mrs. Stokes. Ordering pads. L ballet 10:30. 2 Laurie to Sasha's. Remaining books due at library. Explore dentists. Supper at 5. Call Margot . . .*

Several minutes passed.

"Oh my God, I don't think I can make it," George Carrington said, and put his feet over the side of the bed, and found he could make it, after all. He could bend over and pick up his bathrobe from the floor, and put it on, and find his slippers, and close the window, and turn on the radiator valve. Each act was easier than the one before. He went back to the bed and drew the covers closer around his wife's shoulders.

Yawning, stretching, any number of people got up and started the business of the day. Turning on the shower. Dressing. Putting their hair up in plastic curlers. Squeezing toothpaste out of tubes that were all but empty. Squeezing orange juice. Separating strips of bacon.

The park keepers unlocked the big iron gates that closed the river walk off between Eighty-third and Eighty-fourth Streets. A taxi coming from Doctors Hospital was snagged by a doorman's whistle. The wind picked up the dry filth under the wheels of parked cars and blew it now this way, now that. A child got into an orange minibus and started on the long, devious ride to nursery school and social adjustment.

"Have you been a good girl?" George inquired lovingly, through the closed door of the unused extra maid's room, where the dog slept on a square of carpet. Puppy had not been a good girl. There was a puddle of urine—not on the open newspaper he had left for her, just in case, but two feet away from it, on the black-and-white plastic-tile floor. Her tail quivering with apology, she watched while he mopped the puddle up and disposed of the wet newspaper in the garbage can in the back hall. Then she followed him through the apartment to the foyer, and into the elevator when it came.

There were signs all along the river walk:

> No Dogs
> No Bicycles
> No This
> No That

He ignored them with a clear conscience. If he curbed the dog beforehand, there was no reason not to turn her loose and let her run—except that sometimes she stopped and arched her back a second time. When shouting and waving his hands didn't discourage her from moving her bowels, he took some newspaper from a trash container and cleaned up after her.

At the flagpole, he stood looking out across the river. The lights went off all the way up the airplane beacon, producing an effect of silence—as if somebody had started to say something and then decided not to. The tidal current was flowing south. He raised his head and sniffed, hoping for a breath of the sea, and smelled gasoline fumes instead.

Coming back, the dog stopped to sniff at trash baskets, at cement copings, and had to be restrained from greeting the only other person on the river walk—a grey-haired man who jogged there every morning in a gym suit and was afraid of dogs. He smiled pleasantly at George, and watched Puppy out of the corner of his eyes, so as to be ready when she leapt at his throat.

A tanker, freshly painted, all yellow and white, and flying the flag of George had no idea what country until he read the lettering on the stern, overtook him, close in to shore—so close he could see the captain talking to a sailor in the wheelhouse. To be sailing down the East River on a ship that was headed for open water . . . He waved to them and they waved back, but they didn't call out to him *Come on, if you want to,* and it was too far to jump. It came to him with the seriousness of a discovery that there was no place in the world he would not like to see. Concealed in this statement was another that he had admitted to himself for the first time only recently. There were places he would never see, experiences of the first importance that he would never have. He might die without ever having heard a nightingale.

When they stepped out of the elevator, the dog hurried off to the kitchen to see if there was something in her dish she didn't know about, and George settled down in the living room with the *Times* on his lap and waited for a glass of orange juice to appear at his place at the dining-room table. The rushing sound inside the walls, as of an underground river, was Iris running her bath. The orange juice was in no hurry to get to the dining-room table. Iris had been on the phone daily with the employment agency and for the moment this was the best they could offer: twenty-seven years old, pale, with dirty blond hair, unmarried, overattached to her mother, and given to burning herself on the antiquated gas stove. She lived on tea and cigarettes. Breakfast was all the cooking she was entrusted with; Iris did the rest. Morning after morning his boiled egg was hard enough to take on a picnic. A blind man could not have made a greater hash of half a grapefruit. The coffee was indescribable. After six weeks there was a film of grease over everything in the kitchen. Round, jolly, neat, professionally trained, a marvellous cook, the mother was everything that is desirable in a servant except that, alas, she worked for somebody else. She drifted in and out of the apartment at odd hours, deluding Iris with the hope that some of her accomplishments would, if one were only patient, rub off on her daughter.

"Read," a voice said, bringing him all the way back from Outer Mongolia.

"Tonight, Cindy."

"Read! Read!"

He put the paper down and picked her up, and when she had settled comfortably in his lap he began: " 'Emily was a guinea pig who loved to travel. Generally she stayed home and looked after her brother Arthur. But every so often she grew tired of cooking and mending and washing and ironing; the day would seem too dark, and the house too small, and she would have a great longing to set out into the distance. . . .' "

Looking down at the top of her head as he was reading, he felt an impulse to put his nose down and smell her hair. Born in a hurry she was. Born in one hell of a hurry, half an hour after her mother got to the hospital.

Laurie Carrington said, "What is the difference, what is the difference between a barber and a woman with several children?" Nobody answered, so she asked the question again.

"I give up," Iris said.

"Do you know, Daddy?"

"I give up too, we all give up."

"A barber . . . has razors to shave. And the woman has shavers to raise."

He looked at her over the top of his half-glasses, wondering what ancestor was responsible for that reddish-blond hair.

"That's a terribly funny one, Laurie," he said. "That's the best one yet," and his eyes reverted to the editorial page. A nagging voice inside his head informed him that a good father would be conversing intelligently with his children at the breakfast table. But about what? No intelligent subject of conversation occurred to him, perhaps because it was Iris's idea in the first place, not his.

He said, "Cindy, would you like a bacon sandwich?"

She thought, long enough for him to become immersed in the *Times* again, and then she said, "I would like a piece of bacon and a piece of toast. But not a bacon sandwich."

He dropped a slice of bread in the toaster and said, "Py-rozz-quozz-gill"—a magic word, from one of the Oz books. With a grinding noise the bread disappeared.

"Stupid Cindy," Laurie remarked, tossing her head. But Cindy wasn't fooled. Laurie used to be the baby and now she wasn't anymore. She was the oldest. And what she would have liked to be was the oldest *and* the baby. About lots of things she was very piggy. But she couldn't whistle. Try though she might, *whhih, whhih, whhih,* she couldn't. And Cindy could.

The toast emerged from the toaster and Iris said, "Not at the breakfast table, Cindy." The morning was difficult for her, clouded with amnesia, with the absence of energy, with the reluctance of her body to take on any action whatever. Straight lines curved unpleasantly, hard surfaces presented the look of softness. She saw George and the children and the dog lying at her feet under the table the way one sees rocks and trees and cottages at the seashore through the early-morning fog; just barely recognizable they were.

W hy is a church steeple—"
"My gloves," he said, standing in the front hall, with his coat on.

"They're in the drawer in the lowboy," Iris said.

"Why is a church steeple—"

"Not those," he said.

"Why is a—"

"Laurie, Daddy is talking. Look in the pocket of your chesterfield."

"I did."

"Yes, dear, why is a church steeple."

"Why is a church steeple like a maiden aunt?"

"I give up."

"Do you know, Daddy?"

"No. I've looked in every single one of my coats. They must be in my raincoat, because I can't find that either."

"Look in your closet."

"I did look there." But he went into the bedroom and looked again anyway. Then he looked all through the front-hall closet, including the mess on the top shelf.

Iris passed through the hall with her arms full of clothes for the washing machine. "Did you find your raincoat?" she asked.

"I must have left it somewhere," he said. "But where?"

He went back to the bedroom and looked in the engagement calendar on her desk, to see where they had been, and it appeared that they hadn't been anywhere.

"Where did we go when we had Andrea to babysit?"

"I don't remember."

"We had her two nights."

"Did we? I thought we only went out one night last week."

She began to make the bed. Beds—for it was not one large bed, as it appeared to be in the daytime, but twin beds placed against each other with a king-sized cotton spread covering them both. When they were first married they slept in a three-quarter bed from his bachelor apartment. In time this became a double bed, hard as a rock because of the horsehair mattress. Then it also proved to be too small. For he developed twitches. While he was falling asleep his body beside her would suddenly flail out, shaking the bed and waking her completely. Six or seven times this would happen. After which he would descend at last into a deep sleep and she would be left with insomnia. So now there were twin beds, and even then her bed registered the seismic disturbances in his, though nothing like so much.

"We went to that benefit. With Francis," she said.

"Oh . . . I think I did wear my raincoat that night. No, I wore the coat with the velvet collar."

"The cleaner's?"

"No."

"I don't see how you could have left your raincoat somewhere," she said. "I never see you in just a suit. Other men, yes, but never you."

He went into the hall and pulled open a drawer of the lowboy and took out a pair of grey gloves and drew them on. They had been his father's and they were good gloves but too small for him. His fingers had burst open the seams at the end of the fingers. Iris had mended them, but they would not stay sewed, and so he went to Brooks and bought a new pair—the pair he couldn't find.

"The Howards' dinner party?" he said.

"That was the week before. Don't worry about it," Iris said. "Cindy, what have you been doing?"—meaning hair full of snarls, teeth unbrushed, at twenty-five minutes past eight.

"It makes me feel queer not knowing where I've been," George said, and went out into the foyer and pressed the elevator button. From that moment, he was some other man. Their pictures were under his nose all day but he had stopped seeing them. He did not even remember that he had a family, until five o'clock, when he pushed his chair back from his desk, reached for his hat and coat, and came home, cheerfully unrepentant. She forgave him now because she did not want to deal with any failure, including his, until she had had her second cup of coffee. The coffee sat on the living-room mantelpiece, growing cold, while she brushed and braided Cindy's hair.

"Stand still! I'm not hurting you."

"You are too."

The arm would not go into the sweater, the leggings proved to be on backwards, one mitten was missing. And Laurie wild because she was going to be late for school.

The girls let the front door bang in spite of all that had been said on the subject, and in a moment the elevator doors opened to receive them. The quiet then was unbelievable. With the *Times* spread out on the coffee table in the living room, and holes in the Woman's Page where she had cut out recipes, she waited for her soul, which left her during the night, to return and take its place in her body. When this happened she got up suddenly and went into the bedroom and started telephoning: Bloomingdale's, Saks, the Maid-to-Order service, the children's school, the electrician, the pediatrician, the upholsterer—half the population of New York City.

Over the side of the bed Cindy went, eyes open, wide awake. In her woolly pyjamas with feet in them. Even though it was dark outside—the middle of the night—it was only half dark in the bedroom. There was a blue night-light in the wall plug by the doll's house, and a green night-light in the bathroom, beside the washbasin, and the door to the bathroom was partly open. The door to the hall was wide open and the hall light was on, but high up where it wasn't much comfort, and she had to pass the closed door of Laurie's room and the closed door to the front hall. Behind both these doors the dark was very dark, unfriendly, ready to spring out and grab her, and she would much rather have been back in her bed except it was not safe there either, so she was going for help.

When she got to the door at the end of the hall, she stood still, afraid to knock and afraid not to knock. Afraid to look behind her. Hoping the door would open by itself and it did. Her father—huge, in his pyjamas, with his hair sticking up and his face puffy with sleep. "Bad dream?" he asked.

Behind him the room was all dark except for a little light from the hall. She could see the big windows—just barely— and the great big bed, and her mother asleep under a mound of covers. And if she ran past him and got into the bed she would be safe, but it was not allowed. Only when she was sick. She turned and went back down the hall, without speaking but knowing that he would pick up his bathrobe and follow her and she didn't have to be brave anymore.

"What's Teddy doing on the floor?" he said, and pulled the covers up around her chin, and put his warm hand on her cheek. So nice to have him do this—to have him there, sitting on the edge of her bed.

"Can you tell me what you were dreaming about?"

"Tiger."

"Yes? Well, that's too bad. Were you very frightened?"

"Yes."

"Was it a big tiger?"

"Yes."

"You know it was only a dream? It wasn't a real tiger. There aren't any tigers in New York City."

"In the zoo there are."

"Oh yes, but they're in cages and can't get out. Was this tiger out?"

"Yes."

"Then it couldn't have been a real tiger. Turn over and let me rub your back."

"If you rub my back I'll go to sleep."

"Good idea."

"If I go to sleep I'll dream about the tiger."

"I see. What do you want me to do?"

"Get in bed with me."

What with Teddy and Raggedy Ann and Baby Dear, and books to look at in the morning, and the big pillow and the little pillow, things were a bit crowded. He put his hand over his eyes to shut out the hall light and said, "Go to sleep," but she didn't, even though she was beginning to feel drowsy. She was afraid he was going to leave her—if not right this minute then pretty soon. He would sit up in bed and say *Are you all right now?* and she would have to say *Yes*, because that was what he wanted her to say. Sometimes she said no and they stayed a little longer, but they always went away in the end.

After a while, her eyes closed. After still another while, she felt the bed heave under her as he sat up. He got out of bed slowly and carefully and fixed the covers and put the little red chair by the bed so she wouldn't fall out. She tried to say *Don't go*, but nothing happened. The floorboards creaked under the carpeting as he crossed the room. In the doorway he turned and looked at her, one last look, and she opened her eyes wide so he would know she wasn't asleep, and he waved her a kiss, and that was the last of him, but it wasn't the last of her. Pretty soon, even though there wasn't a sound, she knew something was in the room. Hiding. It was either hiding behind the curtains or it was hiding in the toy closet or it was hiding behind the doll's house or it was behind the bathroom door or it was under the bed. But wherever it was it was being absolutely still, waiting for her to close her eyes and go to sleep. So she kept them open, even though her eyelids got heavier and heavier. She made them stay open. And when they closed she opened them again right afterward. She kept opening them as long as she could, and once she cried out *Laurie!* very loud, but in her mind only. There was no sound in the room.

The thing that was hiding didn't make any sound either, which made her think maybe it wasn't a tiger after all, because tigers have a terrible roar that they roar, but it couldn't have been anything else, for it had stripes and a tail and terrible teeth and eyes that were looking at her through the back of the little red chair. And her heart was pounding and the tiger knew this, and the only friend she had in the world was Teddy, and Teddy couldn't move, and neither could Raggy, and neither could she. But the tiger could move. He could do anything he wanted to except roar his terrible roar, because then the bedroom door would fly open and they would come running.

She looked at the tiger through the back of the little red chair, and the tiger looked at her, and finally it thrashed its tail once or twice and then went and put its head in the air-conditioner.

That isn't possible. . . . But it was. More and more of his body disappeared into the air-conditioner, and finally there was only his tail, and then only the tip of his tail, and when that was gone so was she.

The young policeman who stood all night on the corner of East End Avenue and Gracie Square, eight stories below, was at the phone box, having a conversation with the sergeant on the desk. This did not prevent him from keeping his eyes on an emaciated junkie who stood peering through the window of the drugstore, past the ice-cream bin, the revolving display of paperbacks, the plastic toys, hair sprays, hand creams, cleansing lotions, etc., at the prescription counter. The door had a grating over it but the plate-glass window did not. One good kick would do it. It would also bring the policeman running.

The policeman would have been happy to turn the junkie in, but he didn't have anything on him. Vagrancy? But suppose he had a home? And suppose it brought the Civil Liberties Union running? The policeman turned his back for a minute and when he looked again the junkie was gone, vanished, nowhere.

Though it was between three and four in the morning, people were walking their dogs in Carl Schurz Park. Amazing. Dreamlike. And the sign on the farther shore of the river that changed back and forth continually was enough to unhinge the mind: PEARLWICK HAMPERS became BATHROOM HAMPERS, which in turn became PEARLWICK HAMPERS, and sometimes for a fraction of a second BATHWICK HAMPERS.

In the metal trash containers scattered here and there along the winding paths of the park were pieces of waxed paper that had been around food but nothing you could actually eat. The junkie didn't go into the playground because the gates were locked and it had a high iron fence around it. He could have managed this easily by climbing a tree and dropping to the cement on the other side. Small boys did it all the time. And maybe in there he would have found something—a half-eaten Milky Way or Mounds bar that a nursemaid had taken from a child with a finicky appetite—but then he would have been locked in instead of out, and he knew all there was to know about that: Rikers Island, Sing Sing, Auburn, Dannemora. His name is James Jackson, and he is a figure out of a nightmare— unless you happen to know what happened to him, the steady rain of blows about his unprotected head ever since he was born, in which case it is human life that seems like a nightmare. The dog walkers, supposing—correctly—that he had a switch-blade in his pocket and a certain amount of experience in using it, chose a path that detoured around him. The wind was out of the southeast and smelled of the sea, fifteen miles away on the other side of Long Beach and Far Rockaway. The Hell Gate section of the Triborough Bridge was a necklace of sickly-green incandescent pearls. When the policeman left his post and took a turn through the south end of the park, the junkie was sitting innocently on a bench on the river walk. He was keeping the river company.

And when the policeman got back to his post a woman in a long red coat was going through the trash basket directly across the street from him. She was harmless. He saw her night after night. And in a minute she would cross over and tell him about the doctor at Bellevue who said she probably dreamed that somebody picked the lock of her door while she was out buying coffee and stole her mother's gold thimble.

The threads that bound the woman in the long red coat to a particular address, to the family she had been born into, her husband's grave in the Brooklyn cemetery, and the children who never wrote except to ask for money, had broken, and she was now free to wander along the street, scavenging from trash containers. She did not mind if people saw her, or feel that what she was doing was in any way exceptional. When she found something useful or valuable, she stuffed it in her dirty canvas bag, the richer by a pair of sandals with a broken strap or a perfectly clean copy of "Sartor Resartus." What in the beginning was only an uncertainty, an uneasiness, a sense of the falsity of appearances, a suspicion that the completely friendly world she lived in was in fact secretly mocking and hostile, had proved to be true. Or rather, had become true—for it wasn't always. And meanwhile, in her mind, she was perpetually composing a statement, for her own use and understanding, that would cover this situation.

Three colored lights passed overhead, very high up and in a cluster, blinking. There were also lights strung through the park at intervals, and on East End Avenue, where taxicabs cruised up and down with their roof-lights on. Nobody wanted them. As if they had never in their life shot through a red light, the taxis stopped at Eighty-third Street, and again at Eighty-fourth, and went on when the light turned green. East End Avenue was as quiet as the grave. So were the side streets.

With the first hint of morning, this beautiful quiet came to an end. Stopping and starting, making a noise like an electric toaster, a Department of Sanitation truck made its way down Eighty-fourth Street, murdering sleep. Crash. Tinkle. More grinding. Bump. Thump. Voices. A brief silence and then the whole thing started up again farther down the street. This was followed by other noises—a parked car being warmed up, a maniac in a sports car with no muffler. And then suddenly it was the policeman's turn to be gone. A squad car drove by, with the car radio playing an old Bing Crosby song, and picked him up.

Biding his time, the junkie managed to slip past the service entrance of one of the apartment buildings on East End Avenue without being seen. Around in back he saw an open window on the ground floor with no bars over it. On the other hand he didn't know who or what he would find when he climbed through it, and he shouldn't have waited till morning. He stood flattened against a brick wall while a handyman took in the empty garbage cans. The sound of retreating footsteps died away. The door to the service entrance was wide open. In a matter of seconds James Jackson was in and out again, wheeling a new ten-speed Peugeot. He straddled the bicycle as if he and not the overweight insurance broker in 7E had paid good money for it, and rode off down the street.

Cloudy with rain or showers . . .' Cindy, did you know you dreamt about a tiger last night?"

"Cindy dreamt about a tiger?" Iris said.

"Yes. What happened after I left?"

"Nothing."

"Congratulations. I dreamt the air-conditioner in our room broke and we couldn't get anybody to come and fix it."

"Is it broken?" Iris asked.

"I don't know. We'll have to wait till next summer to find out."

Good morning, Laurie. Good morning, Cindy," Jimmy the daytime elevator man said cheerfully. No answer. But no rudeness intended either. They did not know they were in the elevator.

The red-haired doorman at No. 7 Gracie Square stretched out his arms and pretended he was going to capture Cindy. This happened morning after morning, and she put up with it patiently.

"Taxi!" people wailed. "*Taxi!*" But there were no taxis. Or if one came along there was somebody in it. The doorman of No. 10 stood in the middle of East End Avenue and blew his whistle at nothing. On a balcony five stories above the street, a man lying on his back with his hips in the air was being put through his morning exercises by a Swedish masseur. The tired middle-aged legs went up and down like pistons. Like pistons, the elevators rose and fell in all the buildings overlooking the park, bringing the maids and laundresses up, taking men with briefcases down. The stationery store and the cleaners were now open. So was the luncheonette.

The two little girls stopped, took each other by the hand, and looked carefully both ways before they crossed the car tunnel at No. 10. On the river walk Laurie saw an acquaintance and ran on ahead. Poor Cindy! At her back was the park—very agreeable to play in when she went there with her mother or the kindergarten class, but also frequented by rough boys with water pistols and full of bushes it could be hiding in—and on her right was the deep pit alongside No. 10; it could be down there, below the sidewalk and waiting to spring out when she came along. She did not look to see if it was there but kept well over to the other side, next to the outer railing and the river. A tug with four empty barges was nosing its way upstream. The Simpsons' cook waved to Cindy from their kitchen window, which looked out on the river walk, and Cindy waved back.

In the days when George used to take Laurie to kindergarten because she was too small to walk to school by herself, he had noticed her—a big woman with blond braids in a crown around her head. And one day he said, "Shall we wave to her and see what happens?" Sometimes her back was turned to the window and she didn't know that Cindy and Laurie were there. They did not ever think of her except when they saw her, and if they had met her face to face she would have had to do all the talking.

Laurie was waiting at the Eighty-third Street gate. "Come on," she said.

"Stupid-head," Cindy said.

They went into the school building together, ignoring the big girls in camel's-hair coats who held the door open for them. But it wasn't like Jimmy the elevator man; they knew the big girls were there.

Sitting on the floor of her cubby, with her gym sneakers under her bottom and her cheek against her green plaid coat, Cindy felt safe. But Miss Nichols kept trying to get her to come out. The sandbox, the blocks, the crayons—Cindy said no to them all, and sucked her thumb. So Miss Nichols sat down on a little chair and took Cindy on her lap.

"If there was a (   )?" Cindy asked finally.

In a soft coaxing voice Miss Nichols said, "If there was a what?"

Cindy wouldn't say what.

The fire engines raced down Eighty-sixth Street, sirens shrieking and horns blowing, swung south through a red light, and came to a stop by the alarm box on the corner of East End Avenue and Gracie Square. The firemen jumped down and stood talking in the middle of the street. The hoses remained neatly folded and the ladders horizontal. It was the second false alarm that night from this same box. A county fair wouldn't have made more commotion under their windows but it had happened too often and George and Iris Carrington went on sleeping peacefully, flat on their backs, like stone figures on a medieval tomb.

In the trash basket on the corner by the park gates there was a copy of the *Daily News* which said, in big letters, "TIGER ESCAPES," but that was a different tiger; that tiger escaped from a circus in Jamestown, R.I.

What *is* it?" Iris asked, in the flower shop. "Why are you pulling at my skirt?"

The flower-shop woman (pink-blond hair, Viennese accent)

offered Cindy a green carnation, and she refused to take it. "You don't like flowers?" the woman asked, coyly, and the tiger kept on looking at Cindy from behind some big, wide rubbery green leaves. "She's shy," the flower-shop woman said.

"Not usually," Iris said. "I don't know what's got into her today."

She gave the woman some money, and the woman gave her some money and some flowers, and then she and Cindy went outside, but Cindy was afraid to look behind her. If the tiger was following them, it was better not to know. For half a block she had a tingling sensation in the center of her back, between her shoulder blades. But then, looking across the street, she saw that the tiger was not back there in the flower shop. It must have left when they did, and now it was looking at her from the round hole in a cement mixer.

The lights changed from red to green, and Iris took her hand and started to cross over.

"I want to go that way," Cindy said, holding back, until the light changed again. Since she was never allowed on the street alone, she was not really afraid of meeting the tiger all by herself. But what if some day it should walk into the elevator when Jimmy wasn't looking, and get off at their floor, and hide behind Laurie's bicycle and the scooters. And what if the front door opened and somebody came out and pressed the elevator button and the tiger got inside when they weren't looking. And what if—

"Oh, please don't hold back, Cindy! I'm late as anything!"

So, dangerous as it was, she allowed herself to be hurried along home.

T*ap, tap, tap* . . .
    In the night this was, just after Iris and George had got to sleep.

"Oh, no!" Iris moaned.

But it was. When he opened the door, there she stood.

T*ap, tap* . . .
   That same night, two hours later. Sound asleep but able to walk and talk, he put on his bathrobe and followed her down the hall. Stretched out beside her, he tried to go on sleeping but he couldn't. He said, "What were you dreaming about this time?"

"Sea-things."

"What kind of seethings?"

"Sea-things under the sea."

"Things that wiggled?"

"Yes."

"Something was after you?"

"Yes."

"Too bad. Go to sleep."

T*ap, tap* . . .
   This time as he heaved himself up, Iris said to him, "*You* lie still."

She got up and opened the door to the hall and said, "Cindy, we're tired and we need our sleep. I want you to go back to your bed and stay there."

Then they both lay awake, listening to the silence at the other end of the hall.

I came out of the building," Iris said, "and I had three letters that Jimmy had given me, and it was raining hard, and the wind whipped them right out of my hand."

He took a sip of his drink and then said, "Did you get them?"

"I got two of them. One was from the Richards children,

thanking me for the toys I sent when Lonnie was in the hospital.
And one was a note from Mrs. Mills. I never did find the third.
It was a small envelope, and the handwriting was Society."

"A birthday party for Cindy."

"No. It was addressed to Mr. and Mrs. George Carrington.
Cocktail party, probably."

He glanced at the windows. It was already dark. Then, the
eternal optimist (also remembering the time he found the
button that flew off her coat and rolled under a parked car
on Eighty-fifth Street): "Which way did it blow? I'll look for
it tomorrow."

"Oh, there's no use. You can see by the others. They were
reduced to pulp by the rain, in just that minute. And anyway,
I did look, this afternoon."

In the morning, he took the Seventy-ninth Street crosstown
bus instead of the Eighty-sixth, so that he could look for the
invitation that blew away. No luck. The invitation had already
passed through a furnace in the Department of Sanitation building on Ninety-first Street and now, in the form of ashes, was
floating down the East River on a garbage scow, on its way
out to sea.

The sender, rebuffed in this first tentative effort to get to
know the Carringtons better, did not try again. She had met
them at a dinner party, and liked them both. She was old
enough to be Iris's mother, and it puzzled her that a young
woman who seemed to be well-bred and was quite lovely-
looking and adored "Middlemarch" should turn out to have
no manners, but she didn't brood about it. New York is full of
pleasant young couples, and if one chooses to ignore your invitation the chances are another won't.

D id you hear Laurie in the night?" Iris said.
    "No. Did Laurie have a nightmare?"
"Yes. I thought you were awake."

"I don't think so."

He got up out of bed and went into the children's rooms and turned on the radiators so they wouldn't catch cold. Laurie was sitting up in bed reading.

"Mommy says you had a bad dream last night."

"There were three dreams," she said, in an overdistinct voice, as if she were a grown woman at a committee meeting. "The first dream was about Miss Stevenson. I dreamed she wasn't nice to me. She was like the wicked witch."

"Miss Stevenson loves you."

"And the second dream was about snakes. They were all over the floor. It was like a rug made up of snakes, and· very icky, and there was a giant, and Cathy and I were against him, and he was trying to shut me in the room where the snakes were, and one of the snakes bit me, but he wasn't the kind of snake that kills you, he was just a mean snake, and so it didn't hurt. And the third dream was a happy dream. I was with Cathy and we were skating together and pulling our mommies by strings."

With his safety razor ready to begin a downward sweep, George Carrington studied the lathered face in the mirror of the medicine cabinet. He shook his head. There was a fatal flaw in his character: Nobody was ever as real to him as he was to himself. If people knew how little he cared whether they lived or died, they wouldn't want to have anything to do with him.

The dog moved back and forth between the two ends of the apartment, on good terms with everybody. She was in the dining room at mealtimes, and in the kitchen when Iris was getting dinner (when quite often something tasty fell off the edge of the kitchen table), and she was there again just after dinner, in case the plates were put on the floor for her to lick before they went into the dishwasher. In the late afternoon, for an hour before it was time for her can of beef-and-beef-byproducts, she sat with her front paws crossed, facing the kitchen clock, a reminding statue. After she had been fed, she went to the living room and lay down before the unlit log fire in the fireplace and slept until bedtime. In the morning, she followed Iris back and forth through room after room, until Iris was dressed and ready to take her out. "Must you nag me so?" Iris cried, but the dog was not intimidated. There was something they were in agreement about, though only one of them could have put it in words: It is a crime against Nature to keep a hunting dog in the city. George sometimes gave her a slap on her haunches when she picked up food in the gutter or lunged at another dog. And if she jerked on her leash he jerked back, harder. But with Iris she could do anything—she could even stand under the canopy and refuse to go anywhere because it was raining.

Walking by the river, below Eightieth Street, it wasn't necessary to keep her on a leash, and while Iris went on ahead Puppy sniffed at the godforsaken grass and weeds that grew between the cement walk and the East River Drive. Then she overtook Iris, at full speed, overshot the mark, and came charging back, showing her teeth in a grin. Three or four times she did this, as a rule—with Iris applauding and congratulating her and cheering her on. It may be a crime against Nature to keep a hunting dog in the city, but this one was happy anyway.

After a series of dreams in which people started out as one person and ended up another and he found that there was no provision for getting from where he was to where he wanted to go and it grew later and later and even after the boat had left he still went on packing his clothes and what he thought was his topcoat turned out to belong to a friend he had not seen for seventeen years and naked strangers came and went, he woke and thought he heard a soft tapping on the bedroom door. But when he got up and opened it there was no one there.

"Was that Cindy?" Iris asked as he got back into bed.

"No. I thought I heard her, but I must have imagined it."

"I thought I heard her too," Iris said, and turned over.

At breakfast he said, "Did you have any bad dreams last night?" but Cindy was making a lake in the middle of her oatmeal and didn't answer.

"I thought I heard you tapping on our door," he said. "You didn't dream about a wolf, or a tiger, or a big black dog?"

"I don't remember," she said.

Y ou'll never guess what I just saw from the bedroom window," Iris said.

He put down his book.

"A police wagon drove down Eighty-fourth Street and stopped, and two policemen with guns got out and went into a building and didn't come out. And after a long while two more policemen came and *they* went into the building and pretty soon they all came out with a big man with black hair, handcuffed. Right there on Eighty-fourth Street, two doors from the corner."

"Nice neighborhood we live in," he said.

D addy, Daddy, Daddy, Daddy!" came into his dreams without waking him, and what did wake him was the heaving of the other bed as Iris got up and hurried toward the bedroom door.

"It was Cindy," she said when she came back.

"Dream?" he asked.

"Yes."

"I heard her but went on dreaming myself."

"She doesn't usually cry out like that."

"Laurie used to."

Why all these dreams, he wondered, and drifted gently back to sleep, as if he already knew the answer. She turned and turned, and finally, after three-quarters of an hour, got up and filled the hot-water bottle. What for days had been merely a half-formed thought in the back of her mind was now suddenly, in the middle of the night, making her rigid with anxiety. She needed to talk, and couldn't bring herself to wake him. What she wanted to say was they were making a mistake in bringing the children up in New York City. Or even in America. There was too much that there was no way to protect them from, and the only sensible thing would be to pull up stakes now, before Laurie reached adolescence. They could sublet the apartment until the lease ran out, and take a house somewhere in the South of France, near Aix perhaps, and the children could go to a French school, and they could all go skiing in Switzerland in the winter, and Cindy could have her own horse, and they both would acquire a good French accent, and be allowed to grow up slowly, in the ordinary way, and not be jaded by one premature experience after another, before they were old enough to understand any of it.

With the warmth at her back, and the comforting feeling that she had found the hole in the net, gradually she fell asleep too.

But when she brought the matter up two days later he looked at her blankly. He did not oppose her idea but neither did he accept it, and so her hands were tied.

As usual, the fathers' part in the Christmas program had to be rehearsed beforehand. In the small practice room on the sixth floor of the school, their masculinity—their grey flannel or dark-blue pin-striped suits, their size 9, 10, 11, 11½, and 12 shoes, their gold cufflinks, the odor that emanated from their bodies and from their freshly shaved cheeks, their simple assurance, based on, among other things, the *Social Register* and the size of their income—was incongruous. They were handed sheets of music as they came in, and the room was crammed with folding chairs, all facing the ancient grand piano. With the two tall windows at their backs they were missing the snow, which was a pity. It went up, down, diagonally, and in centrifugal motion—all at once. The fact that no two of the star-shaped crystals were the same was a miracle, of course, but it was a miracle that everybody has long since grown accustomed to. The light outside the windows was cold and grey.

"Since there aren't very many of you," the music teacher said, "you'll have to make up for it by singing enthusiastically." She was young, in her late twenties, and had difficulty keeping discipline in the classroom; the girls took advantage of her good nature, and never stopped talking and gave her their complete attention. She sat down at the piano now and played the opening bars of "O come, O come, Emmanuel/And ransom captive I-i-i-zrah-el . . ."

Somebody in the second row exclaimed, "Oh God!" under his breath. The music was set too high for men's voices.

"The girls will sing the first stanza, you fathers the second—"

The door opened and two more fathers came in.

"—and all will sing the third."

With help from the piano (which they would not have downstairs in the school auditorium) they achieved an approximation of the tune, and the emphasis sometimes fell in the right place. They did their best, but the nineteenth-century words and the ninth-century plainsong did not go well together. Also, one of the fathers had a good strong clear voice, which only made the others more self-conscious and apologetic. They would have been happier without him.

The music teacher made a flip remark. They all laughed and began again. Their number was added to continually as the door opened and let in the sounds from the hall. Soon there were no more vacant chairs; the latecomers had to stand. The snow was now noticeably heavier, and the singing had more volume. Though they were at some pains to convey, by their remarks to one another and their easy laughter, that this was not an occasion to be taken seriously, nevertheless the fact that they were here was proof of the contrary; they all had offices where they should have been and salaries they were not at this moment doing anything to earn. Twenty-seven men with, at first glance, a look of sameness about them, a round, composite, youngish, unrevealing, New York face. Under closer inspection, this broke down. Not all the eyes were blue, nor were the fathers all in their middle and late thirties. The thin-faced man at the end of the second row could not have been a broker or a lawyer or in advertising. The man next to him had survived incarceration in a Nazi prison camp. There was one Negro. Here and there a head that was not thickly covered with hair. Their speaking voices varied, but not so much as they conceivably might have—no Texas drawl, for instance. And all the fingernails were clean, all the shoes were shined, all the linen was fresh.

Each time they went over the hymn it was better. They clearly needed more rehearsing, but the music teacher glanced nervously at the clock and said, "And now 'In Dulci Jubilo.' "

Those who had forgotten their Latin, or never had any, eavesdropped on those who knew how the words should be pronounced. The tune was powerful and swept everything before it, and in a flush of pleasure they finished together, on the beat, loudly, making the room echo. They had forgotten about the telephone messages piling up on their desks beside the unopened mail. They were enjoying themselves. They could have gone on singing for another hour. Instead, they had to get up and file out of the room and crowd into the elevators.

In spite of new costumes, new scenery, different music, and

—naturally—a different cast, the Christmas play was always the same. Mary and Joseph proceeded to Bethlehem, where the inns were full, and found shelter in the merest suggestion of a stable. An immature angel announced to very unlikely shepherds the appearance of the Star. Wise Men came and knelt before the plastic Babe in Mary's arms. And then the finale: the Threes singing and dancing with heavenly joy.

"How did it sound?" George asked, in the crowd on the stairs.

"Fine," Iris said.

"Really? It didn't seem to me—maybe because we were under the balcony—it didn't seem as if we were making any sound at all."

"No, it was plenty loud enough. What was so nice was the two kinds of voices."

"High and low, you mean?"

"The fathers sounded like bears. Adorable."

In theory, since it was the middle of the night, it was dark, but not the total suffocating darkness of a cloudy night in the country. The city, as usual, gave off light—enough so that you could see the island in the middle of the river, and the three bridges, and the outlines of the little houses on East End Avenue and the big apartment buildings on Eighty-sixth Street, and the trees and shrubs and lampposts and comfort station in the park. Also a woman standing by the railing of the river walk.

There was no wind. The river was flowing north and the air smelled of snow, which melted the moment it touched any solid object, and became the shine on iron balustrades and on the bark of trees.

The woman had been standing there a long time, looking out over the water, when she began awkwardly to pull herself up and over the curved iron spikes that were designed, by their size and shape, to prevent people from throwing themselves into the river. In this instance they were not enough. But it took some doing. There was a long tear in the woman's coat and she was gasping for breath as she let herself go backward into space.

The sun enters Aquarius January 20th and remains until February 18th. "*An extremely good friend can today put into motion some operation that will be most helpful to your best interest, or else introduce you to some influential person. Go out socially in the evening on a grand scale. Be charming.*"

The cocktail party was in a penthouse. The elevator opened directly into the foyer of the apartment. And the woman he was talking to—or rather, who was talking to him—was dressed all in shades of brown.

"I tried to get you last summer," she said, "but your wife said you were busy that day."

"Yes," he said.

"I'll try you again."

"Please do," somebody said for him, using his mouth and tongue and vocal cords—because it was the last thing in the world he wanted, to drive halfway across Long Island to a lunch party. "We hardly ever go anywhere," he himself said, but too late, after the damage had been done.

His mind wandered for an instant as he took in—not the room, for he was facing the wrong way, but a small corner of it. And in that instant he lost the thread of the story she was telling him. She had taken her shoe off in a movie theatre and put her purse down beside it, and the next thing he knew they refused to do anything, even after she had explained what happened and that she must get in. Who "they" were, get in where, he patiently waited to find out, while politely sharing her indignation.

"But imagine!" she exclaimed. "They said, 'How valuable was the ring?'"

He shook his head, commiserating with her.

"I suppose if it hadn't been worth a certain amount," she went on, "they wouldn't have done a thing about it."

The police, surely, he thought. Having thought at first it was the manager of the movie theatre she was talking about.

"And while they were jimmying the door open, people were walking by, and nobody showed the slightest concern. Or interest."

So it wasn't the police. But who was it, then? He never found out, because they were joined by another woman, who smiled at him in such a way as to suggest that they knew each other. But though he searched his mind and her face—the plucked eyebrows, the reserved expression in the middle-aged eyes— and considered her tweed suit and her diamond pin and her square figure, he could not imagine who she was. Suppose somebody—suppose Iris came up and he had to introduce her?

The purse was recovered, with the valuable ring still in it, and he found himself talking about something that had occupied his thoughts lately. And in his effort to say what he meant, he failed to notice what happened to the first woman. Suddenly she was not there. Somebody must have carried her off, right in front of his unseeing eyes.

". . . but it isn't really distinguishable from what goes on in dreams," he said to the woman who seemed to know him and to assume that he knew her. "People you have known for twenty or thirty years, you suddenly discover you didn't really know how they felt about you, and in fact you don't know how anybody feels about anything—only what they *say* they feel. And suppose that isn't true at all? You decide that it is better to act as if it is true. And so does everybody else. But it is a kind of myth you are living in, wide awake, with your eyes open, in broad daylight."

He realized that the conversation had become not only personal but intimate. But it was too late to back out now.

To his surprise she seemed to understand, to have felt what he had felt. "And one chooses," she said, "between this myth and that."

"Exactly! If you live in the city and are bringing up children, you decide that this thing is not safe—and so you don't let them do it—and that thing *is* safe. When, actually, neither one is safe and everything is equally dangerous. But for the sake of convenience—"

"And also so that you won't go out of your mind," she said.

"And so you won't go out of your mind," he agreed. "Well," he said after a moment, "that makes two of us who are thinking about it."

"In one way or another, people live by myths," she said.

He racked his brain for something further to say on this or any other subject.

Glancing around at the windows which went from floor to ceiling, the woman in the tweed suit said, "These vistas you have here."

He then looked and saw black night, with lighted buildings far below and many blocks away. "From our living room," he said, "you can see all the way to the North Pole."

"We live close to the ground," she said.

But where? Cambridge? Princeton? Philadelphia?

"In the human scale," he said. "Like London and Paris. Once, on a beautiful spring day, four of us—we'd been having lunch with a visiting Englishman who was interested in architecture —went searching for the sky. Up one street and down the next."

She smiled.

"We had to look for it, the sky is so far away in New York."

They stood nursing their drinks, and a woman came up to them who seemed to know her intimately, and the two women started talking and he turned away.

On her way into the school building, Laurie joined the flood from the school bus, and cried, "Hi, Janet . . . Hi, Connie . . . Hi, Elizabeth . . ." and seemed to be enveloped by her schoolmates, until suddenly, each girl having turned to some other girl, Laurie is left standing alone, her expression unchanged, still welcoming, but nobody having responded. If you collect reasons, this is the reason she behaved so badly at lunch, was impertinent to her mother, and hit her little sister.

He woke with a mild pain in his stomach. It was high up, like an ulcer pain, and he lay there worrying about it. When he heard the sound of shattered glass, his half-awake, oversensible mind supplied both the explanation and the details: two men, putting a large framed picture into the trunk compartment of a parked car, had dropped it, breaking the glass. Too bad . . . And with that thought he drifted gently off to sleep.

In the morning he looked out of the bedroom window and saw three squad cars in front of the drugstore. The window of the drugstore had a big star-shaped hole in it, and several policemen were standing around looking at the broken glass on the sidewalk.

The sneeze was perfectly audible through two closed doors. He turned to Iris with a look of inquiry.

"Who sneezed? Was that you, Laurie?" she called.

"That was Cindy," Laurie said.

In principle, Iris would have liked to bring them up in a

Spartan fashion, but both children caught cold easily and their colds were prolonged, and recurring, and overlapping, and endless. Whether they should or shouldn't be kept home from school took on the unsolvability of a moral dilemma—which George's worrying disposition did nothing to alleviate. The sound of a child coughing deep in the chest in the middle of the night would make him leap up out of a sound sleep.

She blamed herself when the children came down with a cold, and she blamed them. Possibly, also, the school was to blame, since the children played on the roof, twelve stories above the street, and up there the winds were often much rawer, and teachers cannot, of course, spend all their time going around buttoning up the coats of little girls who have got too hot from running.

She went and stood in the doorway of Cindy's room. "No sneezing," she said.

Sneeze, sneeze, sneeze.

"Cindy, if you are catching another cold, I'm going to shoot myself," Iris said, and gave her two baby-aspirin tablets to chew, and some Vitamin C drops, and put an extra blanket on her bed, and didn't open the window, and in the morning Cindy's nose was running.

"Shall I keep her home from school?" Iris asked, at the breakfast table.

Instead of answering, George got up and looked at the weather thermometer outside the west window of their bedroom. "Twenty-seven," he said, when he came back. But he still didn't answer her question. He was afraid to answer it, lest it be the wrong answer, and she blame him. Actually, there was no answer that was the right answer: They had tried sending Cindy to school and they had tried not sending her. This time, Iris kept her home from school—not because she thought it was going to make any difference but so the pediatrician, Dr. de Santillo, wouldn't blame her. Not that he ever said anything.

And Cindy got to play with Laurie's things all morning. She played with Laurie's paper dolls until she was tired, and left them all over the floor, and then she colored in Laurie's coloring book, and Puppy chewed up one of the crayons but not one of Laurie's favorites—not the pink or the blue—and then Cindy rearranged the furniture in Laurie's doll house so it was much nicer, and then she lined up all Laurie's dolls in a row on her bed and played school. And when it was time for Laurie to come home from school she went out to the kitchen and played with the eggbeater. Laurie came in, letting the front door slam behind her, and dropped her mittens in the hall and her coat on the living-room rug and her knitted cap on top of her coat, and started for her room, and it sounded as if she had hurt herself. Iris came running. What a noise Laurie made. And stamping her foot, Cindy noted disapprovingly. And tears.

"Stop screaming and tell me what's the matter!" Iris said.

"Cindy, I hate you!" Laurie said. "I hate you, I hate you!" *Horrible old Laurie* . . .

But in the morning when they first woke up it was different. She heard Laurie in the bathroom, and then she heard Laurie go back to her room. Lying in bed, Cindy couldn't suck her thumb because she couldn't breathe through her nose, so she got up and went into Laurie's room (entirely forgetting that her mother had said that in the morning she was to stay out of Laurie's room because she had a cold) and got in Laurie's bed and said, "Read, read." Laurie read her the story of "The Tinder Box," which has three dogs in it—a dog with eyes as big as saucers, and a dog with eyes as big as millwheels, and a third dog with eyes as big as the Round Tower of Copenhagen.

T*ap, tap, tap* on the bedroom door brought him entirely awake. "What's Laurie been reading to her?" he asked, turning over in bed. That meant it was Iris's turn to get up.

While she was pulling herself together, they heard *tap, tap, tap* again. The bed heaved.

"What's Laurie been reading to you?" she asked as she and Cindy went off down the hall together. When she came back into the bedroom, the light was on and he was standing in front of his dresser, with the top drawer open, searching for Gelusil tablets.

"Trouble?" she said.

S tanding in the doorway of Cindy's room, in her blue dressing gown, with her hairbrush in her hand, Iris said, "Who sneezed? Was that you, Cindy?"

"That was Laurie," Cindy said.

So after that Laurie got to stay home from school too.

I saw Phyllis Simpson in Gristede's supermarket," Iris said. "Their cook committed suicide."

"How?"

"She threw herself in the river."

"No!"

"They think she must have done it sometime during the night, but they don't know exactly when. They just came down to breakfast and she wasn't there. They're still upset about it."

"When did it happen?"

"About a month ago. Her body was found way down the river."

"What a pity. She was a nice woman."

"You remember her?"

"Certainly. She always waved to the children when I used to walk them to school. She waved to me too, sometimes. From the kitchen window. What made her do such a thing?"

"They have no idea."

"She was a big woman," he said. "It must have been hard

for her to pull herself up over that railing. It's quite high. No
note or anything?"

"No."

"Terrible."

O n St. Valentine's Day, the young woman who lived on tea
and cigarettes and was given to burning herself on the
gas stove eloped to California with her mother, and now there
was no one in the kitchen. From time to time, the employment
agency went through the formality of sending someone for
Iris to interview—though actually it was the other way round.
And either the apartment was too large or they didn't care
to work for a family with children or they were not accustomed
to doing the cooking as well as the other housework. Sometimes
they didn't give any reason at all.

A young woman from Haiti, who didn't speak English, was
willing to give the job a try. It turned out that she had never
seen a carpet sweeper before, and she asked for her money at
the end of the day.

W alking the dog at seven-fifteen on a winter morning, he
suddenly stopped and said to himself, "Oh God, somebody's been murdered!" On the high stone stoop of one of the
little houses on East End Avenue facing the park. Somebody
in a long red coat. By the curve of the hip he could tell it was
a woman, and with his heart racing he considered what he
ought to do. From where he stood on the sidewalk he couldn't
see the upper part of her body. One foot—the bare heel and the
strap of her shoe—was sticking out from under the hem of the
coat. If she'd been murdered, wouldn't she be sprawled out in
an awkward position instead of curled up and lying on her side
as though she was in bed asleep? He looked up at the house.
Had they locked her out? After a scene? Or she could have

come home in the middle of the night and discovered that she'd forgotten to take her key. But in that case she'd have spent the night in a hotel or with a friend. Or called an all-night locksmith.

He went up three steps without managing to see any more than he had already. The parapet offered some shelter from the wind, but even so, how could she sleep on the cold stone, with nothing over her?

"Can I help you?"

His voice sounded strange and hollow. There was no answer. The red coat did not stir. Then he saw the canvas bag crammed with the fruit of her night's scavenging, and backed down the steps.

N ow it was his turn. The sore throat was gone in the morning, but it came back during the day, and when he sat down to dinner he pulled the extension out at his end and moved his mat, silver, and glass farther away from the rest of them.

"If you aren't sneezing, I don't think you need to be in Isolation Corner," Iris said, but he stayed there anyway. His colds were prolonged and made worse by his efforts to treat them; made worse still by his trying occasionally to disregard them, as he saw other people doing. In the end he went through box after box of Kleenex, his nose white with Noxzema, his eyelids inflamed, like a man in a subway poster advertising a cold remedy that, as it turned out, did not work for him. And finally he took to his bed, with a transistor radio for amusement and company. In his childhood, being sick resulted in agreeable pampering, and now that he was grown he preferred to be both parties to this pleasure. No one could make him as comfortable as he could make himself, and Iris had all but given up trying.

On a rainy Sunday afternoon in March, with every door in the school building locked and the corridor braced for the shock of Monday morning, the ancient piano demonstrated for the benefit of the empty practice room that it is one thing to fumble through the vocal line, guided by the chords that accompany it, and something else again to be genuinely musical, to know what the composer intended—the resolution of what cannot be left uncertain, the amorous flirtation of the treble and the bass, notes taking to the air like a flock of startled birds.

The faint clicking sounds given off by the telephone in the pantry meant that Iris was dialling on the extension in the master bedroom. And at last there was somebody in the Carringtons' kitchen again—a black woman in her fifties. They were low on milk, and totally out of oatmeal, canned dog food, and coffee, but the memo pad that was magnetically attached to the side of the Frigidaire was blank. Writing down things they were out of was not something she considered part of her job. When an emergency arose, she put on her coat and went to the store, just as if she were still in North Carolina.

The sheet of paper that was attached to the clipboard hanging from a nail on the side of the kitchen cupboard had the menus for lunch and dinner all written out, but they were for yesterday's lunch and dinner. And though it was only nine-thirty, Bessie already felt a mounting indignation at being kept in ignorance about what most deeply concerned her. It was an old-fashioned apartment, with big rooms and high ceilings, and the kitchen was a considerable distance from the master bedroom; nevertheless, it was just barely possible for the two women to live there. Nature had designed them for mutual tormenting, the one with an exaggerated sense of time, always hurrying to meet a deadline that did not exist anywhere but in her own fancy, and calling upon the angels or whoever is in charge of amazing grace to take notice that she had put the food on the hot tray in the dining room at precisely one minute before the moment she had been told to have dinner ready; the other with not only a hatred of planning meals but also a childish reluctance to come to the table. When the minute hand of the electric clock in the kitchen arrived at seven or seven-fifteen or whatever, Bessie went into the dining room and announced in an inaudible voice that dinner was ready. Two rooms away, George heard her by extrasensory perception and leapt to his feet, and Iris, holding out her glass to him, said, "Am I not going to have a second vermouth?"

To his amazement, on Bessie's day off, having cooked dinner and put it on the hot plate, Iris drifted away to the front of the apartment and read a magazine, fixed her hair, God knows what, until he discovered the food sitting there and begged her to come to the table.

They said they lived in Boys Town, and I thought Jimmy let them in because he's Irish and Catholic," Iris said. "There was nothing on the list I wanted, so I subscribed to *Vogue*, to help them out. When I spoke to Jimmy about it, he said he had no idea they were selling subscriptions, and he never lets solicitors get by him—not even nuns and priests. Much as he might want to. So I don't suppose it will come."

"It might," George said. "Maybe they were honest."

"He thought they were workmen because they asked for the eleventh floor. The tenants on the eleventh floor have moved out and Jimmy says the people who are moving in have a five years' lease and are spending fifty thousand dollars on the place, which they don't even *own*. But anyway, what they did was walk through the apartment and then down one floor and start ringing doorbells. The super took them down in the back elevator without asking what they were doing there, and off they went. They tried the same thing at No. 7 and the doorman threw them out."

Walking the dog before breakfast, if he went by the river walk he saw in the Simpsons' window a black-haired woman who did not wave to him or even look up when he passed. That particular section of the river walk was haunted by an act of despair that nobody had been given a chance to understand. Nothing that he could think of—cancer, thwarted love, melancholia—seemed to fit. He had only spoken to her once, when he and Iris went to a dinner party at the Simpsons' and she smiled at him as she was helping the maid clear the table between courses. If she didn't look up when he passed under her window it was as though he had been overtaken by a cloud shadow—until he forgot all about it, a few seconds later. But he could have stopped just once, and he hadn't. When the window was open he could have called out to her, even if it was only "Good morning," or "Isn't it a beautiful day?"

He could have said, *Don't do it. . . .*

Sometimes he came back by the little house on East End Avenue where he had seen the woman in the red coat. He invariably glanced up, half expecting her to be lying there on the stoop. If she wasn't there, where was she?

In the psychiatric ward of Bellevue Hospital was the answer. But not for long. She and the doctor got it straightened out about her mother's gold thimble, and he gave her a prescription and told her where to go in the building to have it filled, and hoped for the best—which, after all, is all that anybody has to hope for.

The weather thermometer blew away one stormy night and after a week or two George brought home a new one. It was round and encased in white plastic, and not meant to be screwed to the window frame but to be kept inside. It registered the temperature outside by means of a wire with what looked like a small bullet attached to the end of it. The directions said to drill a hole through the window frame, but George backed away from all that and, instead, hung the wire across the sill and closed the window on it. What the new thermometer said bore no relation to the actual temperature, and drilling the hole had a high priority on the list of things he meant to do.

There was also a racial barometer in the apartment that registered *Fair* or *Stormy*, according to whether Bessie had spent several days running in the apartment or had just come back from a weekend in her room in Harlem.

The laundress, so enormously fat that she had to maneuver her body around, as if she were the captain of an ocean liner, was a Muslim and hated all white people and most black people as well. She was never satisfied with the lunch Bessie cooked for her, and Bessie objected to having to get lunch for her, and the problem was solved temporarily by having her eat in the luncheonette across the street.

She quit. The new laundress was half the size of the old one, and sang alto in her church choir, and was good-tempered, and fussy about what she had for lunch. Bessie sometimes considered her a friend and sometimes an object of derision, because she believed in spirits.

So did Bessie, but not to the same extent or in the same way. Bessie's mother had appeared to her and her sister and brother, shortly after her death. They were quarrelling together, and her mother's head and shoulders appeared up near the ceiling, and she said they were to love one another. And sometimes when Bessie was walking along the street she felt a coolness and knew that a spirit was beside her. But the laundress said, "All right, go ahead, then, if you want to," to the empty air and, since there wasn't room for both of them, let the spirit precede her through the pantry. She even knew who the spirit was.

It was now spring on the river, and the river walk was a Chinese scroll which could be unrolled, by people who like to do things in the usual way, from right to left—starting at Gracie Square and walking north. Depicted were:

A hockey game between Loyola and St. Francis de Sales

Five boys shooting baskets on the basketball court

A seagull

An old man sitting on a bench doing columns of figures

A child drawing a track for his toy trains on the pavement with a piece of chalk

A paper drinking cup floating on the troubled surface of the water

A child in pink rompers pushing his own stroller

A woman sitting on a bench alone, with her face lifted to the sun

A Puerto Rican boy with a transistor radio

Two middle-aged women speaking German

A bored and fretful baby, too hot in his perambulator, with nothing to look at or play with, while his nurse reads

The tugboat Chicago pulling a long string of empty barges upstream

A little girl feeding her mother an apple

A helicopter

A kindergarten class, in two sections

Clouds in a blue sky

A flowering cherry tree

Seven freight cars moving imperceptibly, against the tidal current, in the wake of the Herbert E. Smith

A man with a pipe in his mouth and a can of Prince Albert smoking tobacco on the bench beside him

A man sorting his possessions into two canvas bags, one of which contains a concertina

Six very small children playing in the sandpile, under the watchful eyes of their mothers or nursemaids

An oil tanker

A red-haired priest reading a pocket-size New Testament
A man scattering bread crumbs for the pigeons
The Coast Guard cutter CG 40435 turning around just north of the lighthouse and heading back toward Hell Gate Bridge
A sweeper with his bag and a ferruled stick
A little boy pointing a red plastic pistol at his father's head
A pleasure yacht
An airplane
A man and a woman speaking French
A child on a tricycle
A boy on roller skates
A reception under a striped tent on the lawn of the mayor's house
The fireboat station
The Franklin Delano Roosevelt Drive, a cinder path, a warehouse, seagulls, and so on
Who said *Happiness is the light shining on the water. The water is cold and dark and deep. . . .*

It's perfectly insane," George said when he met Iris coming from Gristede's with a big brown-paper bag heavy as lead under each arm and relieved her of them. "Don't we still have that cart?"

"Nobody in the building uses them."

"But couldn't you?"

"No," Iris said.

All children," Cindy said wisely, leaning against him, with her head in the hollow of his neck, "all children think their mommy and daddy are the nicest."

"And what about you? Are you satisfied?"

She gave him a hug and a kiss and said, "I think you and Mommy are the nicest mommy and daddy in the whole world."

"And I think you are the nicest Cindy," he said, his eyes moist with tears.

They sat and rocked each other gently.

After Bessie had taken the breakfast dishes out of the dishwasher, she went into the front, dragging the vacuum cleaner, to do the children's rooms. She stood sometimes for five or ten minutes, looking down at East End Avenue—at the drugstore, the luncheonette, the rival cleaning establishments (side by side and, according to rumor, both owned by the same person), the hairstyling salon, and the branch office of the Chase Manhattan Bank. Together they made a canvas backdrop for a procession of people Bessie had never seen before, or would not recognize if she had, and so she couldn't say to herself, "There goes old Mrs. Maltby," but she looked anyway, she took it all in. The sight of other human beings nourished her mind. She read them as people read books. Pieces of toys, pieces of puzzles that she found on the floor she put on one shelf or another of the toy closet in Cindy's room, gradually introducing a disorder that Iris dealt with periodically, taking a whole day out of her life. But nobody told Bessie she was supposed to find the box the piece came out of, and it is questionable whether she could have anyway. The thickness of the lenses in her eyeglasses suggested that her eyesight was poorer than she let on.

She was an exile, far from home, among people who were not like the white people she knew and understood. She was here because down home she was getting forty dollars a week and she had her old age to think of. She and Iris alternated between irritation at one another and sudden acts of kindness. It was the situation that was at fault. Given halfway decent circumstances, men can work cheerfully and happily for other men, in offices, stores, and even factories. And so can women. But if Iris opened the cupboard or the icebox to see what they did or didn't contain, Bessie popped out of her room and said, "Did you want something?" And Iris withdrew, angry because she had been driven out of her own kitchen. In her mind, Bessie always thought of the Carringtons as "my people," but until she had taught them to think of themselves as her people her profound capacity for devotion would go unused; would not even be suspected.

You can say that life is a fountain if you want to, but what it more nearly resembles is a jack-in-the-box.

Half awake, he heard the soft whimpering that meant Iris was having a nightmare, and he shook her. "I dreamt you were having a heart attack," she said.

"Should you be dreaming that?" he said. But the dream was still too real to be joked about. They were in a public place. And he couldn't be moved. He didn't die, and she consulted with doctors. Though the dream did not progress, she could not extricate herself from it but went on and on, feeling the appropriate emotions but in a circular way. Till finally the sounds she made in her sleep brought about her deliverance.

The conversation at the other end of the hall continued steadily—not loud but enough to keep them from sleeping, and he had already spoken to the children once. So he got up and went down the hall. Laurie and Cindy were both in their bathroom, and Cindy was sitting on the toilet. "I have a stomach ache," she said.

He started to say, "You need to do bizz," and then remembered that the time before she had been sitting on the toilet doing just that.

"And I feel dizzy," Laurie said.

"I heard it," Iris said as he got back into bed.

"That's why she was so pale yesterday."

And half an hour later, when he got up again, Iris did too. To his surprise. Looking as if she had lost her last friend. So he took her in his arms.

"I hate everything," she said.

O n the top shelf of his clothes closet he keeps all sorts of things—the overflow of phonograph records, and the photograph albums, which are too large for the bookcases in the living room. The snapshots show nothing but joy. Year after year of it.

O n the stage of the school auditorium, girls from Class Eight, in pastel-colored costumes and holding arches of crêpe-paper flowers, made a tunnel from the front of the stage to the rear right-hand corner. The pianist took her hands from the keys, and the headmistress, in sensible navy blue, with her hair cut short like a man's, announced, "Class B becomes Class One."

Twenty very little girls in white dresses marched up on the stage two by two, holding hands.

George and Iris Carrington turned to each other and smiled, for Cindy was among them, looking proud and happy as she hurried through the tunnel of flowers and out of sight.

"Class One becomes Class Two." Another wave of little girls left their place in the audience and went up on the stage and disappeared into the wings.

"Class Two becomes Class Three."

Laurie Carrington, her red hair shining from the hairbrush, rose from her seat with the others and started up on the stage.

"It's too much!" George said, under his breath.

Class Three became Class Four, Class Four became Class

Five, Class Five became Class Six, and George Carrington took a handkerchief out of his right hip pocket and wiped his eyes. It was their eagerness that undid him. Their absolute trust in the Arrangements. Class Six became Class Seven, Class Seven became Class Eight. The generations of man, growing up, growing old, dying in order to make room for more.

"Class Eight becomes Class Nine, and is now in the Upper School," the headmistress said, triumphantly. The two girls at the front ducked and went under the arches, taking their crêpe-paper flowers with them. And then the next two, and the next, and finally the audience was left applauding an empty stage.

C ome here and sit on my lap," he said, by no means sure Laurie would think it worth the trouble. But she came. Folding her onto his lap, he was aware of the length of her legs, and the difference of her body; the babyness had departed forever, and when he was affectionate with her it was always as if the moment were slightly out of focus; he felt a restraint. He worried lest it be too close to making love to her. The difference was not great, and he was not sure whether it existed at all.

"Would you like to hear a riddle?" she asked.

"All right."

"Who was the fastest runner in history?"

"I don't know," he said, smiling at her. "Who was?"

"Adam. He was the first in the human race. . . . Teeheehee-heehee, wasn't that a good one?"

W aking in the night, Cindy heard her mother and father laughing behind the closed door of their room. It was a sound she liked to hear, and she turned over and went right back to sleep.

What was that?"

He raised his head from the pillow and listened.

"Somebody crying 'Help!'" Iris said.

He got up and went to the window. There was no one in the street except a taxi-driver brushing out the back seat of his hack. Again he heard it. Somebody being robbed. Or raped. Or murdered.

"Help . . ." Faintly this time. And not from the direction of the park. The taxi-driver did not look up at the sound, which must be coming from inside a building somewhere. With his face to the window, George waited for the sound to come again and it didn't. Nothing but silence. If he called the police, what could he say? He got back into bed and lay there, sick with horror, his knees shaking. In the morning maybe the *Daily News* would have what happened.

But he forgot to buy a *News* on his way to work, and days passed, and he no longer was sure what night it was that they heard the voice crying "Help!" and felt that he ought to go through weeks of the *News* until he found out what happened. If it was in the *News*. And if something happened.

The Trojan Women

The business district of Draperville, Illinois (population
12,000), was built around a neo-Roman courthouse and
the courthouse square. Adjoining the railroad station, in the
center of a small plot of ground, a bronze tablet marked the
site of the Old Alton Depot where the first Latham County
Volunteers entrained for the Civil War, and where the funeral
train of Abraham Lincoln halted briefly at sunrise on May
3rd, 1865. Other towns within a radius of a hundred miles
continued to prosper, but Draperville stopped growing. It was
finished by 1900. The last civic accomplishment was the laying
of the tracks for the Draperville Street Railway. The population stayed the same and the wide residential streets were
lined with trees that every year grew larger and more beautiful,
as if to conceal by a dense green shade the failure of men of
enterprise and sound judgment to beget these same qualities in
their sons.

The streetcar line started at the New Latham Hotel and
ran past the baseball park and the county jail, past the state
insane asylum, and on out to the cemetery and the lake. The
lake was actually an abandoned gravel pit, half a mile long and
a quarter of a mile wide, fed by underground springs. Its
water was very deep and very cold. The shoreline was dotted
with summer cottages and between the cottages and an expanse
of cornfields was a thin grove of oak trees. Every summer two
or three dozen families moved out here in June, to escape the
heat, and stayed until the end of August, when the reopening
of school forced them to return to town. After Labor Day,

with the cottages boarded up and the children's voices stilled, the lake was washed in equinoctial rains, polished by the October sun, and became once more a part of the wide empty landscape.

On a brilliant September day in 1912 the streetcar stopped in front of the high school, and a large tranquil colored woman got on. She was burdened with a shopping bag and several parcels, which she deposited on the seat beside her. There were two empty seats between the colored woman and the nearest white passengers, who nodded to her but did not include her in their conversation. The streetcar was open on the sides, with rattan seats. It rocked and swayed, and the passengers, as though they were riding on the back of an elephant, rocked and swayed with it. The people who had flowers—asters or chrysanthemums wrapped in damp news-paper—rode as far as the cemetery where, among acres of monuments and gravestones (Protestant on the right, Catholic on the left), faded American flags marked the final resting place of those who had fallen in the Civil or Spanish-American wars. It was a mile farther to the end of the line. There the conductor switched the trolley for the return trip, and the colored woman started off across an open field.

A winding path through the oak trees led her eventually to a cottage resting on concrete blocks, with a peaked roof and a porch across the front, facing the lake. Wide wooden shutters hinged at the top and propped up on poles gave the cottage a curious effect, as of a creosote-colored bird about to clap its wings and fly away.

The colored woman entered by the back door, into a kitchen so tiny that there was barely room for her to move between the kerosene stove and the table. She put her pack-ages down and dipped a jelly glass into a bucket of water and drank. Through the thin partition came the sound of a child crying and then a woman's voice, high and clear and excitable.

"Is that you, Adah Belle?"

"Yes'm."

"I thought you'd never come."

The colored woman went into the front part of the cottage, a single disorderly room with magazine covers pasted on the walls, odds and ends of wicker furniture, a grass rug, and two cots. Japanese lanterns hung from the rafters, as if the cottage were in the throes of some shoddy celebration, and the aromatic wood smell from the fireplace was complicated by other odors, kerosene, camphor, and pennyroyal. A little boy a year and a half old was standing in a crib, his face screwed up and red with the exertion of crying. On his neck and arms and legs were the marks of mosquito bites.

"What's he crying about now?" the colored woman asked.

"I wish I knew." The woman's voice came from the porch. "I'll be glad when he can talk. Then we'll at least know what he's crying about."

"He's crying because he miss his Adah Belle," the colored woman said and lifted the little boy out of the crib. The crying subsided and the child's face, streaked with dirt and tears, took on a look of seriousness, of forced maturity. "Don't nobody love you like Adah Belle," she said, crooning over him.

"Virginia saw a snake," the voice called from the porch.

"You don't mean that?"

"A water moccasin. At least I think it was a water moccasin. Anyway it was huge. I threw a stick at it and it went under the porch and now I'm afraid to set foot out of the house."

"You leave that snake alone and he leave you alone," the colored woman said.

"Anything could happen out here," the voice said, "and we haven't a soul to turn to. There isn't even a place to telephone. . . . Was it hot in town?"

"I didn't have no time to notice."

"It was hot out here. I think it's going to storm. The flies have been biting like crazy all afternoon."

A moment later the woman appeared in the doorway. She

was thirty years old, small-boned and slender, with dark hair piled on top of her head, and extraordinarily vivid blue eyes. Her pallor and her seriousness were like the little boy's. "Adah Belle," she said, putting her white hand on the solid black arm, "if it weren't for you—if you didn't come just when I think the whole world's against me, I don't know what I'd do. I think I'd just give up."

"I knows you need me," the colored woman said.

"Sometimes I look at the lake, and then I think of my two children and what would happen to them if I weren't here, and then I think, Adah Belle would look after them. And you would, Adah Belle."

The little boy, seeing his mother's eyes fill with tears, puckered his face up and began to cry again. She took him from the colored woman's arms and said, "Never you mind, my angel darling! Never you mind!" her voice rich with maternal consolation and pity for the lot of all children in a world where harshness and discipline prevail. "This has been going on all day."

"Don't you worry, honey," Adah Belle said. "I look after them and you, too. I got you some pork chops."

"Then you'll have to cook them tonight. They won't keep without ice. The first of the week I'm going in and have things out with the ice company." The white woman's voice and manner had changed. She was in the outer office of the Draperville Ice & Coal Co., demanding that they listen to her, insisting on her rights.

"That flying squirrel been into the spaghetti again," Adah Belle said.

"You should have been here last night. Such a time as I had! I lit the lamp and there he was, up on the rafter—" The woman put her hands to her head, and for the moment it was night. The squirrel was there, ready to swoop down on them, and Adah Belle saw and was caught up in the scene that had taken place in her absence.

"I was terrified he'd get in my hair or knock the lamp over and set fire to the cottage."

"And then what?"

"I didn't know what to do. The children were sitting up in bed watching it. They weren't as frightened as I was, and I knew they oughtn't to be awake at that time of night, so I made them put their heads under the covers, and turned out the light—"

"That squirrel getting mighty bold. Some one of these days he come out in the daytime and I get him with a broom. That be the end of the squirrel. What happen when you turn out the light?"

"After that nothing happened. . . . Adah Belle, did you see Mr. Gellert?"

The colored woman shook her head. "I went to the back door and knock, like I ain't never work there, and after a while *she* come."

"Then she's still there?"

"Yes'm, she's there. She say, 'Adah Belle, is that you?' and I say, 'That's right, it's me. I come to get some things for Miz Gellert.' "

"And she let you in?"

"I march in before she could stop me."

"Weren't you afraid?"

"I march through the kitchen and into the front part of the house with her after me every step of the way."

"Oh, Adah Belle, you're wonderful!"

"I come to get them things for you and ain't no old woman going to stop me."

"She didn't dare not let you in, I guess. She knows I've been to see a lawyer. If I decide to take the case into court—"

With the single dramatic gesture that the white woman made with her bare arm, there was the crowded courtroom, the sea of faces, now friendly, now hostile to the colored woman on the witness stand.

"You going to do that, Miz Gellert?" she asked anxiously.

"I don't know, Adah Belle. I may. Sometimes I think it's the only solution."

From her voice it was clear that she also had reason to be afraid of what would happen in the courtroom. *If anybody is to blame, Mildred is,* her friends were saying over the bridge tables in town, women grown stout on their own accomplished cooking, wearing flowered dresses and the ample unwieldy straw hats of the period. Their faces flushed with the excitement of duplicate bridge and the combinations and permutations of gossip, they said, *If she can't stand to live with Harrison, then why doesn't she get a divorce?* Behind this attack was the voice of fear (in a high-keyed Middle Western accent), the voice of doubt.

They were not, like Mildred Gellert, having trouble with their husbands. Their marriages were successful, their children took music lessons and won prizes at commencement, and they had every reason in the world to be satisfied (new curtains for the living room, a glassed-in sun porch), every reason to be happy. It was only that sometimes when they woke in the middle of the night and couldn't get to sleep for a while, and so reviewed their lives, something (what, exactly, they couldn't say) seemed missing. The opportunity that they had always assumed would come to them hadn't come after all. *You mark my words*, the women said to each other (the words of fear, the counsel of doubt), *when cold weather comes, she'll go back to him.*

But could Mildred go back to him? After all, with his mother staying there keeping house for him, he might not want her back.

Oh he'll take her back, the women said, on the wide verandah of the brick mansion on College Avenue. *All you have to do is look at him to tell that. . . .*

The hangdog expression, they meant; the pale abject look of apology that didn't prevent him from nagging her about the grocery bills or from being insanely jealous whenever they were in mixed company and she showed the slightest sign of enjoying herself.

But it really was not fair to the friends who had stood by her again and again. The first two times Mildred Gellert left her husband, the women one and all stopped speaking to him, out of loyalty to her, they said. And then when she went back to him, it was very embarrassing to go to the house on Eighth Street and have to act as if nothing had happened. This time when he tipped his hat to them, they spoke. *There's no use fighting other people's battles*, they said, slipping their pumps off surreptitiously under the bridge table. *They never thank you for it. Besides, I like Harrison. I always have. I know he's difficult, but then Mildred isn't the easiest person in the world to get along with, either, and I think he tries to do what is right and she ought to take that into consideration.*

The tragic heroine takes everything into consideration. That is her trouble, the thing that paralyzes her. While her lawyer is explaining to her the advantages of separate maintenance over an outright divorce, she considers the shape of his hands and how some people have nothing but happiness while they are young, and then, later, nothing but unhappiness.

Much as I like Mildred, the women said, driving back from the lake after listening to a three-hour monologue that had been every bit as good as a play, *I can't get worked up over it any more. Besides, it's bad for the children. And if you ask me, I don't think she knows what she wants to do.*

This was quite right. Mildred Gellert left her husband and took a cottage out at the lake, in September, when all the other cottages were empty and boarded up, and this, of course, didn't solve anything but merely postponed the decision that could not be made until later in the fall, when some other postponement would have to be found, some new half measure.

Did you hear her ask me if I'd seen Harrison? the women said as the carriage reached the outskirts of town.

She wanted to know if he'd been at our house and I said right out that Ralph and I had been to call on his mother. She knows the old lady is there, and I thought I might as well be truthful with her because she might find it out some other way. I was all set to say, "Well, Mildred, if we all picked up our children and left our husbands every six months—" but she didn't say anything, so naturally I couldn't. But I know one thing. I'm not going all the way out there again in this heat just to hear the same old story about how Harrison wouldn't let her go to Peoria. And besides she did go, so what's there to get excited about? If she wants to see me, she can just get on the streetcar and come into town. After all, there's a limit.

The limit is boredom. Unless the tragic heroine can produce new stories, new black-and-blue marks, new threats and outrages that exceed in dramatic quality the old ones, it is better that she stay, no matter how unhappily, with her husband. So says the voice of doubt, the wisdom of fear.

In the front room of the cottage out at the lake Adah Belle said, "She's been changing things around some."

"What?"

"She's got the sofa in the bay window where the table belong, and the table is out in the center of the room."

"I tried them that way but it doesn't work," Mildred Gellert said.

"It don't look natural," the colored woman agreed. "It was better the way you had it. She asked me did I know where to look for what I wanted and I said I could put my hands right on everything, so she sat down and commenced to read, and I took myself off upstairs."

"When Virginia was a baby, Mother Gellert came and stayed with her so Mr. Gellert and I could go to Chicago. When I got back she'd straightened all the dresser drawers and I thought I'd go out of my mind trying to figure out where she could have put things. She'd even got into the cedar chest and wrapped everything up in newspaper. She smiles at you and looks as though butter wouldn't melt in her mouth, and then the minute your back is turned— Did she ask for me?"

"No'm, I can't say she did."

"Or about the children?"

The colored woman shook her head.

"You'd think she might at least ask about her own grand-children," Mildred Gellert said. Her eagerness gave way to disappointment. There was something that she had been expecting from this visit of Adah Belle's to the house on Eighth Street, something besides the woollens that Adah Belle had been instructed to get. "Was there any mail?"

"Well, they was this postcard for little Virginia. It was upstairs on the table beside the bed in her room. I don't know how that child's going to get it if she's out here. But anyway, I stick it inside my dress without asking."

"It's from her Sunday school teacher," Mildred Gellert said, and put the postcard—a view of stalagmites and stalactites in Mammoth Cave, Kentucky—on the mantel.

"While I was at it, I took a look around," Adah Belle said.

"Yes?"

"Judging from the guest-room closet, she's move in to stay."

"That's all right with me," Mildred Gellert said, her voice suddenly harsh with bitterness. "From now on it's her house. She can do anything she likes with it." As she put the little boy in the crib, her mind was filled with possibilities. She would force Harrison to give her the house on Eighth Street; or, if that proved too expensive for her to manage on the money the court allowed her, she could always rent those four upstairs rooms over old Mrs. Marshall. Adah Belle would look after the children in the daytime, and she could get a job in Lembach's selling dresses or teach domestic science in the high school.

"She save brown-paper bags. And string."

"Don't get me started on that," Mildred Gellert said. "Did she say anything when you left?"

"I call out to her I was leaving," Adah Belle said, "and when she come out of the library she had these two boxes in her hand."

"What two boxes?"

"I got them with me in the kitchen. 'Will you give these to the children,' she says. 'They're from Mr. Gellert. I don't know whether Mrs. Gellert will want them to have presents from their father or not, but you can ask her.' "

"As a matter of fact, I don't," Mildred Gellert said.

Out in the kitchen she broke the string on the larger package and opened it. "Building blocks," she said. The other box was flat and square and contained a child's handkerchief with a lavender butterfly embroidered in one corner. "I wish he wouldn't do things like that. With Edward it doesn't matter, but the sooner Virginia forgets her father, the better. He ought to realize that."

"He don't mean no harm by it," the colored woman said.

Mildred Gellert looked at her. "Are you going to turn against me, too?"

"No'm," Adah Belle said. "I ain't turning against you, honey. All I say is he don't mean no harm."

"Well, what he means is one thing," Mildred Gellert said, her eyes fever-bright. "And what he does is just exactly the opposite!" The next time they drove out, her intimate friends, to see her, she would have something to tell them that would make them sit up and take notice. It wasn't enough that Harrison had driven her from the house, forcing her to take refuge out here, in a place with no heat, and fall coming on; that didn't satisfy him. Now he was going to win the children away from her with expensive gifts, so that in the end he'd have everything and she'd be left stranded, with no place to go and no one to turn to. He'd planned it all out, from the very beginning. That would be his revenge.

"What you aim to do with them? Send them back?" Adah Belle asked, looking at the two boxes she had carried all the way out from town.

"Put this on the trash pile and burn it," Mildred Gellert said and left the kitchen.

Outside, under a large oak tree, a little girl of five, her hair in two blond braids, was playing with a strawberry box. She had lined the box with a piece of calico and in it lay a small rubber doll, naked, with a whistle in its stomach. "Now you be quiet," the little girl said to the doll, "and take your nap or I'll slap you."

From her place under the oak tree she watched the colored woman go out to the trash pile with the flat square box, set a match to the accumulation of paper and garbage, and return to the kitchen. The little girl waited a moment and then got up and ran to the fire. She found a stick, pulled the burning box onto the grass, and blew out the flames that were licking at it. Then she ran back to the oak tree with her prize. Part of the linen handkerchief was charred and fell apart in her hands, but the flames hadn't reached the lavender butterfly. The little girl hid the handkerchief under the piece of calico and looked around for a place to put the strawberry box.

When she came into the house, five minutes later, her eyes were blank and innocent. She had learned that much in a year and a half. Her eyes could keep any secret they wanted to. And the box was safe under the porch, where her mother wouldn't dare look for it, because of the snake.

The Pilgrimage

In a rented Renault, with exactly as much luggage as the back seat would hold, Ray and Ellen Ormsby were making a little tour of France. It had so far included Vézelay, the mountain villages of Auvergne, the roses and Roman ruins of Provence, and the gorges of the Tarn. They were now on their way back to Paris by a route that was neither the most direct nor particularly scenic, and that had been chosen with one thing in mind —dinner at the Hôtel du Domino in Périgueux. The Richardsons, who were close friends of the Ormsbys in America, had insisted that they go there. "The best dinner I ever had in my entire life," Jerry Richardson had said. "Every course was something with truffles." "And the dessert," Anne Richardson had said, "was little balls of various kinds of ice cream in a beautiful basket of spun sugar with a spun-sugar bow." Putting the two statements together, Ray Ormsby had persisted in thinking that the ice cream also had truffles in it, and Ellen had given up trying to correct this impression.

At seven o'clock, they were still sixty-five kilometres from Périgueux, on a winding back-country road, and beginning to get hungry. The landscape was gilded with the evening light. Ray was driving. Ellen read aloud to him from the "Guide Gastronomique de la France" the paragraph on the Hôtel du Domino: *"Bel et confortable établissement à la renommée bien assise et que Mme. Lasgrezas dirige avec beaucoup de bonheur. Grâce à un maître queux qualifié, vous y ferez un repas de grande classe qui vous sera servi dans une élégante salle à manger ou dans un délicieux jardin d'été. . . ."*

As they drove through village after village, they saw, in addition to the usual painted Cinzano and Rasurel signs, announcements of the *spécialité* of the restaurant of this or that Hôtel des Sports or de la Poste or du Lion d'Or—always with truffles. In Montignac, there were so many of these signs that Ellen said anxiously, "Do you think we ought to eat *here?*"

"No," Ray said. "Périgueux is the place. It's the capital of Périgord, and so it's bound to have the best food."

Outside Thenon, they had a flat tire—the seventh in eight days of driving—and the casing of the spare tire was in such bad condition that Ray was afraid to drive on until the inner tube had been repaired and the regular tire put back on. It was five minutes of nine when they drove up before the Hôtel du Domino, and they were famished. Ray went inside and found that the hotel had accommodations for them. The car was driven into the hotel garage and emptied of its formidable luggage, and the Ormsbys were shown up to their third-floor room, which might have been in any plain hotel anywhere in France. "What I'd really like is the roast chicken stuffed with truffles," Ellen said from the washstand. "But probably it takes a long time."

"What if it does," Ray said. "We'll be eating other things first."

He threw open the shutters and discovered that their room looked out on a painting by Dufy—the large, bare, open square surrounded by stone buildings, with the tricolor for accent, and the sky a rich, stained-glass blue. From another window, at the turning of the stairs on their way down to dinner, they saw the delicious garden, but it was dark, and no one was eating there now. At the foot of the stairs, they paused.

"You wanted the restaurant?" the concierge asked, and when they nodded, she came out from behind her mahogany railing and led them importantly down a corridor. The maître d'hôtel, in a grey business suit, stood waiting at the door of the dining room, and put them at a table for two. Then he handed them the menu with a flourish. They saw at a glance how expensive the dinner was going to be. A waitress brought plates, glasses, napkins, knives, and forks.

While Ellen was reading the menu, Ray looked slowly around the room. The "*élégante salle à manger*" looked like a hotel coffee shop. There weren't even any tablecloths. The walls were painted a dismal shade of off-mustard. His eyes came to rest finally on the stippled brown dado a foot from his face. "It's a perfect room to commit suicide in," he said, and reached for the menu. A moment later he exclaimed, "I don't see the basket of ice cream!"

"It must be there," Ellen said. "Don't get so excited."

"Well, where? Just show me!"

Together they looked through the two columns of desserts, without finding the marvel in question. "Jerry and Anne were here several days," Ellen said. "They may have had it in some other restaurant."

This explanation Ray would not accept. "It was the same dinner, I remember distinctly." The full horror of their driving all the way to Périgueux in order to eat a very expensive meal at the wrong restaurant broke over him. In a cold sweat he got up from the table.

"Where are you going?" Ellen asked.

"I'll be right back," he said, and left the dining room. Upstairs in their room, he dug the "Guide Michelin" out of a duffel-bag. He had lost all faith in the "Guide Gastronomique," because of its description of the dining room; the person who wrote that had never set eyes on the Hôtel du Domino or, probably, on Périgueux. In the "Michelin," the restaurant of the Hôtel du Domino rated one star and so did the restaurant Le Montaigne, but Le Montaigne also had three crossed forks and spoons, and suddenly it came to him, with the awful clarity of a long-submerged memory at last brought to the surface through layer after layer of consciousness, that it was at Le Montaigne and not at the Hôtel du Domino that the Richardsons had meant them to eat. He picked up Ellen's coat and, still carrying the "Michelin," went back downstairs to the dining room.

"I've brought you your coat," he said to Ellen as he sat down opposite her. "We're in the wrong restaurant."

"We aren't either," Ellen said. "And even if we were, I've *got* to have something to eat. I'm starving, and it's much too late now to go looking for—"

"It won't be far," Ray said. "Come on." He looked up into the face of the maître d'hôtel, waiting with his pencil and pad to take their order.

"You speak English?" Ray asked.

The maître d'hôtel nodded, and Ray described the basket of spun sugar filled with different kinds of ice cream.

"And a spun-sugar bow," Ellen said.

The maître d'hôtel looked blank, and so Ray tried again, speaking slowly and distinctly.

"*Omelette?*" the maître d'hôtel said.

"No—ice cream!"

"*Glace*," Ellen said.

"*Et du sucre*," Ray said. "*Une—*" He and Ellen looked at each other. Neither of them could think of the word for "basket."

The maître d'hôtel went over to a sideboard and returned with another menu. "*Le menu des glaces*," he said coldly. "*Vanille*," they read, "*chocolat, pistache, framboise, fraise, tutti-frutti, praliné . . .*"

Even if the spun-sugar basket had been on the *menu des glaces* (which it wasn't), they were in too excited a state to have found it—Ray because of his fear that they were making an irremediable mistake in having dinner at this restaurant and Ellen because of the dreadful way he was acting.

"We came here on a pilgrimage," he said to the maître d'hôtel, in a tense, excited voice that carried all over the dining room. "We have these friends in America who ate in Périgueux, and it is absolutely necessary that we eat in the place they told us about."

"This is a very good restaurant," the maître d'hôtel said. "We have many *spécialités. Foie gras truffé, poulet du Périgord noir, truffes sous la cendre—*"

"I know," Ray said, "but apparently it isn't the right one." He got up from his chair, and Ellen, shaking her head—because there was no use arguing with him when he was like this—got up, too. The other diners had all turned around to watch.

"Come," the maître d'hôtel said, taking hold of Ray's elbow. "In the lobby is a lady who speaks English very well. She will understand what it is you want."

In the lobby, Ray told his story again—how they had come to Périgueux because their friends in America had told them about a certain restaurant here, and how it was this restaurant and no other that they must find. They had thought it was the restaurant in the Hôtel du Domino, but since the restaurant of the Hôtel du Domino did not have the dessert that their friends in America had particularly recommended, little balls of ice cream in—

The concierge, her eyes large with sudden comprehension, interrupted him. "You wanted truffles?"

Out on the sidewalk, trying to read the "Michelin" map of Périgueux by the feeble light of a tall street lamp, Ray said, "Le Montaigne has a star just like the Hôtel du Domino, but it also has three crossed forks and spoons, so it must be better than the hotel."

"All those crossed forks and spoons mean is that it is a very comfortable place to eat in," Ellen said. "It has nothing to do with the quality of the food. I don't care where we eat, so long as I don't have to go back there."

There were circles of fatigue under her eyes. She was both

exasperated with him and proud of him for insisting on getting what they had come here for, when most people would have given in and taken what there was. They walked on a couple of blocks and came to a second open square. Ray stopped a man and woman.

"*Pardon, m'sieur,*" he said, removing his hat. "*Le restaurant La Montagne, c'est par là*"—he pointed—"*ou par là?*"

"*La Montagne? Le restaurant La Montagne?*" the man said dubiously. "*Je regrette, mais je ne le connais pas.*"

Ray opened the "Michelin" and, by the light of the nearest neon sign, the man and woman read down the page.

"*Ooh,* LE MONTAIGNE*!*" the woman exclaimed suddenly.

"LE MONTAIGNE*!*" the man echoed.

"*Oui, Le Montaigne,*" Ray said, nodding.

The man pointed across the square.

Standing in front of Le Montaigne, Ray again had doubts. It was much larger than the restaurant of the Hôtel du Domino, but it looked much more like a bar than a first-class restaurant. And again there were no tablecloths. A waiter approached them as they stood undecided on the sidewalk. Ray asked to see the menu, and the waiter disappeared into the building. A moment later, a second waiter appeared. "*Le menu,*" he said, pointing to a standard a few feet away. Le Montaigne offered many specialties, most of them *truffés,* but not the Richardsons' dessert.

"Couldn't we just go someplace and have an ordinary meal?" Ellen said. "I don't think I feel like eating anything elaborate any longer."

But Ray had made a discovery. "The restaurant is upstairs," he said. "What we've been looking at is the café, so naturally there aren't any tablecloths."

Taking Ellen by the hand, he started up what turned out to be a circular staircase. The second floor of the building was dark. Ellen, convinced that the restaurant had stopped serving dinner, objected to going any farther, but Ray went on, and, protesting, she followed him. The third floor was brightly lighted—was, in fact, a restaurant, with white tablecloths, gleaming crystal, and the traditional dark-red plush upholstery, and two or three clients who were lingering over the end of dinner. The maître d'hôtel, in a black dinner jacket, led them to a table and handed them the same menu they had read downstairs.

"I don't see any roast chicken stuffed with truffles," Ellen said.

"Oh, I forgot that's what you wanted!" Ray said, conscience-stricken. "Did they have it at the Domino?"

"No, but they had *poulet noir*—and here they don't even have that."

"I'm so sorry," he said. "Are you sure they don't have it here?" He ran his eyes down the list of dishes with truffles and said suddenly, "There it is!"

"Where?" Ellen demanded. He pointed to "*Tournedos aux truffes du Périgord.*" "That's not chicken," Ellen said.

"Well, it's no good, then," Ray said.

"No good?" the maître d'hôtel said indignantly. "It's *very* good! *Le tournedos aux truffes du Périgord* is a *spécialité* of the restaurant!"

They were only partly successful in conveying to him that that was not what Ray had meant.

No, there was no roast chicken stuffed with truffles.

No chicken of any kind.

"I'm very sorry," Ray said, and got up from his chair.

He was not at all sure that Ellen would go back to the restaurant in the Hôtel du Domino with him, but she did. Their table was just as they had left it. A waiter and a busboy, seeing them come in, exchanged startled whispers. The maître d'hôtel did not come near them for several minutes after they had sat down, and Ray carefully didn't look around for him.

"Do you think he is angry because we walked out?" Ellen asked.

Ray shook his head. "I think we hurt his feelings, though. I think he prides himself on speaking English, and now he will never again be sure that he does speak it, because of us."

Eventually, the maître d'hôtel appeared at their table. Sickly smiles were exchanged all around, and the menu was offered for the second time, without the flourish.

"What is *les truffes sous la cendre?*" Ellen asked.

"It takes forty-five minutes," the maître d'hôtel said.

"*Le foie gras truffé,*" Ray said. "For two."

"*Le foie gras,* O.K.," the maître d'hôtel said. "*Et ensuite?*"

"*Œufs en gelée,*" Ellen said.

"*Œufs en gelée,* O.K."

"*Le poulet noir,*" Ray said.

"*Le poulet noir,* O.K."

"*Et deux Cinzano,*" Ray said, on solid ground at last, "*avec un morceau de glace et un zeste de citron. S'il vous plaît.*"

The apéritif arrived, with ice and lemon peel, but the wine list was not presented, and Ray asked the waitress for it. She spoke to the maître d'hôtel, and that was the last the Ormsbys ever saw of her. The maître d'hôtel brought the wine list, they ordered the dry white *vin du pays* that he recommended, and their dinner was served to them by a waiter so young that Ray looked to see whether he was in knee pants.

The pâté was everything the Richardsons had said it would be, and Ray, to make up for all he had put his wife through in the course of the evening, gave her a small quantity of his, which, protesting, she accepted. The maître d'hôtel stopped at their table and said, "Is it good?"

"Very good," they said simultaneously.

The *œufs en gelée* arrived and were also very good, but were they any better than or even as good as the *œufs en gelée* the Ormsbys had had in the restaurant of a hotel on the outskirts of Aix-en-Provence was the question.

"Is it good?" the maître d'hôtel asked.

"Very good," they said. "So is the wine."

The boy waiter brought in the *poulet noir*—a chicken casserole with a dark-brown Madeira sauce full of chopped truffles.

"Is it good?" Ray asked when the waiter had finished serving them and Ellen had tasted the *pièce de résistance*.

"It's very good," she said. "But I'm not sure I can taste the truffles."

"I think I can," he said, a moment later.

"With the roast chicken, it probably would have been quite easy," Ellen said.

"Are you sure the Richardsons had roast chicken stuffed with truffles?" Ray asked.

"I think so," Ellen said. "Anyway, I know I've read about it."

"Is it good?" the maître d'hôtel, their waiter, and the waiter from a neighboring table asked, in succession.

"Very good," the Ormsbys said.

Since they couldn't have the little balls of various kinds of ice cream in a basket of spun sugar with a spun-sugar bow for dessert, they decided not to have any dessert at all. The meal came to an abrupt end with *café filtre*.

Intending to take a short walk before going to bed, they heard dance music in the square in front of Le Montaigne, and found a large crowd there, celebrating the annual fair of Périgueux. There was a seven-piece orchestra on a raised platform under a canvas, and a few couples were dancing in the street. Soon there were more.

"Do you feel like dancing?" Ray asked.

The pavement was not as bad for dancing as he would have

supposed, and something happened to them that had never happened to them anywhere in France before—something remarkable. In spite of their clothes and their faces and the "Michelin" he held in one hand, eyes constantly swept over them or past them without pausing. Dancing in the street, they aroused no curiosity and, in fact, no interest whatever.

At midnight, standing on the balcony outside their room, they could still hear the music, a quarter of a mile away.

"Hasn't it been a lovely evening!" Ellen said. "I'll always remember dancing in the street in Périgueux."

Two people emerged from the cinema, a few doors from the Hôtel du Domino. And then a few more—a pair of lovers, a woman, a boy, a woman and a man carrying a sleeping child.

"The pâté was the best I ever ate," Ellen said.

"The Richardsons probably ate in the garden," Ray said. "I don't know that the dinner as a whole was all *that* good," he added thoughtfully. And then, "I don't know that we need tell them."

"The poor people who run the cinema," Ellen said.

"Why?"

"No one came to see the movie."

"I suppose Périgueux really isn't the kind of town that would support a movie theatre," Ray said.

"That's it," Ellen said. "Here, when people want to relax and enjoy themselves, they have an apéritif, they walk up and down in the evening air, they dance in the street, the way people used to do before there were any movies. It's another civilization entirely from anything we're accustomed to. Another world."

They went back into the bedroom and closed the shutters. A few minutes later, some more people emerged from the

movie theatre, and some more, and some more, and then a great
crowd came streaming out and, walking gravely, like people
taking part in a religious procession, fanned out across the
open square.

The Patterns of Love

Kate Talbot's bantam rooster, awakened by the sudden appearance of the moon from behind a cloud on a white June night, began to crow. There were three bantams—a cock and two hens—and their roost was in a tree just outside the guest-room windows. The guest room was on the first floor and the Talbots' guest that weekend was a young man by the name of Arnold, a rather light sleeper. He got up and closed the windows and went back to bed. In the sealed room he slept, but was awakened at frequent intervals until daylight Saturday morning.

Arnold had been coming to the Talbots' place in Wilton sometime during the spring or early summer for a number of years. His visits were, for the children, one of a thousand seasonal events that could be counted on, less exciting than the appearance of the first robin or the arrival of violets in the marsh at the foot of the Talbots' hill but akin to them. Sometimes Duncan, the Talbots' older boy, who for a long time was under the impression that Arnold came to see *him*, slept in the guest room when Arnold was there. Last year, George, Duncan's younger brother, had been given that privilege. This time, Mrs. Talbot, knowing how talkative the boys were when they awoke in the morning, had left Arnold to himself.

When he came out of his room, Mrs. Talbot and George, the apple of her eye, were still at breakfast. George was six, small and delicate and very blond, not really interested in food at any time, and certainly not now, when there was a guest in the house. He was in his pyjamas and a pink quilted bathrobe. He smiled at Arnold with his large and very gentle eyes and said, "Did you miss me?"

"Yes, of course," Arnold said. "I woke up and there was the other bed, flat and empty. Nobody to talk to while I looked at the ceiling. Nobody to watch me shave."

George was very pleased that his absence had been felt. "What is your favorite color?" he asked.

"Red," Arnold said, without having to consider.

"Mine, too," George said, and his face became so illuminated with pleasure at this coincidence that for a moment he looked angelic.

"No matter how much we disagree about other things," Arnold said, "we'll always have that in common, won't we?"

"Yes," George said.

"You'd both better eat your cereal," Mrs. Talbot said.

Arnold looked at her while she was pouring his coffee and wondered if there wasn't something back of her remark—jealousy, perhaps. Mrs. Talbot was a very soft-hearted woman, but for some reason she seemed to be ashamed—or perhaps afraid—to let other people know it. She took refuge continually behind a dry humor. There was probably very little likelihood that George would be as fond of anyone else as he was of his mother for many years to come. There was no real reason for her to be jealous.

"Did the bantams keep you awake?" she asked.

Arnold shook his head.

"Something tells me you're lying," Mrs. Talbot said. "John didn't wake up, but he felt his responsibilities as a host even so. He cried 'Oh!' in his sleep every time a bantam crowed. You'll have to put up with them on Kate's account. She loves them more than her life."

Excluded from the conversation of the grownups, George finished his cereal and ate part of a soft-boiled egg. Then he asked to be excused and, with pillows and pads which had been brought in from the garden furniture the night before, he made a train right across the dining-room floor. The cook had to step over it when she brought a fresh pot of coffee, and Mrs. Talbot and Arnold had to do likewise when they went out through the dining-room door to look at the bantams. There were only two—the cock and one hen—walking around under the Japanese cherry tree on the terrace. Kate was leaning out of an upstairs window, watching them fondly.

"Have you made your bed?" Mrs. Talbot asked.

The head withdrew.

"Kate is going to a houseparty," Mrs. Talbot said, looking at the bantams. "A sort of houseparty. She's going to stay all night at Mary Sherman's house and there are going to be some boys and they're going to dance to the victrola."

"How old is she, for heaven's sake?" Arnold asked.

"Thirteen," Mrs. Talbot said. "She had her hair cut yesterday and it's too short. It doesn't look right, so I have to do something about it."

"White of egg?" Arnold asked.

"How did you know that?" Mrs. Talbot asked in surprise.

"I remembered it from the last time," Arnold said. "I remembered it because it sounded so drastic."

"It only works with blonds," Mrs. Talbot said. "Will you be able to entertain yourself for a while?"

"Easily," Arnold said. "I saw 'Anna Karenina' in the library and I think I'll take that and go up to the little house."

"Maybe I'd better come with you," Mrs. Talbot said.

The little house was a one-room studio halfway up the hill, about a hundred feet from the big house, with casement windows on two sides and a Franklin stove. It had been built several years before, after Mrs. Talbot had read "A Room of One's Own," and by now it had a slightly musty odor which included lingering traces of wood smoke.

"Hear the wood thrush?" Arnold asked, as Mrs. Talbot threw open the windows for him. They both listened.

"No," she said. "All birds sound alike to me."

"Listen," he said.

This time there was no mistaking it—the liquid notes up and then down the same scale.

"Oh, that," she said. "Yes, I love that," and went off to wash Kate's hair.

From time to time Arnold raised his head from the book he was reading and heard not only the wood thrush but also Duncan and George, quarrelling in the meadow. George's voice was shrill and unhappy and sounded as if he were on the verge of tears. Both boys appeared at the window eventually and asked for permission to come in. The little house was out of bounds to them. Arnold nodded. Duncan, who was nine, crawled in without much difficulty, but George had to be hoisted. No sooner were they inside than they began to fight over a wooden gun which had been broken and mended and was rightly George's, it seemed, though Duncan had it and refused to give it up. He refused to give it up one moment, and the next moment, after a sudden change of heart, pressed it upon George—*forced* George to take it, actually, for by that time George was more concerned about the Talbots' dog, who also wanted to come in.

The dog was a Great Dane, very mild but also very enormous. He answered to the name of Satan. Once Satan was admitted to the little house, it became quite full and rather noisy, but John Talbot appeared and sent the dog out and made the children leave Arnold in peace. They left as they had come, by the window. Arnold watched them and was touched by the way Duncan turned and helped George, who was too small to jump. Also by the way George accepted this help. It was as if their hostility had two faces and one of them was the face of love. Cain and Abel, Arnold thought, and the wood thrush. All immortal.

John Talbot lingered outside the little house. Something had been burrowing in the lily-of-the-valley bed, he said, and had also uprooted several lady's slippers. Arnold suggested that it might be moles.

"More likely a rat," John Talbot said, and his eyes wandered to a two-foot espaliered pear tree. "That pear tree," he said, "we put in over a year ago."

Mrs. Talbot joined them. She had shampooed not only Kate's hair but her own as well.

"It's still alive," John Talbot said, staring at the pear tree, "but it doesn't put out any leaves."

"I should think it would be a shock to a pear tree to be espaliered," Mrs. Talbot said. "Kate's ready to go."

They all piled into the station wagon and took Kate to her party. Her too short blond hair looked quite satisfactory after the egg shampoo, and Mrs. Talbot had made a boutonnière out of a pink geranium and some little blue and white flowers for Kate to wear on her coat. She got out of the car with her suitcase and waved at them from the front steps of the house.

"I hope she has a good time," John Talbot said uneasily as he shifted gears. "It's her first dance with boys. It would be terrible if she didn't have any partners." In his eyes there was a vague threat toward the boys who, in their young callowness, might not appreciate his daughter.

"Kate always has a good time," Mrs. Talbot said. "By the way, have you seen both of the bantam hens today?"

"No," John Talbot said.

"One of them is missing," Mrs. Talbot said.

One of the things that impressed Arnold whenever he stayed with the Talbots was the number and variety of animals they had. Their place was not a farm, after all, but merely a big white brick house in the country, and yet they usually had a dog and a cat, kittens, rabbits, and chickens, all actively involved in the family life. This summer the Talbots weren't able to go in and out by the front door, because a phoebe had built a nest in the porch light. They used the dining-room door instead, and were careful not to leave the porch light on more than a minute or two, lest the eggs be cooked. Arnold came upon some turtle food in his room, and when he asked about it, Mrs. Talbot informed him that there were turtles in the guest room, too. He never came upon the turtles.

The bantams were new this year, and so were the two very small ducklings that at night were put in a paper carton in the sewing room, with an electric-light bulb to keep them warm. In the daytime they hopped in and out of a saucer of milk on the terrace. One of them was called Mr. Rochester because of his distinguished air. The other had no name.

All the while that Mrs. Talbot was making conversation with Arnold, after lunch, she kept her eyes on the dog, who, she explained, was jealous of the ducklings. Once his great head swooped down and he pretended to take a nip at them. A nip would have been enough. Mrs. Talbot spoke to him sharply and he turned his head away in shame.

"They probably smell the way George did when he first came home from the hospital," she said.

"What did George smell like?" Arnold asked.

"Sweetish, actually. Actually awful."

"Was Satan jealous of George when he was a baby?"

"Frightfully," Mrs. Talbot said. "Call Satan!" she shouted to her husband, who was up by the little house. He had found a rat hole near the ravaged lady's slippers and was setting a trap. He called the dog, and the dog went bounding off, devotion in every leap.

While Mrs. Talbot was telling Arnold how they found Satan at the baby's crib one night, Duncan, who was playing only a few yards away with George, suddenly, and for no apparent reason, made his younger brother cry. Mrs. Talbot got up and separated them.

"I wouldn't be surprised if it wasn't time for your nap,

George," she said, but he was not willing to let go of even a small part of the day. He wiped his tears away with his fist and ran from her. She ran after him, laughing, and caught him at the foot of the terrace.

Duncan wandered off into a solitary world of his own, and Arnold, after yawning twice, got up and went into the house. Stretched out on the bed in his room, with the Venetian blinds closed, he began to compare the life of the Talbots with his own well-ordered but childless and animalless life in town. Everywhere they go, he thought, they leave tracks behind them, like people walking in the snow. Paths crisscrossing, lines that are perpetually meeting: the mother's loving pursuit of her youngest, the man's love for his daughter, the dog's love for the man, the two boys' preoccupation with each other. Wheels and diagrams, Arnold said to himself. The patterns of love.

That night Arnold was much less bothered by the crowing, which came to him dimly, through dreams. When he awoke finally and was fully awake, he was conscious of the silence and the sun shining in his eyes. His watch had stopped and it was later than he thought. The Talbots had finished breakfast and the Sunday *Times* was waiting beside his place at the table. While he was eating, John Talbot came in and sat down for a minute, across the table. He had been out early that morning, he said, and had found a chipmunk in the rat trap and also a nest with three bantam eggs in it. The eggs were cold.

He was usually a very quiet, self-contained man. This was the first time Arnold had ever seen him disturbed about anything. "I don't know how we're going to tell Kate," he said. "She'll be very upset."

Kate came home sooner than they expected her, on the bus. She came up the driveway, lugging her suitcase.

"Did you have a good time?" Mrs. Talbot called to her from the terrace.

"Yes," she said, "I had a beautiful time."

Arnold looked at the two boys, expecting them to blurt out the tragedy as soon as Kate put down her suitcase, but they didn't. It was her father who told her, in such a roundabout way that she didn't seem to understand at all what he was saying. Mrs. Talbot interrupted him with the flat facts; the bantam hen was not on her nest and therefore, in all probability, had been killed, maybe by the rat.

Kate went into the house. The others remained on the terrace. The dog didn't snap at the ducklings, though his mind was on them still, and the two boys didn't quarrel. In spite of the patterns on which they seem so intent, Arnold thought, what happens to one of them happens to all. They are helplessly involved in Kate's loss.

At noon other guests arrived, two families with children. There was a picnic, with hot dogs and bowls of salad, cake, and wine, out under the grape arbor. When the guests departed, toward the end of the afternoon, the family came together again on the terrace. Kate was lying on the ground, on her stomach, with her face resting on her arms, her head practically in the ducklings' saucer of milk. Mrs. Talbot, who had stretched out on the garden chaise longue, discovered suddenly that Mr. Rochester was missing. She sat up in alarm and cried, "Where is he?"

"Down my neck," Kate said.

The duck emerged from her crossed arms. He crawled around them and climbed up on the back of her neck. Kate smiled. The sight of the duck's tiny downy head among her pale ash-blond curls made them all burst out laughing. The cloud that had been hanging over the household evaporated into bright sunshine, and Arnold seized that moment to glance at his watch.

They all went to the train with him, including the dog. At the last moment Mrs. Talbot, out of a sudden perception of his lonely life, tried to give him some radishes, but he refused them. When he stepped out of the car at the station, the boys were arguing and were with difficulty persuaded to say good-bye to him. He watched the station wagon drive away and then stood listening for the sound of the wood thrush. But, of course, in the center of South Norwalk there was no such sound.

What Every Boy
Should Know

Shortly before his twelfth birthday, Edward Gellert's eyes were opened and he knew that he was naked. More subtle than any beast of the field, more rational than Adam, he did not hide himself from the presence of God or sew fig leaves together. The most he could hope for was to keep his father and mother, his teachers, people in general from knowing. He took elaborate precautions against being surprised, each time it was always the last time, and afterward he examined himself in the harsh light of the bathroom mirror. It did not show yet, but when the mark appeared it would be indelible and it would be his undoing.

People asked him, Who is your girl? And he said, I have no girl, and they laughed and his mother said, Edward doesn't care for girls, and they said, All that will change.

People said, Edward is a good boy, and that was because they didn't know.

He touched Darwin and got an electric shock: ". . . the hair is chiefly retained in the male sex on the chest and face, and in both sexes at the juncture of all four limbs with the trunk. . . ." There was more, but he heard someone coming and had to replace the book on the shelf.

He stopped asking questions, though his mind was teeming with them, lest someone question him. And because it was no use; the questions he wanted to ask were the questions grown people and even older boys did not want to answer. This did not interrupt the incessant kaleidoscopic patterns of ignorance and uncertainty: How did they know that people were really dead, that they wouldn't open their eyes suddenly and try to push their way out of the coffin? And how did the worms get to them if the casket was inside an outer casket that was metal? And when Mrs. Spelman died and Mr. Spelman married again, how was it arranged so that there was no embarrassment later on when he and the first Mrs. Spelman met in Heaven?

Harrison Gellert's boy, people said, seeing him go by on his way to school. To get to him, though, you had first to get past his one-tube radio, his experimental chemistry set, his growing ball of lead foil, his correspondence with the Scott Stamp & Coin Co., his automatically evasive answers.

Pure, self-centered, a moral outcast, he sat through church, in his blue serge Sunday suit, and heard the Reverend Harry Blair who baptized him say solemnly from the pulpit that he was conceived in sin. But afterward, at the church door, in the brilliant sunshine, he shook hands with Edward; he said he was happy to have Edward with them.

In the bookcase in the upstairs hall Edward found a book that seemed to have been put there by someone for his enlightenment. It was called "What Every Boy Should Know," and it told him nothing that he didn't know already.

Arrived at the age of exploration, he charted his course by a map that showed India as an island. The Pacific Ocean was overlooked somehow. Greenland was attached to China, and rivers flowed into the wrong sea. The map enabled him to determine his latitude with a certain amount of accuracy, but for his longitude he was dependent on dead reckoning. In his search for an interior passage, he continually mistook inlets for estuaries. The Known World is not, of course, known. It probably never will be, because of those areas the mapmakers have very sensibly agreed to ignore, where the terrain is different for every traveller who crosses them. Or fails to cross them. The Unknown World, indicated by dotted lines or by no lines at all, was based on the reports of one or two boys in little better case than Edward and frightened like him by tales of sea monsters, of abysses at the world's end.

A savage ill at ease among the overcivilized, Edward remembered to wash his hands and face before he came to the table, and was sent away again because he forgot to put on a coat or a sweater. He slept with a stocking top on his head and left his roller skates where someone could fall over them. It was never wise to send him on any kind of involved errand.

He was sometimes a child, sometimes an adult in the uncomfortable small size. He had opinions but they were not listened to. He blushed easily and he had his feelings hurt. His jokes were not always successful, having a point that escaped most people, or that annoyed his father. His sister Virginia was real, but his father and mother he was aware of mostly as generalities, agents of authority or love or discipline, telling him to sit up straight in his chair, to stand with his shoulders back, to pick up his clothes, read in a better light, stop chewing his nails, stop sniffing and go upstairs and get a handkerchief. When his father asked some question at the dinner table and his mother didn't answer, or, looking down at her plate, answered inaudibly, and when his father then, in the face of these warnings, pursued the matter until she left the table and went upstairs, it didn't mean that his mother and father didn't love each other, or that Edward didn't have as happy a home as any other boy.

Meanwhile, his plans made, his blue eyes a facsimile of innocence, he waited for them all to go some place. Who then moved through the still house? No known Edward. A murderer with flowers in his hair. A male impersonator. A newt undergoing metamorphosis. Now this, now that mirror was his accomplice. The furniture was accessory to the fact. The house being old, he could count on the back stairs to cry out at the approach of discovery. When help came, it came from the outside as usual. Harrison Gellert, passing the door of his son's room one November night, seeing Edward with his hand at the knob of his radio and the headphones over his ears, re-flected on Edward's thinness, his pallor, his poor posture, his moodiness of late, and concluded that he did not spend enough time out-of-doors. Edward was past the age when you could tell him to go outside and play, but if he had a job of some kind that would keep him out in the open air, like delivering papers . . . Too shocked to argue with his father (you don't ask some-one to give you a job out of the kindness of their heart when they don't even know you and also when there may not even be any job or if there is they may have somebody else in mind who would be better at it and who deserves it more), Edward went downtown after school and stood beside the wooden railing in the front office of the Draperville *Evening Star*, wait-ing for someone to notice him. He expected to be sent away in disgrace, and instead he was given a canvas bag and a list of names and told to come around to the rear of the building.

From five o'clock on, all over town, all along College Avenue with its overarching elms, Eighth Street, Ninth Street, Fourth Street, in the block of two-story flats backed up against the railroad tracks, and on those unpaved, nameless streets out where the sidewalk ended and the sky took over, old men sitting by the front window and children at a loss for some-thing to do waited and listened for the sound of the paper striking the porch, and the cry—disembodied and forlorn—of "Pay-er!" Women left their lighted kitchens or put down their sewing in upstairs rooms and went to the front door and looked to see if the evening paper had come. Sometimes spring had come instead, and they smelled the sweet syringa in the next yard. Or the smell was of burning leaves. Sometimes they saw their breath in the icy air. A few minutes later they went to the door and looked again. Left too long, the paper blew out into the yard, got rained on, was covered with snow. Their persistence rewarded at last, they bent down and picked up the paper, opened it, and read the headline, while the paper boy rode on rapidly over lawns he had been told not to ride over, as if he were bent on overtaking lost time or some other paper boy who was not there.

In a place where everybody could easily be traced back to his origin, people did not always know who the paper boy was or care what time he got home to supper. They assumed from a general knowledge of boys that if the paper was late it was because the paper boy dawdled somewhere, shooting marbles, throwing snowballs, when he should have been delivering their paper.

Every afternoon after school the boys rode into the alley behind the *Star* Building, let their bicycles fall with a clatter, and gathered in the cage next to the pressroom. They were dirty-faced, argumentative, and as alike as sparrows. Their pockets sagged with pieces of chalk, balls of string, slingshots, marbles, jackknives, deified objects, trophies they traded. Boasting and being called on to produce evidence in support of what ought to have been true but wasn't, they bet large sums of unreal money or passed along items of misinformation that were gratefully received and stored away in a safe place. Easily deflated, they just as easily recovered their powers of pretending. With the press standing idle, the linotype machine clicking and lisping, the round clock on the wall a torment to them every time they glanced in that direction, they asked, What time is the press going to start?—knowing that the printing press of the Draperville *Evening Star* was all but done for, and that it was a question not of how soon it would start printing but of whether it could be prevailed upon to print at all. When the linotype machines stopped, there was a quarter of an hour of acute uncertainty, during which late-news bulletins were read in reverse, corrections were made in the price of laying mash and ladies' ready-to-wear, and the columns of type were locked in place. The boys waited. The pressroom waited. The front office waited and listened. And suddenly the clean white paper began to move, to flow like a waterfall. Words appeared on one side and then on the other. The clittering clattering discourse gained momentum. The paper was cut, the paper was folded. Smelling of damp ink, copies of the Draperville *Evening Star* slid down a chute and were scooped up and counted by a young man named Homer West, who never broke down or gave trouble to anyone. Cheerful, even-tempered, he handed the papers through a wicket to the seventeen boys who waited in line with their canvas bags slung over one shoulder and their bicycles in a tangle outside. One of them was Homer's brother Harold, but Homer was a brother to all of them. He teased them, eased the pressure of their high-pitched impatience with joking, kept them from fighting each other during that ominous quarter of an hour after the linotype machines fell silent, and listened for the first symptoms of disorder in the press. When it began chewing paper instead of printing, he pulled the switch, and a silence of a deeply discouraging import succeeded the whir and the clitter-clit-clatter. The boys who were left said, I can't wait around here all night, I have homework to do. And Homer, waiting also, for the long day to end and for the time still far in the future when he could afford to get married, said, Do your homework now, why don't you? They said, Here? and he said, Why not? What's the matter with this place? It's warm. You've got electric light. They said, I can't concentrate. And Homer said, Neither can I with you talking to me. He said, It won't be long now. And when they insisted on knowing how long, he said, Pretty soon.

The key to age is patience; and the key to patience is unfortunately age, which cannot be hurried, which takes time (in which to be disappointed); and time is measured by what happens; and what happens is printed (some of it) in the evening paper.

Just when it seemed certain that there would be no more copies of that evening's *Star*, the waterfall resumed its flowing —slowly at first, and then with a kind of frantic confidence.

One after another the boys received their papers through the wicket, counted them, and, with their canvas bags weighted, ran out of the building to mount their bicycles and ride off to the part of town that depended on them for its knowledge of what was going on in the outside world in the year 1922.

After their first mild surprise at finding Eddie Gellert in the cage with them, the other boys accepted his presence there, serene in the knowledge that they could lick him if he started getting wise, and that they had thirty-seven or forty-two or fifty-one customers in a good neighborhood to his thirteen in the poorest-paying section of town. His route had been broken off one of the larger ones, with no harm to the loser, who, that first evening, went with him to point out the houses that took the *Star*, and showed him how to fold the papers as he went along and how to toss them so they landed safely on the porch. After that, Edward was on his own.

The boys received their papers from Homer in rotation, and it was better to be second or third or fourth or even fifth than it was to be first, because if you were first it meant that the next night you would be last. "Pay-er . . ." Edward called, like the others. "Pay-er?"—with his mind on home. His last paper delivered, he turned toward the plate kept warm for him in the oven, the place it would have been so pleasant to come to straight from school. But he was twelve now, and out in the world. He had put the unlimited leisure of childhood behind him. As his father said, he was learning the value of money, his stomach empty, his nostrils burning with the cold, his chin deep in the collar of his Mackinaw.

How much money his father had, Edward did not know. It was one of those interesting questions that grown people do not care to answer. Since his mother was also kept in the dark about this, there was no reason to assume he could find out by asking. But he knew he was expected to do as well some day, and own a nice home and provide decently for the wife and children it was as yet impossible for him to imagine. If all this were easy to manage, then his father would not be upset about lights that were left burning in empty rooms or mention the coal bill every time somebody complained that the house was chilly. Life is serious and without adequate guarantees, whether your mother takes in washing or belongs to the Friday Bridge Club. Poverty is no joke—but neither is the fear of poverty never experienced. Every evening Edward saw, like a lantern slide of failure, the part of town he must never live in, streets that weren't ever going to be paved, in all probability, houses that year after year the banks or the coal company or old Mr. McIvor saw no need for repainting or doing anything about, beyond seeing to it that the people who lived in them paid their rent promptly on the first day of the month.

On Saturday mornings he came with his metal collection book and knocked and the door was opened by a solemn, filthy child or a woman who had no corset on under her housedress and whose hair had not been combed since she got out of bed. The women gave him a dime and took the coupon he held out to them as if that were the commodity in question. If they asked him to step inside he held his breath, ignoring the bad air and an animal odor such as might have been left by foxes or raccoons or wolves in their lair. The women wadded the coupon into a ball or, if they were of a suspicious turn of mind, saved it for the day when he would try to cheat them, and they could triumphantly confront him with the proof of his dishonesty. If they didn't have a dime (often the case in that part of town) or were simply afraid, on principle, to part with money, they put him off with every appearance of not remembering that they had put him off the week before and the week before that. He turned away, disappointed but trying desperately to be polite, and the paper kept on coming.

Regardless of how many customers paid or put off paying the paper boy, the *Evening Star* claimed its percentage every Saturday morning. Any other arrangement would have complicated the bookkeeping, and the owners of the paper did not consider themselves responsible for the riot that broke out, one Friday afternoon, in the cage next to the pressroom. The boys refused to take the papers Homer held out to them through the wicket, and nothing that he said to them had any effect, because their grievances were suddenly intolerable and they themselves were secure in the knowledge (why had they never thought of this before?) that the *Star* was helpless without them. The word "strike" was heard above the sound of the press, which had started on time, for once, and which went right on printing editorial after editorial advising the President of the United States to take over the coal mines—with troops if necessary, since the public welfare was threatened.

At quarter of five, home was not as Edward had remembered it. There was nothing to do, nobody to talk to except Old Mary, and she said, Now don't go spoiling your supper! when all in the world he wanted was company. He went back through the empty uneasy rooms and settled in a big chair in the library with a volume of "Battles and Leaders of the Civil War" on his lap. He didn't read; he only looked at the pictures (a farmhouse near Shiloh, the arsenal at Harper's Ferry) and listened for the sound of a step on the front porch. It was dark outside, and people all over town were beginning to look for the evening paper. His mind was still filled with remembered excitement, triumph that blurred and threatened to turn into worry. But then he turned a page. This had the same effect as when a dreamer, waking, escapes from the nightmare by changing his position in bed.

Virginia came in, and Edward called out to her, but she rushed upstairs, too absorbed in her own world of spit curls and charm bracelets, of what Ossie Dempsey said to Elsie McNish, of TL's and ukuleles, to answer her own brother. And where was his mother?

Mildred Gellert, unable to get along with her husband, unable to bear his bad temper, his nagging, had tried leaving him. Sometimes she took the children with her and sometimes, with her suitcases in the front hall, she clung to them and told them they mustn't forget her, and that when they were older they would understand. The trouble was, they did understand already. For a time it was very exciting, full of subtle moves (she communicated with Harrison through her lawyer) and countermoves (his mother came and kept house for him) like a chess game. The Gellerts' house, no matter who ordered the meals and sat at the opposite end of the dining-room table from Harrison Gellert, had a quality of sadness. This was partly architectural, having to do with the wide overhanging eaves, and partly because the shrubbery—the bridal wreath and barberry—had been allowed to become spindly and the trees kept the sunlight from the lawn. Neither surprised by its own prosperity, like the Tudor and Dutch Colonial houses in the new addition to Draperville, nor frankly shabby, like other old houses of its period, the Gellerts' house and yard were at a standstill, having reached their final look, which owed so much, apparently, to accident, and so little to design or intention or thought.

When Edward walked into Virginia's room she was lying on the bed reading a movie magazine, and she implied that she would just as soon he went somewhere else. Not that he cared. He sat slumped in a chair until she said, "Do you have to breathe like that?"

"Like what?"

"With your mouth open like a fish."

Nothing made him so uncomfortable as being reminded of some part of himself that there was no need to be reminded of. It took all the joy out of life. "This is the way you breathe," he said indignantly. "Just let me give you an imitation."

She laughed scornfully at his attempt to fasten on her a failing she did not have, and so he reminded her—a thing he had meant not to do—that she owed him thirty cents. This led to more insinuations and denials, in the heat of which he forgot he was home early until his mother, standing in the doorway with her hat on, said, "If you children don't stop this eternal arguing, I don't know what I will do!" Neither of them had heard her come upstairs. They looked at each other, conspirators, on the same side. "We're not arguing."

Convicted without a hearing (their mother went on to her own room), they drew apart from each other again. Virginia said, "That was all your fault. I didn't ask you in here, and you're not supposed to come in my room unless I ask you in." Which was a rule she made up, along with a lot of others.

Before they even realized they were arguing again, a voice called, "Children, please! please!" Their mother's voice, so nervous, unhappy, and remote after the Friday Bridge Club. It embarrassed them, reminding them of scenes at the dinner table and conversations between their mother and father that floated up the stairs late at night after they were in bed.

Edward went into the bathroom and ran lukewarm water into the washbasin. It takes patience and some native skill to make a pumice stone float. Absorbed in this delicate task, Edward forgot about his grimy hands and also about the hands of the clock. A warning from his mother as she started down the stairs (how did she know he was in the bathroom?) woke him from a dream of argosies, and the stone boat sank. He arrived in the dining room out of breath, his blond hair slicked down and wet, his hands clean but not his wrists, and an excuse ready on his tongue. He had decided not to mention the strike but it came out just the same. Halfway through dinner it burst out of him, and he felt better immediately.

"How did it start?" Harrison Gellert asked. The lamp that used to hang low over the dining-room table, with its red and green stained glass, its beaded glass fringe, had been replaced, in the last year or two, by glaring wall brackets, a white light in which nothing could be concealed.

"I don't know," Edward said. He passed his plate for a second helping. The plate was filled and passed back to him, and then his father said, "You were there, weren't you?"

"Yes."

"Well, all I'm asking you to tell me is what happened. Something must have happened. How did the strike get started in the first place?"

"I don't remember," Edward said.

He glanced at his sister, across the table. She had stopped eating and with a lurking smile, as if to say *You're going to catch it*, waited for him to flounder in deeper and deeper. He did not hold this against her. The shoe was often enough on the other foot.

"It seemed like it just happened," Edward said, hoping that this explanation, which satisfied him, was truthful and accurate, would also satisfy his father. "I left my arithmetic book in my desk at school and had to go back and get it."

Pleased to have recalled this detail, he stopped and then saw that his father was waiting for him to go on.

"When did the boys decide they weren't going to deliver their papers, before you got there or after?"

"After."

"But the trouble had already started?"

"Not exactly."

"You mean it was like any other evening."

Edward shook his head. What he could not explain was that the boys were always threatening to strike, to quit, to make trouble of one kind or another.

"What are you striking about?"

"The collection. We're supposed to go around collecting on Saturday morning. And people are supposed to pay us, and we're supposed to pay the *Star*. We pay Mrs. Sinclair seven cents and keep three. Only lots of times when we ask for the money, they— You want to see my collection book?"

"No. Just tell me about it."

There were times when, if it hadn't been for the reassurance of Edward's monthly report card, Harrison Gellert would have been forced to wonder if his son were a mental defective. No doubt he was passing through a stage, but it was a very tire-some one.

"Sometimes we have to wait five or six weeks for the money," Edward said.

"But you get it eventually?"

Edward nodded. "But she takes her share right away, out of whatever we do collect, and it's not fair."

"What's unfair about it?"

"She has lots of money and we don't."

"What else are the boys striking for?"

"When the press breaks down, sometimes we don't get home until after seven o'clock. One night it was nearly eight."

"It isn't Mrs. Sinclair's fault that the press breaks down."

To this Edward made no answer.

"What else?"

"We want more money."

"How much more?"

"Oh, let the poor child alone!" Mildred Gellert exclaimed, raising her wan, unhappy face from her salad and looking at her husband.

"He's not a child," Harrison Gellert said. "And I'm not picking on him. How much did you make this week?"

"Thirty-three cents," Edward said. "But some of it was back pay. I only have thirteen customers. Barney Lefferts has the most. He has fifty-two. He makes about a dollar and a half a week when he gets paid."

"That's very good, for a boy."

"I guess so," Edward said.

"Did anybody take the trouble to explain to Mrs. Sinclair why you were refusing to deliver the paper?"

"Oh, yes, but she didn't listen to us. She was awful mad. And Homer was standing there, too."

"What did she say to you?"

"She was inside, where the press and the linotype machines are."

"But what did she say?"

"She tried to get us to deliver the papers. So we all went outside and left her."

"And then what happened?"

"The other guys jumped on their bicycles and rode off."

"And what did you do?"

"I came on home."

"Who's going to deliver our paper?" Virginia asked.

"Nobody, I guess. They can't, if we're all on strike." Edward turned back to his father. "Do you think I did wrong?"

"It's something you're old enough to decide for yourself," Harrison Gellert said. Edward was relieved. On the other hand, it wasn't the same thing as being told that he had his father's complete and wholehearted approval to take part in a strike any time there was one. If he hadn't gone on strike with the others, it would have been uncomfortable. He would have had enemies. The school yard would not have been a very safe place for him, and neither would the alley in the back of the *Star* Building, but actually he had wanted to go out on strike and he had enjoyed the excitement.

"They'll have to take us all back, won't they?" he asked. "Since we all did it together?"

"Finish your potato, dear," Mildred Gellert said. "You're keeping Mary waiting." She was not young any more; she had given up searching for her destiny and had come home, for the sake of the children. Acceptance has its inevitable meager rewards. The side porch was now enclosed, and it was generally agreed that the new green brocade curtains in the living room had cost Harrison plenty.

During dessert, Edward remembered suddenly that he was saving his money to buy a bicycle, and the rice pudding stuck in his throat and would not for the longest time go down. When the others left the dining room, he lingered until Old Mary finished clearing the table and with her hand on the light switch said, "You figure on sitting here in the dark?"

Edward got up and went into the library, where his mother and Virginia were. His mother was sewing. She was changing the hem on Virginia's plaid skirt. Edward sat down, like a visitor waiting to be entertained. He heard the front door open and close, and then his father came in and sat down in his favorite chair and (quite as if he hadn't understood a word of all that Edward had been telling him) opened the evening paper.

When the paper boys ran out of the building, Harold West got as far as the door when Homer called to him. Homer said, "You stay here, Harold," and Harold stayed. After he had delivered his own papers, he rode back downtown and with a list supplied by the front office, he and Homer had started out together. Ever so many houses had no street numbers beside the front steps or on the porch roof; or else the numbers, corroded, painted over five or six times, could not be seen in the dark. Not every subscriber to the Draperville *Evening Star* got a paper that night. The lists were incomplete, and there is no adequate substitution for habit. The office stayed open until ten, and there were a few telephone calls, but most people were not surprised that the evening paper, arriving at such different times every night, should finally have failed to arrive at all.

On Saturday morning, Edward went downtown. He saw a knot of boys standing on the sidewalk in front of the *Star* Building. The riot was over, the strike had collapsed, and though they had counted on him to act with them, they had not bothered to inform him of their surrender. If he hadn't been led there by curiosity, he would have been the only one not now apologizing and asking to have his route given back to him.

Riot, in the soul or in an alley, wears off. It is not self-sustaining. Reason waits, worry bides its time. The recording angel assigned to mark the sparrow's fall took a little extra space in order to record the fact that George Gibbs, Harry Lathrop, John Weiner, Bert Savage, Dave O'Connell, Marvin Shapiro, Barney Lefferts, Edward Gellert, and nine other sparrows were flying and fluttering against a net of their own devising.

One at a time the boys were allowed to go inside. Through the plate-glass window Edward saw Barney Lefferts, sitting in a straight chair beside Mrs. Sinclair's desk, with his eyes lowered, anxiously twisting his dirty old cap while she talked on and on. Once, with an odd gesture of pleading, he interrupted her; he said something that she brushed aside. When Edward looked in the window again, Barney Lefferts was crying. While you are learning the value of money, you learn also—you can't, in fact, help learning—that whoever has it has the right to withhold it. Courage doesn't count, in these circumstances.

When Barney Lefferts came out of the building, all that was behind him and he was triumphant. He said, "Jesus, I got my route back!"

Edward's interview with Mrs. Sinclair was short, and the scolding he got from her was restrained, out of respect for his father's credit and certain social distinctions that both Edward and Mrs. Sinclair were aware of.

"I'm very disappointed in you, Edward," she said. "I know, of course, that you wouldn't have done what you did if you hadn't been led astray by the others. But there was somebody who didn't let himself be led astray. Harold West delivered papers until eleven o'clock, last night, and Mr. Sinclair and I are very grateful to him." She played with a paper clip, and then said, "I know you are sorry, but that isn't the same as if you had behaved in an honorable way, is it? I've decided to let you have your route back, but I want you to promise me, on your word of honor, that if such a thing ever happens again around here, you will be on the side of the Newspaper."

Edward promised, conscious of the fact that her thin, flat chest would not be comforting to put his head on, in time of trouble. He was grateful, but not to her. While he was waiting his turn outside, he had made a bargain: he had offered to give up, from now on, for the rest of his life, the secret, sinful practices that would fill people with horror if they knew and that made God (who did know) sad, if God would give him back his paper route, and God had done it.

"We were thinking of giving you a larger route, Edward," Mrs. Sinclair said, "but I'm afraid, in the light of what happened yesterday . . . Well, we won't talk about it any more. What's done is done. Suppose you go and do your Saturday-morning collecting."

The promise to Mrs. Sinclair, Edward never had an opportunity to keep. The promise to God he broke, over and over and over. He prayed, he made new promises, he offered acts of kindness, acts of self-denial, in place of the one renunciation he could not manage. And though he knew it could not be so, it almost seemed at times as if God did not mind what he did as soon as he had the house all to himself; or else He was trying to make Edward feel worse, because he did get the larger paper route, with fifty-three customers, in a much better part of town, and the total in his bankbook rose higher and higher, with compound interest in red, and finally, on a clear bright windy day in September, Edward went to his father's office after school and a few minutes later they walked around the courthouse square to the bank, and from there they went to Kohler's bicycle shop, where Edward, with his father's solemn approval, parted gladly with his savings and rode off on his heart's delight. The new bicycle was blue and silver, and stood out conspicuously among all the other bicycles in the two long racks in the school yard. It had a headlight and a tool case. He adjusted the handlebars so they were low like the handlebars of a racing bike, and then rode without using them at all, unless it was a matter of keeping the front wheel out of the streetcar track. Boys asked to try his new bicycle out, and rather than get into a fight about it he let them have a brief ride, but it was agony to him until they jumped off and let him have his Blue Racer again. When the bicycle got rained on, he dried it with a rag he kept in his canvas bag. At night he stood it in the woodshed, out of the dew. He would have taken it into his bed if this had been at all practical.

The bicycle was still new, he had only had it a few weeks, when it was run over. It happened on a Saturday noon. Hungry, in a hurry to get home for lunch, he rode up in front of the *Star* Building. A voice in his head reminded him that the boys were not allowed to leave their bicycles in front of the building, and another voice said promptly, She won't see it, and even if she does, this once won't matter. . . . He leaned his bicycle carefully against the high curbing and went inside. There were two boys ahead of him. While he was counting the money in his change purse, a boy opened the street door and shouted, "You better come out here, Gellert! Somebody just ran over your new bicycle!"

Without any feeling whatever, as if he were dreaming, Edward went outside, and a man he'd never seen before said, "I didn't know it was there, and I backed over it."

Edward kept right on, without looking at the man, until he reached the edge of the sidewalk and could look down at what ought to have been somebody else's ruined bicycle, not (oh, please not) his.

His mouth began to quiver.

The man said, "I'm sorry," and Edward burst into tears. What had happened was so terrible, and he felt such pity for the mangled spokes, the tires torn from their rims.

Mrs. Sinclair, seeing that there was trouble of some kind in front of the building, left her desk and went to the door. She looked at the bicycle and then at Edward standing there blindly, with the tears streaming down his face. "You're not supposed to leave your wheels in front of the building," she said, and went inside. People gathered around Edward, trying to console him. The man who had run over Edward's bicycle got into his car and drove away. Someone told Edward his name, and where he lived.

That night Harrison Gellert backed the car out of the garage and, with Edward in the front seat beside him, drove out to the edge of town and stopped in front of a one-story frame house in a poor neighborhood. "You wait here," he said, and got out and went up the brick walk. A man came to the door, and Edward saw a lighted room. His father said something and the man said something. Then he held the screen door open, and his father stepped inside and the door closed. Edward waited in perfect confidence that his father would tell him that it was all settled and the man was going to buy him a new bicycle. Instead, his father came out, after about five minutes, and got in the car and started the engine without saying a word. They were halfway down the block before he turned to Edward and explained that the man didn't know anything about his bicycle.

"But they *said* it was him!"

"I know," Harrison Gellert said. "He may not have been telling the truth."

Conscious of how quiet it had become in the front seat, he added, "Would you like to drive downtown for an ice-cream soda?"

They parked in front of the ice-cream parlor, and his father honked and a high-school boy came out, with a white apron around his hips, and took their order. A few minutes later he reappeared with two tin trays and two tall chocolate sodas. The soda was as good a comfort as any, if Edward had been allowed to eat it in silence, but Harrison Gellert was genuinely distressed and sorry for his son, and his sympathy took the form (as it had in the past when he tried to comfort his wife) of feeling sorry for himself. "As you get older," he said, "you will find that a great many things happen that aren't easy to bear. Things you can't change, no matter how you try. You have to accept them and go right on, doing the best you can."

"But it isn't right!" Edward burst out. "He ran over it. It's his fault!"

"I know all that."

"Then why doesn't he have to pay for it?"

"If it was his fault, he *ought* to pay for having your bicycle repaired. But you can't make him do it if he doesn't want to."

A year earlier, Edward would have cried out, "But *you* can!" He thought it now, but he didn't say it.

"We'll find out from Mr. Kohler how much it will cost to have your bicycle fixed, and I'll go fifty-fifty with you, when it comes to paying for it."

Edward thanked his father politely, but there was no use talking about having his bicycle fixed. It would never be the same. The frame was sprung, and you could always tell a re-painted bike from one that was straight from the factory. His father could go to court if necessary, and the judge would make the man pay for ruining his bicycle, and maybe fine him besides.

"It may be cheaper in the end to get a secondhand bicycle," Mr. Gellert said.

With an effort Edward kept the tears from spilling over. He didn't want a secondhand bicycle. He wanted not to leave his new bicycle in front of the *Star* Building where it would be run over.

And Mr. Gellert wanted to say and didn't say, "I hope this will be a lesson to you."

It was a lesson, of course, in the sense that everything that happens, good or bad, is a lesson.

Edward Gellert was thirteen going on fourteen when the paper boys went on strike against the *Evening Star*, and he was fourteen going on fifteen when his bicycle was run over.

One half the individual nature never seems any different, from the cradle to the grave; the other half is pathetically in step with the slightest physical change. Edward's voice had deepened, hairs had appeared on his body where Darwin said they should appear, his feet and hands were noticeably large for the rest of him, and something would not allow him to kneel in the dark beside his bed and ask God to give him back his new bicycle. People might be raised from the dead, as it said in the Bible, but a ruined bicycle could not by any power on earth or in Heaven be made shining and whole again.

The French Scarecrow

*I spied John Mouldy in his cellar
Deep down twenty steps of stone;
In the dusk he sat a-smiling,
Smiling there alone.*
                    —*Walter de la Mare.*

Driving past the Fishers' house on his way out to the public road, Gerald Martin said to himself absent-mindedly, "There's Edmund working in his garden," before he realized that it was a scarecrow. And two nights later he woke up sweating from a dream, a nightmare, which he related next day, lying tense on the analyst's couch.

"I was in this house, where I knew I oughtn't to be, and I looked around and saw there was a door, and in order to get to it I had to pass a dummy—a dressmaker's dummy without any head."

After a considerable silence the disembodied voice with a German accent said, "Any day remnants?"

"I can't think of any," Gerald Martin said, shifting his position on the couch. "We used to have a dressmaker's dummy in the sewing room when I was a child, but I haven't thought of it for years. The Fishers have a scarecrow in their garden, but I don't think it could be that. The scarecrow looks like Edmund. The same thin shoulders, and his clothes, of course, and the way it stands looking sadly down at the ground. It's a caricature of Edmund. One of those freak accidents. I wonder if they realize it. Edmund is not sad, exactly, but there was a period in his life when he was neither as happy or as hopeful as he is now. Dorothy is a very nice woman. Not at all maternal, I would say. At least, she doesn't mother Edmund. And when you see her with some woman with a baby, she always seems totally indifferent. Edmund was married before, and his first wife left him. Helena was selfish but likable, the way selfish people sometimes are. And where Edmund was concerned, completely heartless. I don't know why. She used to turn the radio on full blast at two o'clock in the morning, when he had to get up at six-thirty to catch a commuting train. And once she sewed a ruffle all the way around the bed he was trying to sleep in. Edmund told me that her mother preferred her older sister, and that Helena's whole childhood had been made miserable because of it. He tried every way he could think of to please her and make her happy, and with most women that would have been enough, I suppose, but it only increased her dissatisfaction. Maybe if there had been any children . . . She used to walk up and down the road in a long red cloak, in the wintertime when there was snow on the ground. And she used to talk about New York. And it was as if she was under a spell and waiting to be delivered. Now she blames Edmund for the divorce. She tells everybody that he took advantage of her. Perhaps he did, unconsciously. Consciously, he wouldn't take advantage of a fly. I think he needs analysis, but he's very much opposed to it. Scared to death of it, in fact . . ."

Step by step, Gerald Martin had managed to put a safe distance between himself and the dream, and he was beginning to breathe easier in the complacent viewing of someone else's failure to meet his problems squarely when the voice said, "Well—see you again?"

"I wish to Christ you wouldn't say that! As if I had any choice in the matter."

His sudden fury was ignored. A familiar hypnotic routine obliged him to sit up and put his feet over the side of the couch. The voice became attached to an elderly man with thick glasses and a round face that Gerald would never get used to. He got up unsteadily and walked toward the door. Only when he was outside, standing in front of the elevator shaft, did he remember that the sewing room had a door opening into his mother and father's bedroom, and at one period of his life he had slept there, in a bed with sides that could be let down, a child's bed. This information was safe from the man inside—unless he happened to think of it while he was lying on the couch next time.

That evening he stopped when he came to the Fishers' vegetable garden and turned the engine off and took a good look at the scarecrow. Then, after a minute or two, afraid that he would be seen from the house, he started the car and drove on.

The Fishers' scarecrow was copied from a scarecrow in France. The summer before, they had spent two weeks as paying guests in a country house in the Touraine, in the hope that this would improve their French. The improvement was all but imperceptible to them afterward, but they did pick up a number of ideas about gardening. In the *potager*, fruit trees, tree roses, flowers, and vegetables were mingled in a way that aroused their admiration, and there was a more than ordinarily fanciful scarecrow, made out of a blue peasant's smock, striped morning trousers, and a straw hat. Under the hat the stuffed head had a face painted on it; and not simply two eyes, a nose, and a mouth but a face with a sly expression. The scarecrow stood with arms upraised, shaking its white-gloved fists at the sky. Indignant, self-centered, half crazy, it seemed to be saying: *This is what it means to be exposed to experience.* The crows were not taken in.

Effects that had needed generations of dedicated French gardeners to bring about were not, of course, to be imitated successfully by two amateur gardeners in Fairfield County in a single summer. The Fishers gave up the idea of marking off the paths of their vegetable garden with espaliered dwarf apple and pear trees, and they could see no way of having tree roses without also having to spray them, and afterward having to eat the spray. But they did plant zinnias, marigolds, and blue pansies in with the lettuce and the peas, and they made a very good scarecrow. Dorothy made it, actually. She was artistic by inclination, and threw herself into all such undertakings with a childish pleasure.

She made the head out of a dish towel stuffed with hay, and was delighted with the blue stripe running down the face. Then she got out her embroidery thread and embroidered a single eye, gathered the cloth in the middle of the face into a bulbous nose, made the mouth leering. For the body she used a torn pair of Edmund's blue jeans she was tired of mending, and a faded blue workshirt. When Edmund, who was attached to his old clothes, saw that she had also helped herself to an Army fatigue hat from the shelf in the hall closet, he exclaimed, "Hey, don't use that hat for the scarecrow! I wear it sometimes."

"*When* do you wear it?"

"I wear it to garden in."

"You can wear some other old hat to garden in. He's got to have something on his head," she said lightly, and made the hat brim dip down over the blank eye.

"When winter comes, I'll wear it again," Edmund said to himself, "if it doesn't shrink too much, or fall apart in the rain."

The scarecrow stood looking toward the house, with one arm limp and one arm extended stiffly, ending in a gloved hand holding a stick. After a few days the head sank and sank until it was resting on the straw breastbone, and the face was concealed by the brim of the hat. They tried to keep the head up with a collar of twisted grass, but the grass dried, and the head sank once more, and in that attitude it remained.

The scarecrow gave them an eerie feeling when they saw it from the bedroom window at twilight. A man standing in the vegetable garden would have looked like a scarecrow. If he didn't move. Dorothy had never lived in the country before she married Edmund, and at first she was afraid. The black windows at night made her nervous. She heard noises in the basement, caused by the steam circulating through the furnace pipes. And she would suddenly have the feeling—even though she knew it was only her imagination—that there was a man outside, looking through the windows at them. "Shouldn't we invite him in?" Edmund would say when her glance strayed for a second. "Offer him a drink and let him sit by the fire? It's not a very nice night out."

He assumed that The Man Outside represented for her all the childish fears—the fear of the dark, of the burglar on the stairs, of what else he had no way of knowing. Nor she either, probably. The Man Outside was simply there, night after night, for about six weeks, and then he lost his power to frighten, and finally went away entirely, leaving the dark outside as familiar and safe to her as the lighted living room. It was Edmund, strangely, who sometimes, as they were getting ready for bed, went to the front and back doors and locked them. For he was aware that the neighborhood was changing, and that things were happening—cars stolen, houses broken into in broad daylight—that never used to happen in this part of the world.

The Fishers' white clapboard house was big and rambling, much added onto at one time or another, but in its final form still plain and pleasant-looking. The original house dated from around 1840. Edmund's father, who was a New York banker until he retired at the age of sixty-five, had bought it before the First World War. At that time there were only five houses on this winding country road, and two of them were farmhouses. When the Fishers came out from town for the summer, they were met at the railroad station by a man with a horse and carriage. The surrounding country was hilly and offered many handsome views, and most of the local names were to be found on old tombstones in the tiny Presbyterian churchyard. Edmund's mother was a passionate and scholarly gardener, the founder of the local garden club and its president for twenty-seven years. Her regal manner was quite unconscious, and based less on the usual foundations of family, money, etc., than on the authority with which she could speak about the culture of delphinium and lilies, or the pruning of roses. The house was set back from the road about three hundred yards, and behind it were the tennis courts, the big three-story barn, a guesthouse overlooking the pond where all the children in the neighborhood skated in winter, and, eventually, a five-car garage. Back of the pond, a wagon road went off into the woods and up onto higher ground. In the late twenties, when Edmund used to bring his school friends home for spring and fall weekends and the Easter vacation, the house seemed barely large enough to hold them all. During the last war, when the taxes began to be burdensome, Edmund's father sold off the back land, with the guesthouse, the barn, and the pond, to a Downtown lawyer, who shortly afterward sold it to a manufacturer of children's underwear. The elder Mr. and Mrs. Fisher started to follow the wagon road back into the woods one pleasant Sunday afternoon, and he ordered them off his property. He was quite within his rights, of course, but nevertheless it rankled. "In the old days," they would say whenever the man's name was mentioned, "you could go anywhere, on anybody's land, and no one ever thought of stopping you."

Edmund's father, working from his own rough plans and supervising the carpenters and plumbers and masons himself, had converted the stone garage into a house, and he had sold it to Gerald Martin, who was a bachelor. The elder Fishers were now living in the Virgin Islands the year round, because of Mrs. Fisher's health. Edmund and Dorothy still had ten acres, but they shared the cinder drive with Gerald and the clothing manufacturer, and, of course, had less privacy than before. The neighborhood itself was no longer the remote place it used to be. The Merritt Parkway had made all the difference. Instead of five houses on the two-and-a-half-mile stretch of dirt road, there were twenty-five, and the road was macadamized. Cars and delivery trucks cruised up and down it all day long.

In spite of all these changes, and in spite of the considerable difference between Edmund's scale of living and his father's —Dorothy had managed with a part-time cleaning woman where in the old days there had been a cook, a waitress, an upstairs maid, a chauffeur, and two gardeners—the big house still seemed to express the financial stability and social confidence and belief in good breeding of the Age of Trellises. Because he had lived in the neighborhood longer than anyone else, Edmund sometimes felt the impulses of a host, but he had learned not to act on them. His mother always used to pay a call on new people within a month of their settling in, and if she liked them, the call was followed by an invitation to the Fishers' for tea or cocktails, at which time she managed to bring up the subject of the garden club. But in the last year or so that she had lived there, she had all but given this up. Twice her call was not returned, and one terribly nice young couple accepted an invitation to tea and blithely forgot to come. Edmund was friendly when he met his neighbors on the road or on the station platform, but he let them go their own way, except for Gerald Martin, who was rather amusing, and obviously lonely, and glad of an invitation to the big house.

I am sewed to this couch," Gerald Martin said. "My sleeves are sewed to it, and my trousers. I could not move if I wanted to. Oedipus is on the wall over me, answering the spink-spank-sphinx, and those are pussy willows, and I do not like bookcases with glass sides that let down, and the scarecrow is gone. I don't know what they did with it, and I don't like to ask. And today *I* might as well be stuffed with straw. The dream I had last night did it. I broke two plates, and woke up unconfident and nervous and tired. I don't know what the dream means. I had three plates and I dropped two of them, and it was so vivid. It was a short dream but very vivid. I thought at first that the second plate—why *three* plates?—was all right, but while I was looking at it, the cracks appeared. When I picked it up, it gave; it came apart in my hands. It was painted with flowers, and it had openwork, and I was in a hurry, and in my hurry I dropped the plates. And I was upset. I hardly ever break anything. Last night while I was drying the glasses, I thought how I never break any of them. They're Swedish and very expensive. The plates I dreamed about were my mother's. Not actually; I *dreamed* that they were my mother's plates. I broke two things of hers when I was little. And both times it was something she had warned me about. I sat in the teacart playing house, and forgot and raised my head suddenly, and it went right through the glass tray. And the other was an etched-glass hurricane lamp that she prized very highly. I climbed up on a chair to reach it. And after she died, I could have thought—I don't ever remember thinking this, but I could have thought that I did something I shouldn't have, and she died. . . . Thank you, I have matches. . . . I can raise my arm. I turned without thinking. I can't figure out that dream. My stepmother was there, washing dishes at the sink, and she turned into Helena Fisher, and I woke up thinking, Ah, that's it. They're *both* my stepmothers! My stepmother never broke anything that belonged to my mother, so she must have been fond of her. They knew each other as girls. And I never broke anything that belonged to my stepmother. I only broke something that belonged to my mother. . . . Did I tell you I saw her the other day?"

"You saw someone who reminded you of your mother?"

"No, I saw Helena Fisher. On Fifth Avenue. I crossed over to the other side of the street, even though I'm still fond of her, because she hasn't been very nice to Dorothy, and because it's all so complicated, and I really didn't have anything to say to her. She was very conspicuous in her country clothes." He lit another cigarette and then said, after a prolonged silence, "I don't seem to have anything to say now, either." The silence became unbearable, and he said, "I can't think of anything to talk about."

"Let's talk about you—about this dream you had," the voice said, kind and patient as always, the voice of his father (at $20 an hour).

T he scarecrow had remained in the Fishers' vegetable garden, with one arm limp and one arm stiffly extended, all summer. The corn and the tomato vines grew up around it, half obscuring it during the summer months, and then, in the fall, there was nothing whatever around it but the bare ground. The blue workshirt faded still more in the sun and rain. The figure grew frail, the straw chest settled and became a middle-aged thickening of the waist. The resemblance to Edmund disappeared. And on a Friday afternoon in October, with snow flurries predicted, Edmund Fisher went about the yard carrying in the outdoor picnic table and benches, picking up stray flowerpots, and taking one last look around for the pruning shears, the trowel, and the nest of screwdrivers that had all disappeared during the summer's gardening. There were still three or four storm windows to put up on the south side of the house, and he was about to bring them out and hang them when Dorothy, on her hands and knees in the iris bed, called to him.

"What about the scarecrow?"

"Do you want to save it?" he asked.

"I don't really care."

"We might as well," he said, and was struck once more by the lifelike quality of the scarecrow, as he lifted it out of the soil. It was almost weightless. "Did the doctor say it was all right for you to do that sort of thing?"

"I didn't ask him," Dorothy said.

"Oughtn't you to ask him?"

"No," she said, smiling at him. She was nearly three months pregnant. Moonfaced, serenely happy, and slow of movement (when she had all her life been so quick about everything), she went about now doing everything she had always done but like somebody in a dream, a sleepwalker. The clock had been replaced by the calendar. Like the gardeners in France, she was dedicated to making something grow. As Edmund carried the scarecrow across the lawn and around the corner of the house, she followed him with her eyes. Why is it, she wondered, that he can never bear to part with anything, even though it has ceased to serve its purpose and he no longer has any interest in it?

It was as if sometime or other in his life he had lost something, of such infinite value that he could never think of it without grieving, and never bear to part with anything worthless because of the thing he had had to part with that meant so much to him. But what? She had no idea, and she had given some thought to the matter. She was sure it was not Helena; he said (and she believed him) that he had long since got over any feeling he once had for her. His parents were both still living, he was an only child, and death seemed never to have touched him. Was it some early love, that he had never felt he dared speak to her about? Some deprivation? Some terrible injustice done to him? She had no way of telling. The attic and the basement testified to his inability to throw things away, and she had given up trying to do anything about either one. The same with people. At the end of a perfectly pleasant evening he would say "Oh no, it's early still. You mustn't go home!" with such fervor that even though it actually was time to go home and the guests wanted to, they would sit down, confused by him, and stay a while longer. And though the Fishers knew more people than they could manage to see, he would suddenly remember somebody he hadn't thought of or written to in a long time, and feel impelled to do something about them. Was it something that happened to him in his childhood, Dorothy asked herself. Or was it something in his temperament, born in him, a flaw in his horoscope, Mercury in an unsympathetic relation to the moon?

She resumed her weeding, conscious in a way that she hadn't been before of the autumn day, of the end of the summer's gardening, of the leaf-smoke smell and the smell of rotting apples, the hickory tree that lost its leaves before all the other trees, the grass so deceptively green, and the chill that had descended now that the sun had gone down behind the western hill.

Standing in the basement, looking at the hopeless disorder ("A place for everything," his father used to say, "and nothing in its place"), Edmund decided that it was more important to get at the storm windows than to find a place for the scarecrow. He laid it on one of the picnic-table benches, with the head toward the oil burner, and there it sprawled, like a man asleep or dead-drunk, with the line of the hipbone showing through the trousers, and one arm extended, resting on a slightly higher workbench, and one shoulder raised slightly, as if the man had started to turn in his sleep. In the dim light it could have been alive. I must remember to tell Dorothy, he thought. If she sees it like that, she'll be frightened.

The storm windows were washed and ready to hang. As Edmund came around the corner of the house, with IX in one hand and XI in the other, the telephone started to ring, and Dorothy went in by the back door to answer it, so he didn't have a chance to tell her about the scarecrow. When he went indoors, ten minutes later, she was still standing by the telephone, and from the fact that she was merely contributing a monosyllable now and then to the conversation, he knew she was talking to Gerald Martin. Gerald was as dear as the day was long—everybody liked him—but he had such a ready access to his own memories, which were so rich in narrative detail and associations that dovetailed into further narratives, that if you were busy it was a pure and simple misfortune to pick up the telephone and hear his cultivated, affectionate voice.

Edmund gave up the idea of hanging the rest of the storm windows, and instead he got in the car and drove to the village; he had remembered that they were out of cat food and whiskey. When he walked into the house, Dorothy said, "I've just had such a scare. I started to go down in the cellar—"

"I knew that would happen," he said, putting his hat and coat in the hall closet. "I meant to tell you."

"The basement light was burnt out," she said, "and so I took the flashlight. And when I saw the scarecrow I thought it was a man."

"Our old friend," he said, shaking his head. "The Man Outside."

"And you weren't here. I knew I was alone in the house . . ."

Her fright was still traceable in her face as she described it.

On Saturday morning, Edmund dressed hurriedly, the alarm clock having failed to go off, and while Dorothy was getting breakfast, he went down to the basement, half asleep, to get the car out and drive to the village for the cleaning woman, and saw the scarecrow in the dim light, sprawling by the furnace, and a great clot of fear seized him and his heart almost stopped beating. It lay there like an awful idiot, the realistic effect accidentally encouraged by the pair of work shoes Edmund had taken off the night before and tossed carelessly down the cellar stairs. The scarecrow had no feet—only two stumps where the trouser legs were tied at the bottom—

but the shoes were where, if it had been alive, they might have been dropped before the person lay down on the bench. I'll have to do something about it, Edmund thought. We can't go on frightening ourselves like this. . . . But the memory of the fright was so real that he felt unwilling to touch the scarecrow. Instead, he left it where it was, for the time being, and backed the car out of the garage.

On the way back from the village, Mrs. Ryan, riding beside him in the front seat of the car, had a story to tell. Among the various people she worked for was a family with three boys. The youngest was in the habit of following her from room to room, and ordinarily he was as good as gold, but yesterday he ran away, she told Edmund. His mother was in town, and the older boys, with some of the neighbors' children, were playing outside with a football, and Mrs. Ryan and the little boy were in the house. "Monroe asked if he could go outside, and I bundled him up and sent him out. I looked outside once, and saw that he was laying with the Bluestones' dog, and I said, 'Monroe, honey, don't pull that dog's tail. He might turn and bite you.'" While she was ironing, the oldest boy came inside for a drink of water, and she asked him where Monroe was, and he said, "Oh, he's outside." But when she went to the door, fifteen minutes later, the older boys were throwing the football again and Monroe was nowhere in sight. The boys didn't know what had happened to him. He disappeared. All around the house was woods, and Mrs. Ryan, in a panic, called and called.

"Usually when I call, he answers immediately, but this time there was no answer, and I went into the house and telephoned the Bluestones, and they hadn't seen him. And then I called the Hayeses and the Murphys, and they hadn't seen him either, and Mr. Hayes came down, and we all started looking for him. Mr. Hayes said only one car had passed in the last half hour— I was afraid he had been kidnapped, Mr. Fisher—and Monroe wasn't in it. And I thought, When his mother comes home and I have to tell her what I've done . . . And just about that time, he answered, from behind the hedge!"

"Was he there all the time?" Edmund asked, shifting into second as he turned in to his own driveway.

"I don't know where he was," Mrs. Ryan said. "But he did the same thing once before—he wandered off on me. Mr. Ryan thinks he followed the Bluestones' dog home. His mother called me up last night and said that he knew he'd done something wrong. He said 'Mummy, I was bad today. I ran off on Sadie. . . .'·But Mr. Fisher, I'm telling you, I was almost out of my mind."

"I don't wonder," Edmund said soberly.

"With woods all around the house, and as Mr. Hayes said, climbing over a stone wall a stone could fall on him and we wouldn't find him for days."

Ten minutes later, she went down to the basement for the scrub bucket, and left the door open at the head of the stairs. Edmund heard her exclaim, for their benefit, "God save us, I've just had the fright of my life!"

She had seen the scarecrow.

The tramp that ran off with the child, of course, Edmund thought. He went downstairs a few minutes later, and saw that Mrs. Ryan had picked the dummy up and stood it in a corner, with its degenerate face to the wall, where it no longer looked human or frightening.

Mrs. Ryan is frightened because of the nonexistent tramp. Dorothy is afraid of The Man Outside. What am I afraid of, he wondered. He stood there waiting for the oracle to answer, and it did, but not until five or six hours later. Poor Gerald Martin called, after lunch, to say that he had the German measles.

"I was sick as a dog all night," he said mournfully. "I thought I was dying. I wrote your telephone number on a slip of paper and put it beside the bed, in case I *did* die."

"Well, for God's sake, why didn't you call us?" Edmund exclaimed.

"What good would it have done?" Gerald said. "All you could have done was say you were sorry."

"Somebody could have come over and looked after you."

"No, somebody couldn't. It's very catching. I think I was exposed to it a week ago at a party in Westport."

"I had German measles when I was a kid," Edmund said. "We've both had it."

"You can get it again," Gerald said. "I still feel terrible. . . ."

When Edmund left the telephone, he made the mistake of mentioning Gerald's illness to Mrs. Ryan, forgetting that it was the kind of thing that was meat and drink to her.

"Has Mrs. Fisher been near him?" she asked, with quickened interest.

He shook his head.

"There's a great deal of it around," Mrs. Ryan said. "My daughter got German measles when she was carrying her first child, and she lost it."

He tried to ask if it was a miscarriage or if the child was born dead, and he couldn't speak; his throat was too dry.

"She was three months along when she had it," Mrs. Ryan went on, without noticing that he was getting paler and paler. "The baby was born alive, but it only lived three days. She's had two other children since. I feel it was a blessing the Lord took that one. If it had lived, it might have been an imbecile. You love them even so, because they belong to you, but it's better if they don't live, Mr. Fisher. We feel it was a blessing the child was taken."

Edmund decided that he wouldn't tell Dorothy, and then five minutes later he decided that he'd better tell her. He went upstairs and into the bedroom where she was resting, and sat down on the edge of the bed, and told her about Gerald's telephone call. "Mrs. Ryan says it's very bad if you catch it while you're pregnant. . . . And she said some more."

"I can see she did, by the look on your face. You shouldn't have mentioned it to her. What did she say?"

"She said—" He swallowed. "She said the child could be born an imbecile. She also said there was a lot of German measles around. You're not worried?"

"We all live in the hand of God."

"I tell myself that every time I'm really frightened. Unfortunately that's the only time I do think it."

"Yes, I know."

Five minutes later, he came back into the room and said, "Why don't you call the doctor? Maybe there's a shot you can take."

The doctor was out making calls, and when he telephoned back, Dorothy answered, on the upstairs extension. Edmund sat down on the bottom step of the stairs and listened to her half of the conversation. As soon as she had hung up, she came down to tell him what the doctor had said.

"The shot only lasts three weeks. He said he'd give it to me if I should be exposed to the measles anywhere."

"Did he say there was an epidemic of it?"

"I didn't ask him. He said that it was commonly supposed to be dangerous during the first three months, but that the statistics showed that it's only the first two months, while the child is being formed, that you have to worry." Moonfaced and serene again, she went to put the kettle on for tea.

Edmund got up and went down to the basement. He carried the dummy outside, removed the hat and then the head, unbuttoned the shirt, removed the straw that filled it and the trousers, and threw it on the compost pile. The hat, the head, the shirt and trousers, the gloves that were hands, he rolled into a bundle and put away on a basement shelf, in case Dorothy wanted to make the scarecrow next summer. The two crossed sticks reminded him of the comfort that Mrs. Ryan, who was a devout Catholic, had and that he did not have. The hum of the vacuum cleaner overhead in the living room, the sad song of a mechanical universe, was all the reassurance he could hope for, and it left so much (it left the scarecrow, for example) completely unexplained and unaccounted for.

Young Francis Whitehead

The Whiteheads lived on the sheltered side of a New Hampshire hill, less than half a mile from town. Their house was set back from the road, and there were so many low-skirted pine trees on both sides of the drive that Miss Avery, who had a parcel under her arm and was coming to see Mrs. Whitehead, was almost up to the house before she could see the green shutters and the high New England roofline. The driveway went past the garage and up to the front door, then around and down again to the road. Both garage doors were open and the afternoon sun shone upon Mrs. Whitehead's Buick sedan and, beside it, a new and shiny blue convertible. While Miss Avery was admiring it, an Irish setter came bounding out of the shrubbery. The dog barked and whined and stepped on Miss Avery's feet and blocked her way no matter where she turned, so that in desperation she gave him a shove with the flat of her hand.

As soon as she did that, a window flew open upstairs and young Francis Whitehead put his head out. "Go on, beat it!" he said. Apparently he had no clothes on. His hair and his face and shoulders were dripping wet, and for a moment Miss Avery wasn't sure whether Francis was talking to her or to the dog. "You silly creature!" he said, and whistled and gave orders and made threats until finally the dog disappeared around the side of the house. Then for the first time Francis looked at Miss Avery. "Oh," he said. "It's you. Come on in, why don't you?"

"All right," she said. "I was just going to."

"I'm in the shower," Francis explained, "but Mother's around somewhere. She'll be glad to see you." He drew his head in and closed the window.

Miss Avery had stood by, in one capacity or another, while Francis learned to walk and to talk, to cut out strings of paper dolls, and ride a bicycle but they had seen very little of each other the last two or three years. Francis had been away at school much of the time. He was at Cornell. And Miss Avery decided, as she raised the knocker on the big front door, that he probably wouldn't care to be reminded of the fact that she had once sewed buttons on his pantywaists. The knocker made a noise, but no one came. Miss Avery waited and waited, and finally she opened the door and walked in.

The house was dark after the spring sunlight outside. Miss Avery felt blind as a mole. The first thing she saw was herself—her coat with the worn fur at the collar and her thin, unromantic, middle-aged face—reflected in a mirror that ran from floor to ceiling. She turned her eyes away and walked on into the library. Bookcases went nearly around the room. A wood fire was burning in the fireplace and the clock on the mantel was ticking loudly. Over by the French windows a card table had been set up. There was a pile of little baskets on it, and a number of chocolate rabbits and little chickens made out of cotton, and quantities of green and yellow wax-paper straw.

Miss Avery put down her parcel, which contained some mending that Mrs. Whitehead had asked her to do, and stood looking at the confusion on the card table until a voice exclaimed, "Happy Easter!" She turned and found Mrs. Whitehead smiling at her. Mrs. Whitehead had a china dish in one hand and a paper bag in the other. She advanced upon Miss Avery, put both arms about her, and kissed her.

"Easter is still two days off," Miss Avery said. "This is only Good Friday."

"I know it is. I was just indulging myself," Mrs. Whitehead

said, and she carried the dish over to the card table and poured out the sackful of Easter eggs. "I was just thinking about you and here you are." She drew Miss Avery down beside her on the sofa and took both of her hands. "How's your mother? I've been meaning to stop in and see how she was, but we've had so much company lately—Mrs. Howard from Portsmouth and Cousin Ada Sheffield right after that, and I really haven't had a moment. And tell me how *you* are. That's what I really want to know."

"Well," Miss Avery began without enthusiasm, but Mrs. Whitehead had already got up and was searching everywhere for little dishes and jars, lifting the tops and peering into them hopefully.

"I had some ginger, but it looks as if I'd eaten every scrap of it," she said. "There isn't a thing to offer you but Easter eggs."

Miss Avery tried to explain that it was all right; she didn't like ginger any better than she liked Easter eggs, but Mrs. Whitehead paid no attention to her. "I was just going to fix some baskets. My only child is home for his spring vacation, and I'm having eight of his cronies to dinner tomorrow night. And they all have to have Easter baskets." She gave up looking among the dishes and jars and sat down again, at the card table this time. "Francis brought a dog home with him, too," she said as she took one of the baskets and began lining it with green straw. "A perfectly mammoth setter. You know how huge they are. And so beautiful and so dumb!"

Miss Avery nodded, out of politeness. One dog was much like another so far as she was concerned.

"The boy it belonged to got a job somewhere," Mrs. Whitehead said, choosing first a yellow chicken from the pile in front of her, then a rabbit, and then a white chicken small enough to fasten on the rim of the basket. "Boston, I think it was."

"Providence," Francis said from the doorway. He came in and sat down quietly and stretched his long legs out in front of him. His hair was still wet, but it was combed neatly back from his ears. He had flannel trousers on, and a white shirt, and an old tweed coat. He was also wearing heavy leather boots that were laced as far as his ankles and came halfway up his shins. Miss Avery let her eyes wander from boots to coat, to the right-hand pocket of the coat, which had been ripped open by accident last fall when Francis was home for Thanksgiving. The cloth had been torn a little, too, but it was all right now, Miss Avery decided. She had made it as good as new.

"Providence, then," Mrs. Whitehead was saying. "Anyway, they had the dog in their dormitory all year and this boy couldn't take it to work with him, so Francis brought it home, without saying a word to anybody. Red, his name is. And I give you my word, he's as big as a pony. All morning long he's been going around knocking things over, tracking dirt in and out, stealing meat off the kitchen table—all the things boys do in college, I'm sure." She looked at Francis slyly. "And then every time he does something wrong, he comes and apologizes with those great brown eyes of his until I really don't think I can stand it much longer."

Francis drew himself up into his chair. "You exaggerate something awful," he said.

Mrs. Whitehead looked at Miss Avery. "It isn't so," she said meekly. "Is it, Miss Avery? Francis is always saying that I exaggerate." She turned to Francis. "Miss Avery's mother exaggerates, too, Francis, even with her hardening of the arteries." Then back to Miss Avery: "Though I never heard her do it, you understand. I daresay all mothers exaggerate." She looked from one to the other of them and then burst into laughter. "Miss Avery takes me so seriously," she said. "She always did. She never changes a bit. We're the ones who have changed, Francis. There's not one piece of ginger in the house."

She held the Easter basket off, admiring it from this angle and that. Then she put it aside and began on another one, which she lined with yellow straw. Before she had finished the second basket, the maid appeared in the doorway, carrying a wide silver tea tray. The dog followed after her, sniffing. "Annie, how nice of you to think of tea," said Mrs. Whitehead. When Annie tried to put the tray down, the dog came forward, blocking her way completely. Mrs. Whitehead was plunged into despair. "You see, Francis?" she said.

Francis rose and took hold of the dog's collar. "Red," he exclaimed fondly, "did anyone ever tell you you were a nuisance?" and dragged the dog out of the room.

"Don't put him in the pantry," Mrs. Whitehead called. Then she turned to Miss Avery again. "He can open the swinging door with his paw. Besides, he'll just be there for Annie to fall over."

From where Miss Avery sat, she could see into the front hall. Francis was whirling the dog round and round by his front legs and saying "Swing, you crazy dog, swing, swing!"

"Francis is going to leave school," Mrs. Whitehead said. "Last summer nothing would do but he must learn to walk the tightrope. Now he wants to leave school." She began arranging the teacups absent-mindedly in their saucers. "He intends to go back and take his examinations in June. Then he's going to stop. I've talked until I'm blue in the face and it makes no difference to him. Not the slightest. . . What kind of sandwiches are there, Annie?"

"Cream cheese," Annie said, "and guava jelly, and hot cross buns."

"Hot cross buns!" Francis said, coming back into the room. "Do you hear that, Mother?"

Mrs. Whitehead looked at him disapprovingly as he sat down. "The way you twist Annie around your little finger! I don't know what I'll do when you come home to stay."

Francis bent over, and having folded the cuffs of his trousers inside his boots, continued lacing them. "I'm not coming home to stay," he said, with his chin between his knees.

For a moment the room was absolutely still. Without looking at her son, Mrs. Whitehead put the tea-strainer on the tray where the plate of lemon had been, reflected, and changed them back again. "Sugar?" she said to Miss Avery.

"If you please," Miss Avery said.

Annie brought her tea and the plate of sandwiches, the plate of hot cross buns. When Francis also had been taken care of, Annie waited to see whether Mrs. Whitehead wanted anything else of her and then withdrew from the room. Francis went on lacing his boots. After he had finished, he adjusted his trousers so that they hung over like ski pants. Then, quite by accident, he discovered his cup of tea. Nobody spoke. The dog returned, making soft, padded noises on the hardwood floor. Miss Avery thought that Mrs. Whitehead would probably object and that Francis would have to take hold of Red and drag him out again, but it was not that way at all. The dog came and put his head on Mrs. Whitehead's lap and she began to stroke his long, red ears.

"If you're not coming here, Francis," she said suddenly, "where *do* you intend to go?"

"New York."

"Why New York?" Mrs. Whitehead asked.

"I want to get a job," Francis said, and pulled a hot cross bun to pieces and ate it.

Mrs. Whitehead watched him as if it were an altogether new sight. When he had finished, she said, "You can get a job right here. There are plenty of jobs. Your Uncle Frank will probably make a place for you."

"I don't want a job in the mill," Francis said.

In a spasm of exasperation, Mrs. Whitehead turned away from him and poured herself a second cup of tea. "Really, Francis," she said, "I don't know what's come over you."

Miss Avery was ready to get up as soon as she caught Mrs. Whitehead's eye, and go home. But when Mrs. Whitehead did glance in her direction, Miss Avery saw that she was more than exasperated—that she was frightened also. Her look said that, for a few minutes at least, Miss Avery was not to go; that she was to relax and sit back in her chair.

"You do what *you* want, Mother," Francis said reasonably. "You like to have breakfast in bed, so Annie brings it up to you. I want to do the things *I* like. I've had enough school. I want to begin living, like other people."

Mrs. Whitehead pushed the dog's head out of her lap. "Being grown up isn't as interesting as you think. Your father and I always hoped that you would study medicine. He talked so much about it during his last illness. But you don't seem to care for that sort of thing and I suppose there's no reason why you should be made to go on with your studies if you don't want to. There are other things to think of, however. I can't rent this house overnight. People don't want so large a place, you know. It may take all summer. And you may not like it in New York after you get there. You'll miss the country and you'll miss your home and your friends. You may not even be able to keep your car. Had you thought of that?" She waited for him to say something, but he went on intently balancing the heel of one boot on the toe of the other. "We'll have to take a little apartment somewhere," she said, "and it'll be cramped and uncomfortable—"

"I'm sorry, Moth!" He stood up suddenly, and his voice was strained and uncertain. "When I go to New York I'm going alone," he said. "I want to lead my own life." Then he turned and went out of the room, with the dog racing after him.

When Mrs. Whitehead started talking again, it was not about Francis but something else entirely—a book she had read once long ago. The book was about New Orleans after the Civil War. She had forgotten the title of it, and she didn't suppose Miss Avery would remember it either, but it was about a little girl named Dea, who used to carry wax figurines around on a tray in the marketplace and sell them to people from the North.

Annie came in and carried the tea tray out to the kitchen. When they were alone again, Mrs. Whitehead seemed to have forgotten the book, or else she had said all there was to say about it. The moment had come for Miss Avery to bring forth her handiwork. She went and got the brown-paper parcel and sat down with it on her lap. Her fingers trembled slightly as she pulled the knot apart, and when the wrapping fell open she expected exclamations of approval. There were none. Mrs. Whitehead did not even see the mending. She was sitting straight up in her chair, and her eyes were quite blind and overflowing with tears.

"Francis is so young," she said. "Just twenty, you know. Just a boy. And there's really no reason why he should be in such a rush. Most people live a long time. Longer than they need to."

Miss Avery nodded. There was nothing that she could think of to say. She wanted to go home, but she waited until Mrs. Whitehead had found her handkerchief and wiped her eyes and given her nose a little blow and glanced surreptitiously at the clock.

A Final Report

In the matter of the estate of Maud M. Cameron, deceased,
who carried me on a pillow when I was a sickly baby, a
little over fifty years ago, *Probate No. 2762,* for many years
my mother's best friend and our next-door neighbor, a beautiful woman with a knife-edge to her voice and a grievance
against her husband (What? What on earth could it have
been? Everybody loved him): *Final report to the Honorable
Frank Mattein, Judge of the County Court of Latham County,
Illinois: The undersigned, Margaret Wilson, Executor of the
Last Will of Maud M. Cameron, deceased, respectfully states:
1. That on or about the 17th day of June, 1961, Maud M.
Cameron departed this life . . .* though it was far from easy. It
took her almost twenty years of not wanting to live any more.
And if she had been left in her own house, in all that frightful
squalor and filth and no air and the odor of cats' defecation,
she might have needed still more time. But when she was carrying me on a pillow it was not a question of when she would die
but of whether I would live.

It is safe to assume that she shared my mother's fears, com-
forted her, lied to her—comforting lies, about the way I looked
today as compared with the way I looked yesterday; and that
at some point she took my mother in her arms and let her cry.
Though Aunty Cameron lived to be so old, there was no question of her mental competence. She left a will, which was duly
approved and admitted to probate. Letters testamentary were
duly issued; the executor was duly qualified; an inventory of
all estate assets, both real and personal, was filed and approved

by the court; notices for the filing of claims were published, as provided by law; and proof of heirship was made, from which it appears *that the decedent left her surviving no husband* (there is nothing like the law for pointing out what everybody knows) *and the following named person as her only heir at law: Agnes Jones,* an adult cousin, whom I have never heard of.

I don't, of course, remember being carried on the pillow, but I remember the playhouse in Aunty Cameron's back yard. It was made of two upright-piano boxes put together, in the fashion of that period, with windows and a door, and real shingles on the roof. It had belonged to a little girl named Mary King. The Camerons' house used to be the Kings'. And when I got to be five or six years old, my mother, seeing that I loved the playhouse, which was locked, which I never went in, and which I shouldn't have loved, since I was a little boy and playhouses are for little girls—my mother asked if she could buy the playhouse for me and Aunty Cameron said no, she was keeping it for Bun. Bun was her dog—a bulldog. I don't know whether it was at that point that she stopped being my mother's best friend (my mother seldom took offense, but when she did it was usually permanent) or whether Aunty Cameron said that because she had already stopped being my mother's best friend. There is so much that children are not told and that it never occurs to them to ask. Anyway, I went on peering through the windows of the locked playhouse at the things Mary King had left behind when the Kings moved away, and hoping that someday the playhouse would be un-locked and I could go inside. Once I heard my mother mention it to my Aunt Esther, and I realized from the tone of her voice that it was a mildly sore subject with her but not taken so seriously that—that what? That I didn't spend a great many hours in Aunty Cameron's kitchen with the hired girl while my mother and Aunty Cameron were talking in the front part of the house. I don't remember what they talked about. It didn't interest me, and so I went out to the kitchen, where I could do some of the talking. And in return I even listened. The hired girl's name was Mae, and she had a child in the state institution for the feeble-minded, on the outskirts of town. She was not feeble-minded herself, but neither was she terribly bright, I suppose. The men joked about her. My father had seen her leaving the Camerons' house all dressed up, on her afternoon off, and he had not recognized her. From the rear, the men agreed, she was some chicken. When you saw her face, it was a different story. She was about as homely as it is possible to be. Scraggly teeth, a complexion the color of putty, kinky hair, and a slight aura of silliness. What I talked to her about I don't know. Children never seem to suffer from a lack of things to say. What she talked to me about was the fact that Aunty Cameron wouldn't let her have cream in her coffee. This was half a century ago, when hired girls got four or five dollars a week. At our house nobody ever told the hired girl she couldn't have what we had. So far as I know. And I seem to remember telling my mother that Aunty wouldn't let Mae have cream in her coffee, but whether I remember or only think I remember, I undoubtedly did tell my mother this, because I told her everything. It was my way of dealing with facts and with life. The act of telling her made them manageable. I don't suppose I told her anything about Aunty Cameron that she didn't know already. And she was a very good and loving mother, and didn't tell me everything by way of making her facts and her life manageable. She just shone on me like the sun, and in spite of my uncertain beginning I grew. I was not as strong as other children, but I came along. I stayed out of the cemetery.

Of all those times next door during my childhood, there are only four distinct memories. Two of them take place on the Camerons' front porch, in the summertime. It is almost dark, and my father is smoking a cigar, and the women are fanning themselves, and suddenly all this serenity vanishes because of a change in the color of the sky. The sunset is long past, and yet the sky above the houses on the other side of the street is growing pink. There is only one thing it could be. Aunty goes indoors and finds out from the telephone operator where the fire is, but they do not jump in the car, because there is no car, and if you are in your right mind you don't drive to a fire in a horse-and-buggy. Instead, my mother and Aunty Cameron sit taking the catastrophe in from the porch swing. *Creak—creak. Creak—creak* . . . The whole sky is a frightening red now, and in their voices I hear something I have never heard before. It occurs to me that we might be witnessing The End of the World, so often mentioned in the Presbyterian Sunday school. In simple fact, it is the Orphans' Home burning down.

No. 2: One of the things that Aunty Cameron held against her husband was that he spoke with a Scottish accent. He had every right to. (He always referred to Scotland as "the old country," and I thought as a child that it was the only place so called.) In the dusk, sitting on the porch steps, he suddenly exclaimed, "Maud, Maud, there's a speeder on you!" And though she had been married to him for I don't know how long —ten or fifteen years, I would guess—she affected not to understand that a "speeder" was a spider. She was from a little town nearby—Dover, Illinois—and according to the executor's report owned property there at the time of her death, a house that was sold for $1,600, for which somebody had been paying $22 a month rent.

The two other set pieces both happen upstairs. We—my mother and I—are in Aunty's bedroom, and on the big brass double bed there are a great many Christmas presents, wrapped either in white paper with red ribbon or red paper with white ribbon. They are of all shapes and sizes, and interest me very much. Aunty is showing my mother something that still has to be wrapped—a bottle of cologne or some crocheted doilies, that sort of thing—and my mother is admiring whatever it is, and as I stand there, it is borne in on me, by intuition, that in all this collection of presents there is nothing for me.

The final memory is of a nightmare that I had when I was wide awake. I am in bed, in the Camerons' spare room, and the door is open, and I can see out into the hall. At the head of the stairs there is a large picture of a man in a nightshirt on a tumbled bed, by a brook, over which red-coated huntsmen are jumping their horses. The man is asleep and doesn't know the danger he is in. The horses' hoofs are going to come down on him and kill him, and there is nothing I can do to save him. Though it does not take very much to make me cry, this time I do not. I know that Aunty is just down the hall and would hear me and get up out of bed and come to me, and still I do not make a sound. I stare at the picture until I fall asleep and dream about it. What I was doing there I do not know. I had been left with Aunty for the night. My mother and father must have been away, and perhaps they took my brother with them.

Twenty-five or thirty years later, I spoke of the picture to Aunty Cameron, and asked if I could see it. By that time, my mother was dead and we had moved away, like the Kings, and there was a layer of dust over everything. She was no longer the housekeeper that she used to be, but apart from this there was no change in her house, which pleased me, because there was nothing but change everywhere else. Our house, next door, had been sold to strangers and the furniture scattered. The house is still standing, but I have never been inside it since the day the moving men emptied it room by room. To come to see Dr. and Aunty Cameron was to walk straight into the past. Fremont, the street they lived on, was lined with handsome shade trees that kept the houses from seeming ordinary, which they were, Aunty Cameron's house no less than the others. But the inside of her house was not ordinary, it was amazing. When she was a young woman nobody thought her taste pecular, for the simple reason that everyone else's taste was peculiar, too. It was an age that admired individuality, and in most cases individuality was arrived at through the marriage of Grand Rapids and *art nouveau*. Accident and sentiment also played a part. The total effect was usually homelike and comfortable, once the eye got over the shock. But a whole generation after all the other beaded portières in Draperville, Illinois, had been taken down, Aunty Cameron's continued to divide the sitting room from the dark, gloomy dining room, and when you pushed your way through, it made an agreeable rattle. Along with the portière, all sorts of things survived their period. For example, two long peacock feathers in a hand-painted vase on the upright piano that was never tuned and never played on. In an old snapshot that I came upon recently, I saw, to my surprise and pleasure, that most of my mother's friends were, as young women, beautiful. Some of them went on being beautiful, but Aunty Cameron did not. The Camerons had no children. She lost both her parents. And Dr. Cameron lost a good deal of money in a business venture that I never understood. Add to this those grotesque but common deprivations that people don't like to talk about, such as false teeth and bifocals and the fear of falling. Aunty Cameron was sufficiently aware of all that she had lost, and did not want to add to it by throwing things away —even such things as the evening paper and second-class mail. Also clothes that were worn out or long out of fashion. Cups that had lost their handle, saucers that had no cup. The wallpaper had not even been changed, but was allowed to go on fading. In the sitting room, up next to the ceiling, at repeated intervals the same three knights rode up to the same castle that they used to ride up to when I was a small child. So it was reasonable to assume that the picture of the man sprawled out on the tumbled bed by a brook was still hanging at the head of the stairs, but it turned out that the picture was not there. Dr. Cameron had taken it to Chicago, and it was hanging in a club near the stockyards. He had loaned it to them, Aunty said, but she would get it back. From that time on, she nagged him to bring the picture home so I could have it, and he promised to. Each time I went to see them he would say, "Stevie, I haven't forgotten about your picture." And one night the club burned down, and then she had something else to blame him for. One more thing. The truth is, he—The truth is I have no idea what the truth is. Perhaps he gave the picture to the club, and would have been embarrassed to ask for it back, and so pretended that he kept forgetting to ask for it. Anyway, it is preserved forever, the way all lost things are. It is quite safe, from mildew and from the burning pile (*Nov. 19 Virgil Edmonds, George Colby, Roy Miller, Clarence Sylvester, labor for cleaning decedent's residence, $12, $12, $16, $16,* and what a bonfire it must have been).

Whatever the picture was like, it wasn't the picture I remember; I know this much about pictures looked at in childhood. It was in color, perhaps hand-colored but more likely a lithograph. The man on the bed was not being trampled to death but dreaming of the hunt or steeplechase or whatever it was that was going on in the air above his bed. And I am glad I do not have it, because I cannot throw things away, either, and the attic is full of souvenirs of the past from which the magic has long since evaporated. The playhouse, strangely, I still regret. I find myself wondering if it is still there. The executor's report does not list it.

I assumed that Aunty loved me, because of the way her face would light up when she opened the front door and saw me standing there. I know she loved my mother and father. And everybody loved my brother Rex. They loved him with a special love because when he was five years old he got his left leg caught in the wheel of a buggy and it had to be cut off above the knee. But they loved him before that, because he was a beautiful little boy, and because he was so wicked. He gave up cigars when he was five. In the space of five minutes one afternoon, he turned the hose on my mother and my Aunt Hallie and Aunty Cameron (who was, of course, only a courtesy aunt) and my father. The women were starting out to a card party, and retired shrieking into the house, but my father walked right through the stream to the outside faucet and cut the water off at the source. My brother lit out down the alley. My Aunt Esther lived half a block away, and if he got to her he was safe from a whipping—she was excitable and not afraid of my father. On this occasion, she was upstairs combing her hair. She heard him calling, but by the time she got outside it was too late. My father had overtaken him, and there was nothing she could do. Possession is nine-tenths of the law, as my brother used to say when he had one of my toys and I wanted it. Though he gave up cigars, he didn't give up being wicked.

As I say, everybody loved him, but there were two people who worshipped the ground he walked on. The light in their eyes when they spoke to him or about him, the pleasure they took in telling stories about things he did when he was little, the way they said his name made this quite plain. One was my Aunt Esther, and the other was Dr. Cameron. As it happened, they were also devoted to each other. From the beginning of Time all these friendships were; from before I was born. And they lasted out the lifetime of all the people involved, and most of them lived to be very old. Dr. Cameron was a small, compact man, in appearance and in character totally unlike anyone else in Draperville. He was a horse dealer as well as a veterinary, and at one time he had a livery stable on the east side of the courthouse square. During the First World War, he supplied horses to the American Expeditionary Forces. He also, somewhat earlier, supplied my brother with ponies. In the earliest picture I have ever seen of my brother, except baby pictures, he is in a pony cart alone and holding the reins. I don't know whether it was taken before or after his accident. My father was earning a modest salary, and he was not extravagant by nature, and I rather think that the pony cart and the succession of ponies must have come from Dr. Cameron's stable and were eventually returned to it. I was under the impression that I, too, would have a pony, when I was old enough. Perhaps I would have, except for the fact that the world was changing. My father sold the carriage horse when I was six years old, and bought a seven-passenger Chalmers. Where the barn had stood there was now a garage. The change from horses to cars cannot have made Dr. Cameron any happier than it made me. It didn't affect Aunty Cameron one way or the other, because she never went anywhere except to our house, and she didn't come there often. If you wanted to see her, you had to go to her house. She went to my mother's funeral, I have no doubt. And then, just before her own, she went to the hospital and to a nursing home. In between, for forty-one years, she never went out of her front door except to sweep the leaves off the front porch or to open the mailbox, or to pick up the *Evening Star*. The reason she gave for not going anywhere was that it was not suitable for the wife of a horse doctor to accept invitations. The horse doctor was universally loved and admired. People went to him for advice about financial matters and they also went to him when the time had come for them to open their hearts to somebody. In short, it was all in her head.

He lived to be almost ninety, and during his last illness, which went on for months, she took care of him herself. Often she was up all night with him. After he died, the change set in. She looked older, of course, but then she *was* old. In order to sit down, when you went to see her, you had to remove a pile of old newspapers or a party hat with tired-looking cloth roses on it or a box of old letters or, sometimes, it was hard to say exactly what—an object. She would be pleased to see you, but you had the feeling as you were leaving that when the front door closed she would pick up the conversation with herself where it had left off and forget that you'd been there until she got a card from you at Christmastime. A cousin of mine who took care of her legal affairs for a time found that if he wanted to get her signature on a paper it was a good idea to telephone first, because she had stopped answering the door. She was deaf, but not that deaf; she just let the doorbell ring. I have tried this myself. In a little while, sometimes in a surprisingly little while, it stops ringing, leaving instead a silence that is full of obscure satisfaction. The same thing was true for the man who came to read the gas and electric-light meter, and for the salesman who was trying to interest her in a life-insurance policy, and for the minister who was concerned about her soul, and for the neighbors who wanted to bring some warm food over to her in a covered dish—they all took to telephoning first. Sometimes she let the telephone ring and ring.

A young woman turned up who had known Dr. Cameron. I don't know her name or where she came from, but she was a businesswoman, energetic and capable, and with an understanding of financial affairs that most women do not have, and the patience to explain them. Her first visit was followed by others. It is easy to deduce from what happened what must have led up to it. The pleasure of finding a letter in the mailbox instead of the usual circulars, and of putting fresh sheets on the bed in the spare room because someone was coming on the six-fifteen train. What could it have been like except having the child, the affectionate daughter, that she had wanted and been denied? At last, someone was concerned about her. All sorts of people who actually were concerned about her—her husband's friends, the men at the bank, and the neighbors on Fremont Street—were satisfied that she was being taken care of and that they needn't worry about her any more. So they weren't worried about her, until somebody gossiping over the back fence said that Mrs. Cameron had said that the young woman wanted her to sign over to her everything she owned, with the understanding that she would take care of Mrs. Cameron as long as she lived. In a small place, word always gets around—rather quickly, in fact. And small-town people are not in the habit of shrugging off responsibility. Two of Dr. Cameron's friends—much younger men than he was, but he had a gift for friendship and it was not limited to his contemporaries—went to see Aunty Cameron, and shortly afterward the young woman retired from the field.

Unfortunately, though they could protect her from being taken advantage of, they could not protect her from loneliness. She started feeding a stray cat, and then she let the cat into the house one cold night, and the cat had kittens. The dilemma is classical, and how you solve it depends on what kind of person you are. Between five-fifteen and five-thirty every morning, the back door opened and out came the cats. The smell of coffee drifted through the house, and another day was added to the long chain that went back, past the First World War and the Spanish-American War and the assassinations of Garfield and McKinley, to the eighteen-seventies, when things were so much pleasanter and quieter than they are now. The chain is not as strong as it seems: The beaded portière fell down. All by itself. For no reason. In the middle of the night, she told me. It couldn't have been caused by a sudden stirring of air, because the windows were closed. When she came downstairs in the morning, the first thing she saw was the empty doorway, and then she saw the glass beads all over the sitting-room floor.

The rest I know only from hearsay. I never saw her again after this visit. She fell and broke her hip. Out of the kindness of her heart, the woman who lived next door put food out for the cats, but no one expected Aunty Cameron to come home from the hospital. She did come home, looking a lot thinner and older, and she went on as before, except that the experience had taught her something. If an accident could befall her, it could befall her cats. She found it harder and harder to let them out into a world full of vicious dogs, poisoned meat, boys with slingshots and BB guns, and people who don't like cats. She put down some shredded newspaper in a roasting pan in the back hall and showed it to the cats, and they quickly got the idea, and after that she didn't have to let them out of the house at all. At her age one doesn't go around opening windows recklessly in all kinds of weather, and so the house—to put it bluntly—smelled. Since she never went out of it, she had no idea how strong the smell really was. Sometimes when she had neglected to put down fresh paper, the cats retired to a corner somewhere, and this added to the unpleasantness. For she was half blind and could not be expected to go around on her hands and knees searching for the source of the smell. And if she had someone in to clean, as people often urged her to do, what was to prevent the cleaning woman from lifting the piano scarf or the corner of the bedroom rug and finding who knows how much money and putting it quietly in her apron pocket? No thank you.

One day she heard the doorbell ring, and this time it didn't stop ringing. It went on and on until finally, against her better judgment, she opened the door. The caller was not Death, but it might just as well have been. My brother is a forceful, decisive man, with a big heart and a loud, cheerful voice and enough courage for three people, but he had to excuse himself after five minutes and go to the front door for a breath of fresh air. By nightfall she was in bed in a nursing home. She lived on a few weeks, expecting that this time, too, she would go home, and instead she died in her sleep.

The Camerons' house had too many trees around it, and so the grass was thin. The house was heated by hot-air registers, and had its own smell, as all houses did in those days. I don't remember ever having a meal in the dark dining room, though I must have, and I don't remember any flowers, inside or out, unless possibly iris around the foundations. No, I'm sure there weren't any. The flowers were on our side of the fence. Flower beds around a birdbath in the back yard, flower beds all along one side of the house, and vines on trellises—a trumpet vine, clematis, a grape arbor. What I remember cannot be true, if only because the climate of Illinois is not right for it, but the effect is of a full-blown lushness that I associate with Lake Como, which I have never seen, and old-fashioned vaudeville curtains. What can my mother and Aunty Cameron have seen in each other? Something; otherwise the names of my older and younger brothers and my name would not have appeared in her will as beneficiaries—one-seventeenth of the estate each: $1,182.55, less Illinois inheritance tax amounting to $108.72. Or about twice her annual income. How did she live in the nineteen-fifties on $55 a month? On air; she must have subsisted on air and old memories and fear—the fear of something happening to her cats.

She did not ever say that she preferred me to my older brother, but when I was a child and cared one way or the other, I used to think that she would not have said so often that she carried me on a pillow if she hadn't meant that my brother was Dr. Cameron's favorite and I was hers. I understood the principle of equity, even though I had not yet encountered the word. I know now that she loved my brother the way everyone else did—because of what happened to him, and because he was so wicked when he was little, and so bold. How their faces shone with amusement when someone told the story of the hose, or how, totally unafraid, he said to the gypsy, "Mr. Gypsy, what have you got in your *bag*?" After his leg was amputated and he was hobbling around on crutches, the other boys picked on him. It is shocking, but that's the way it was. My father had to hire a colored boy to be his bodyguard—

because he *would* play with the other boys; nothing could frighten him away; he must go where they went, be a part of the gang. I have heard him as a grown man speak affectionately of the bodyguard, on the one hand, and on the other hand defend lynchings in Mississippi. He is like my mother in that he is warm-blooded and generous and not very forgiving. What it is he couldn't forgive his bodyguard I do not know. The indebtedness, perhaps: being protected from the fists of his friends. Or perhaps he only said that to get a rise out of me. Aunty Cameron would not have let anyone but my brother remove her from her house to that nursing home, or have believed anyone else who told her, as he did, that it was only for a week or so. She believed him because he had had his leg cut off when he was five years old and still did everything that other boys could do, including tennis and diving from a high diving board and dancing and golf. To see Dr. Cameron with him when my brother was a grown man was to see, unforgettably, the image of love. We—my brother and his wife and I— went to the races with him in Chicago. Dr. Cameron didn't touch my brother, but his hands fluttered around him. The expression on the old man's face was of someone looking into the sun. It is so curious how the qualities of the parents are shuffled and dealt and redealt among the children, and then redealt among their children.

The balance transferred from the conservator's account to the executor's account was $2,073.04. In Aunty's bank account: $82.55. Half a year's interest on government bonds: $300. The rent from the house in Dover. On October 24th, the executor deposited the first collection of money found in the house: $293 in bills and $51.40 in coins. On November 3rd: $325 in gold pieces, which should have been turned in thirty years before. Thirty years before, Aunty was in her late fifties, and voted the straight Republican ticket, if she voted at all. She was, in any case, strong-minded. She did as she pleased, without regard for fiscal policies. On May 4th, these items: Proceeds from the sale of old car: $25, the standard price for junk. (I didn't know they had a car. I thought of Dr. Cameron as loyal exclusively to horses.) A flower urn brought $15, which means that some woman in Draperville had had her eye on it. $18 in gold, and $12.45 in cash. On June 29th, somebody made a down payment of $500 on the house on Fremont Street, the total sale price being $7,000. A big house for that, but it undoubtedly was run down. On August 7th: *liquidating dividend from German-American National Bank Stock owned by E. D. Cameron,* but no mention of the stock, and the bank hasn't been called that since shortly after the sinking of the Lusitania. An uncashed dividend check turned up somewhere, in a book or in a box of old letters or God knows where. And then, oddly, jewelry not bequeathed in her will. A diamond ring: $175. An amethyst ring with a small pearl: $20. A small pocket watch: $5 (meaning it wouldn't run). A pearl and rhinestone (!) ring: $3. A small locket on a chain (which I have a feeling I remember, the only jewelry I remember her wearing, but perhaps this is imagination). A diamond ring: $150, and a dinner ring with small diamonds: $200. A down payment of $250 on the house in Dover. Proceeds from the sale of cufflinks, tiepins, collar buttons, etc.: $10. An imitation ruby ring: $7. All this in January and February. In March, a pin, another watch, and a ring: $25. They must have turned up in some hiding place, though the house had been cleaned, by four men, several months before. And probably these items were not mentioned in the will because Aunty had forgotten she had them.

The disbursements are less eccentric. It took $817.21 (the Abraham Lincoln Memorial Hospital, St. Joseph's Nursing Home) to help her out of this life. There is a charge for sewerage-system service—stopped-up drain or sink or toilet. And Ernest J. Gottlieb was paid $12 for opening a safe in the basement. Some of the money was probably there; or the jewelry. Or the safe could have been empty. Anything is possible. The spray of flowers for her own casket cost $34, and the funeral expenses were $1,470, so she was buried within the circumference of the middle class. She died in June, and the yard was mowed all through July, August, and September, and the water and gas were not turned off until the following February. The doctor bills were $150.50. In Draperville, doctors still dispense medicine. Apparently she had stopped taking the evening paper; there is no item for the paper boy. But from time to time during the settling of the estate, notices were run in the Draperville *Evening Star* and the Dover *Times*. Carl Simmons was paid $3 for painting a "For Sale" sign. There is no telephone bill. In April the yard was raked, the porch and the windows were repaired. There are two items for real-estate taxes. The First Presbyterian Church received $500, according to the fifteenth clause of the will, and various sums of money were paid out for the recording of affidavits and for appraisals, broker's and auctioneer's commissions, and court costs. The executor's commission was $1,500, the attorney's fee $2,500.

In June the yard was mowed again, and on August 8th the house passed into the hands of somebody else and was no longer Aunty Cameron's. The three knights that for so long rode up to that faded castle have no doubt been covered over. There is no mention in the final report of the peacock feathers or the piano that was never tuned and never played on. My cousin told me that the contents of the house were sold intact to someone from out of town, for $2,000; that the buyer wanted the clothes for theatrical purposes, and also thought they might be of interest to museums and historical societies. It was all carted off to a warehouse somewhere until he had a chance to go over everything and see what was there. It would have been a pleasure to go through Aunty Cameron's things, up to a point, and after that probably nauseating. This is the past unillumined by memory or love. The sediment of days, what covered Troy and finally would have covered her if my brother hadn't come and taken her away.

Haller's Second Home

The doorman, the two elevator men in the lobby all said "Good evening, Mr. Haller" to him and when he stepped off at the fourth floor he didn't ring the bell of the apartment directly in front of the elevator shaft but merely transferred the package he was carrying from his right arm to his left, opened the door, and walked in. A large grey cat was waiting just inside. "Well?" Haller said to it and the cat turned away in disappointment. There was only one human being the cat cared about and it was not Haller. He saw that the lights were on in the living room, but it was always empty at this time of evening. He put his hat and gloves on the front-hall table and, still wearing his raincoat, went in search of whoever he could find.

He had come here for the first time on a winter afternoon, when he was twenty-two years old. With a girl. Somebody else's girl, whom Mrs. Mendelsohn embraced and welcomed into the family. The girl was marrying Mrs. Mendelsohn's nephew, Dick Shields, who was Haller's best friend in high school in Chicago and on into college. And she and Haller were friends also. And she had asked him to come with her because he happened to be in New York—he had come down from Cambridge to go to the opera—and she was nervous about meeting these people who were about to become her relatives. The whole future course of her marriage and of her life might be affected favorably or unfavorably. And then what did she do but explain to them, before she had her coat off, that if she hadn't been marrying Dick she would have been marrying

Haller. No one took this remark seriously, not even Haller. All in the world he wanted, behind those big horn-rimmed glasses, was to be loved, but he had his hands full with the Harvard Graduate School, and a wife would have been more than he could manage.

That first time, he rang the bell politely and, when the girl looked at herself in the round mirror of her compact, said, "Stop fussing. You look fine. You look like the Queen of the May." "I don't feel like the Queen of the May," she said, and they heard footsteps approaching and a woman's high, clear, beautiful voice finishing a remark that was addressed to someone in the apartment. Haller thought he was a spectator sitting on the sidelines, but in fact he was about to acquire a second home. This was eleven years ago: the winter of 1930–31. He was now thirty-three years old and still unmarried.

East Eighty-fourth Street was not noisy then, any more than it is now, and as always in New York a great deal depends on what floor you are on. The Mendelsohns' apartment was three stories above the street. Taxi horns, Department of Sanitation trucks, the air brakes of the Lexington Avenue buses—all such shattering sounds seemed to avoid the fourth floor and to choose a higher or lower level of the air to explode in. Even with the windows open, the Mendelsohns' living room was quiet. It was also rather dark in the daytime. Long folds of heavy red draperies shut out a good deal of the light that came from two big windows, and the glass curtains filtered out some more. These were never drawn, and you had to part them if you wanted to see the brownstones across the way or the street below. It was hard to say whether the room was furnished with very bad taste or no taste at all. With time Haller had grown accustomed to the too bright reds and blues in the big Saruk rug, the queer statuary, the not quite comfortable and in some cases too ornate and in other cases downright rickety furniture. Though he was an aesthetic snob, there was nothing he would have changed. Not even a bronze nymph and satyr that would have been perfectly at home in the window of a Third Avenue thrift shop. What is a feeling for interior decoration compared to a front door that is never locked, day or night?

Through curtained French doors he saw a large female figure moving about the dining-room table and, being nearsighted, thought it was the Mendelsohns' cook. It turned out to be Mrs. Mendelsohn herself. "Hello, Haller darling," she said, and kissed him.

She was a stately woman, with blue eyes and black hair and a fine complexion. She was half Irish and a half English— that is, her grandparents were. She favored the Irish side. The small, oval, tinted photograph of her on the living-room table, taken when she was nineteen, suggested that she had always been beautiful and that the beauty had been improved rather than blurred by the years. The blue eyes were still clear, the black hair had becoming lines of grey in it. She flirted with her husband. Her children admired her appearance, made fun of her conversation, and were careful not to bring down on themselves the full force of her explosive character. Haller had the feeling that her kindness toward him was largely because of his connection with her sister's son. There were flowers on the table—sweet peas—and dubonnet candles in yellow holders, and little arsenic-green crêpe-paper baskets filled with nuts. "Looks like a birthday," he said.

"I don't know whether it is or not," Mrs. Mendelsohn said. "I got home late and there were no preparations of any kind. Ab has forbidden Renée to bake a cake, and so I'm just trying to rustle something together before Father comes up and is angry because dinner isn't ready."

"Where'll I put the present?" Haller asked.

"Present?" Mrs. Mendelsohn said. "You dare to give her a present?"

"Certainly. What are birthdays for if not to get presents?"

"Put it on her chair, then," Mrs. Mendelsohn said with a sigh, "and take the consequences."

He did as she suggested and then left the dining room and walked along the hall, looking in one door after another. Renée was in the kitchen. She was a West Indian, from Barbados, and she had only been with the Mendelsohns a few months, but in this short time she had become the family clearinghouse for all secrets and private messages. Nathan was her favorite; he told her things he told no one else, and made her feel very special indeed, and so was slowly pushing her toward the precipice where the rights of the employer and the obligations of the employed give way, in a moment of too great clarity, to the obligations of the employer and the rights of the employed. But while she lasted, and especially in the beginning, she was a delight to everyone but Mrs. Mendelsohn, who did not like her all that much. The Doctor joked with Renée and praised her cooking. "Enjoy yourselves!" she called when Nathan and Leo and Abbie and their friends went out the front door together, on a Saturday afternoon. "We will, we will," they promised.

Haller was tempted to go in and tell her what he had up his sleeve, but her back was turned and she looked busy, so he went on to the boys' room. The light was on in there but it was empty, like the living room. He took his raincoat off and laid it on one of the beds. Then he walked out again, and down the hall to the next door on the right. It was closed. The door of Abbie Mendelsohn's room was always closed—against what went on in the rest of the apartment and what went on in the world. Her brothers came and went without knocking, and Haller was permitted in there, and one or two other friends. He knocked lightly, and a voice said, "Come in."

The light went on as he pushed the door open and he saw that Nathan was lying on one of the twin beds and Abbie on the other. She sat up and looked at him. Then her blond head drooped. "Oh God," she said. "There's no use trying to sleep. How are you, Haller, dear?"

"I'm fine. Happy birthday."

"Happy what?" she said, sinking back on the bed.

"Would you like me to go someplace else?"

"Don't pay any attention to her," Nathan said. "She's just being difficult."

"I'm so tired my teeth water," Abbie said.

"Are you sure?" Haller asked. "I don't see how that's possible."

"It's what it feels like. I haven't slept for a week, on account of the kittens. They crawl on my face all night long. Be careful you don't step on them."

Haller made his way cautiously to the nearest chair and sat down. The Victorian sofa and chairs had belonged to the great-aunt for whom Abbie was named, and they gave this room an entirely different quality from the family living room. There were flower prints on the walls, the window looked out on a court, and the room was quiet as a tomb. "When are you going to start giving them away?" he asked.

"We gave one of them away this afternoon," Nathan said. "To a patient of Father's."

Officially the Mendelsohns had two cats—the altered male that was waiting at the door and a recently acquired alley cat whose standing in the family was doubtful. Dr. Mendelsohn did not like cats of any description and was convinced that they contributed to his asthma. "Two cats are one more than there is room for in a city apartment," he announced alarmingly from behind the *Evening Sun*, but so far he had done nothing about it.

The cat yowled up at Nathan from the courtyard one snowy night, and he went down in his bathrobe and slippers and rescued her. A month later she had a litter of four, behind the closed door of Abbie's room, and she was raising them without Dr. Mendelsohn's permission; without, in fact, his knowing anything about it. She nursed her kittens in a grocery carton on the floor between the twin beds, and now that they were able to stagger around on their own feet an opening had been cut in the side of the box for them to go in and out by. When they were not pushing at the mother cat's belly they clawed their way up the bedspreads, or collected in all but invisible groups on the mulberry-colored carpet, or went exploring. Except one, which Nathan now brought forth from the carton. This kitten could move, and it was apparently not in pain, but when he put his hand under it and tried to make it stand, the kitten collapsed and lay limp and miserable on the bedspread.

"The girl we gave the other kitten to is an orphan," he said. "First her mother died, and then she went to live with her grandfather and grandmother and *they* died."

"What a sad story," said Haller. "Do you believe it?"

Nathan was dark—dark hair, dark eyes, dark skin—and very handsome. Originally he had his mother's beautiful nose, but when he was a small child a dog bit him. He was playing with the dog, and teasing it, and it bit him on the nose. He had to have several stitches in it, and his nose was not the same shape afterward. His brother and sister mourned over this accident, as if it had been some tragic flaw in his destiny. He himself was resigned to his loss but did not minimize it.

"She's only eighteen," he said. "And her guardian was with her. A very nice woman. When I told her about the kittens she looked at the girl and said, 'Very well, we'll take the sick one.' But they took the one with the black mustache, instead. The one that looked like Hitler." He yawned.

"What you need is a change," Haller said, hanging over the arm of his chair to watch the kittens on the rug. "Why don't we all drive south into the spring. We could be as far south as Richmond, Virginia, the first night. We could see the tulips on the White House lawn."

"How do you know," Nathan asked, "how do you know there will be tulips on the White House lawn?"

"There will be something. If not tulips then there will be dandelions. When Moris Burge and I drove to Santa Fe last year we spent the first night in a wonderful tourist home in Richmond—"

"That Moris Burge," Nathan said.

"—and when we woke up the next morning we heard a cardinal singing in the back yard, and the lilacs were all in bloom. I'm not exaggerating. Why don't we drive south, the three of us, and go straight through the spring? We'll see iris in Alexandria, and in the southern part of New Jersey there will be pine forests with dogwood—white dogwood—all through them. Or we could go down the Shenandoah Valley and pick violets at Harper's Ferry, like I did when I was seventeen."

"You're such a traveller," Nathan said, but not unkindly.

"The West Indies when I was twenty-three. And Santa Fe, last summer. Where else have I been?"

"Boston."

"But you've all been to Europe."

"With Father."

"What were you doing in Harper's Ferry when you were seventeen?" Abbie asked, from her pillow.

"I went to Washington with a special train, from high school. We saw Mount Vernon, and Annapolis, and Fredericksburg, and Gettysburg. We saw George Washington's false teeth. And we had our picture taken in front of the Capitol Building. It was one of those moving cameras, on a track, and I was standing at one end of the group, and the boy who was standing next to me said 'Come on!' and ran around in back, so I did too. We got in the picture twice. I had on an ice-cream suit. Twins is what it looked like. And perfectly plausible, except that I had one leg in the air because I'd just arrived. The next picture, everybody tried it and they had to give the whole thing up."

"Do you still have that picture?" Nathan asked. "I'd like to see it. I'd like to see what you'd be like if you were twins."

"It's somewhere. There isn't anything to look at in Gettysburg but wheat fields, but Harper's Ferry is remarkable. Three states meet there."

"Which three?" Nathan asked skeptically.

"West Virginia, Virginia, and I forget what the other is. But anyway, there are three states right in front of you—three mountains, green all the way to the top, with rivers between them, and the town is on a hill, and it's very old, and the streets are winding, and when I was seventeen I got off the train and ran all through the town and came back and picked violets by the tracks before the train started again. All this was in April."

"Haller, there's no such place, but I love you just the same." Abbie threw the quilt aside and sat up stretching.

"You haven't heard anything?" Nathan said. "No letter, I mean?"

"No," Haller said.

For three weeks, one of the people who was often in this unnaturally quiet room had been missing from it. A rubber stamp descending on a printed form separated Francis Whitehead from his civilian status. It was a grey day, and there was some snow mixed with rain. Governors Island offered a foretaste of things to come. Though now and then someone was sent back, the lines mostly moved one way. He was set down in a muddy Army camp, with a rifle and bayonet to take the place of his Leica and light meter, a footlocker for his earthly possessions—which, as it happened, he was indifferent to—and a serial number. He didn't really need a number to distinguish him from other soldiers, because he was the only one who could tell, in the dark, that the crease in the middle of the sheet he was lying on was not in the exact center of the bed.

There had been two letters from him since he went in the

Army and they didn't say anything. He was not a letter writer, it seemed. He wrote notes, instead—on the backs of envelopes or other people's letters to him or laundry lists or old bank deposit slips. Not because of anything the messages were in themselves but because of something elusive in his character that made any clue seem interesting, Haller could never bear to throw these scraps of paper away. They drifted through his socks and handkerchiefs, in the top dresser drawer: *Why are you never home? If you want to lead a double life it's all right with me but I think you ought to live on the second floor. I'm tired of climbing these stairs. F. . . .* Or, *That new sport jacket is a mistake, you should have asked me to come with you. I can't make it tonight. What about Thursday? F. . . .* Or, *You are so pompous. F.*

When Francis Whitehead laughed his eyes filmed over with tears, but he kept his mouth closed, to cover his receding gums. This condition was apparent to his dentist and to him and to no one else. Like everything about him, his tight-lipped smile was charming. Before he went into the Army he was on the fringe of the world of fashion photography. Before that, he had been in the theatre. His looks, the way he wore his clothes, his jokes, his talent for choosing just the present that would please above all other presents, his tormented smile enslaved people, but he himself did not quite know what he wanted, and so there was little prospect of his getting it.

Haller had written to remind him that today was Abbie's birthday. He didn't say—he didn't need to say—that if Francis could manage to call up from a pay station somewhere it would give her more pleasure than any present possibly could.

"Dinner's ready, children," Mrs. Mendelsohn said through the closed door. Abbie and Nathan scattered to wash. When Haller walked into the dining room, Dr. Mendelsohn was sitting down at the head of the table.

"Good evening, Haller," he said kindly and whisked his napkin into his lap. Mrs. Mendelsohn lit the candles, while

Haller stood behind her chair. The others appeared one by one during the soup course. First Nathan. Then Leo, who had stayed at school for a meeting of the Geographical Society. He came into the dining room quietly, a tall thin youngster with the grey cat balancing serenely on his shoulders. Abbie was the last to turn up. She looked at the dining table and then said, "Mother, how could you?" but she was not really angry. The moroseness was overdone, and deliberately comic. It was true that she hadn't wanted any birthday celebration, but equally true that she was trying hard to grow up. And part of growing up was learning to accept the way her mother and father were, and not to hold it against them that they weren't the things she used to think they ought to be. If her mother wanted to decorate the table and bring home a birthday cake, it surely was possible to treat this as natural and not a crime, though silly.

She saw the package on her chair and said, "What's this?"

"It looks rather like a birthday present," Haller said.

"Do you mind if I don't open it until after dinner?" she said, and put the package on a chair at the far end of the room. And so indicated—rather too subtly for the people present to understand, but the guppies in the fish tank got it and so did the still life over the sideboard—that Haller had done something to her that, even if it was a long time ago, she had no intention ever of forgiving, though from time to time she forgot about it and from time to time she remembered and reminded him of it, and still he didn't understand. There was very little, as she observed to Nathan, that Haller did understand.

Haller didn't mind that his present had ended up in the far corner of the room. That is, he pretended that this, too, was funny and partially succeeded in believing that it was.

When Dr. Mendelsohn talked at the dinner table it was usually to one person only. Tonight it was Haller. He was telling Haller about one of his patients. "She's neurotic and self-pitying, you know what I mean? I gave the same treatment to somebody else that same afternoon and the whole thing was over in half an hour and the woman went home. But this patient was screaming before I ever got her on the table. Finally I had to say to her, 'Mrs. Weinstock,' I said, 'if you don't stop thrashing around, the instrument will pierce your bladder and you'll get peritonitis and die!'"

"Did she quiet down after that?" Haller asked politely.

"Yes, but she wouldn't go home. It was one-thirty and I was supposed to be at the hospital, so I . . ."

Haller didn't feel it was respectful to eat while Dr. Mendelsohn was addressing him, and his plate sat untouched in front of him. He compromised, however, by snitching cashew nuts out of the little crêpe-paper basket. When he had eaten all there were, the two boys passed their paper cups around the table and Abbie slyly emptied them and finally her own into Haller's basket. He ate them all absent-mindedly, and when Dr. Mendelsohn finished his story and took up his knife and fork, Haller saw that the crêpe-paper basket at his place was empty and said indignantly, "Somebody's been stealing my cashew nuts!"

The boys leaned against each other with laughter.

"Mr. Napier called today, Father," Mrs. Mendelsohn said, and the Doctor quickly and furtively raised his napkin and wiped away the particle of food that was clinging to his mouth.

He had his office on the ground floor of the apartment building, and the waiting room, with dark-green walls and uncomfortable, turn-of-the-century oak furniture and dog-eared back numbers of *Time* and *Field and Stream* and the *Saturday Evening Post*, was always full. His working day began at seven and he had every excuse to be tired and cross by six-thirty at night. Actually, the practice of medicine was pure pleasure to him; it was his family, not his patients, that made him irritable. He had grown up on the lower East Side, in extreme poverty—the oldest son of an immigrant couple who did not speak English. When there was nothing to eat he went through the neighborhood searching for food in the refuse cans.

Certain storekeepers knew this and took to leaving something for him. Working at odd jobs before and after school, he earned what money a boy could. He got conspicuously high marks in school, and he cured himself of a speech impediment by imitating Demosthenes—that is to say, he took the Coney Island Express to the end of the line and walked up and down the deserted beach reciting the Gettysburg Address with pebbles in his mouth. The rabbi had no fault to find with him, and neither did his father and mother. But he had no childhood whatever. When his favorite sister died of tuberculosis, the direction of his future was fixed. By a long unbroken chain of miracles he put himself through medical school. And how, lacking the hardships that had shaped his character, his children's characters were to be shaped and made firm was a riddle he could not find the answer to. Abbie had an excellent mind, and she was an affectionate daughter, but she did not know how to cook and keep house and sew, the way his sisters had at her age. When she was just out of college she and a dancer in a Broadway musical stepped into a taxi and got out at the Municipal Building and went inside, to the chapel on the first floor. The marriage lasted ten days. All she ever said, in explanation, was that they couldn't talk to each other. She was now working in a public-relations firm. Nathan didn't finish school. He had a job but could not have lived on his salary. His father considered him immature for his age, and lazy. And Leo had a preference for low company. Loudmouthed roughnecks, and their vulgar girls. When Dr. Mendelsohn looked around the dinner table a spasm of irritation would come over him—at the thought of what his children might be making of themselves and all too obviously weren't—and he would put his napkin beside his plate and push his chair back and go off and eat by himself at Longchamps.

His children understood how he felt, but at the same time there was very little they could do about it. They couldn't very well go and live on the lower East Side, in conditions of extreme poverty. No one would have taken them in. Their Hungarian grandparents were dead and their father's brothers and sisters had, through their own efforts and his, all risen in the world. And if Abbie and Nathan and Leo had tried to sleep in an areaway their father would have come and stood over them, impatient and scolding, and made them come home where they belonged.

Dr. Mendelsohn's irritability was, so far as Haller could see, a matter of pride to his family. It gave him an authority that his physical presence alone—he was smaller than his wife—would not have provided, and it made all their lives more interesting. They never hesitated to provoke him, while pretending to go to considerable lengths to avoid this. His explosions were brief and harmless. But Nathan said that his father didn't like Gentiles, and Haller didn't know whether he came under this proscription or not. On the other hand, Dr. Mendelsohn didn't like most Jews either. This much Haller knew: He was a wonderful doctor.

After dinner, Abbie tore the wrapping off her present, which proved to be an album of Sibelius: "Night Ride and Sunrise" and "The Oceanides."

"I bought them on account of the titles," he said.

"The titles are beautiful," Abbie said. "And I'm sure they are too."

"I haven't the faintest idea what they're like," Haller said.

Unfortunately there was no way of finding out. When they went into the living room to play the records, they discovered that the machine wasn't working. It was connected to the amplifier and speaker of the radio, and where there should have been an empty space on the dial, free from broadcasting, three kinds of music were fighting for first place, none of them Sibelius.

Leo explained that it was a tube, and he and Nathan went

out to buy a new one. Haller and Abbie sat down together on one of the beds in her room. He was expecting the telephone to ring, and his hand was ready to reach out for it as he watched her worrying over the sick kitten.

"You poor thing," she said, holding the kitten's head against her cheek. "Probably it's nothing but imagination—because he's only been this way since last night—but he seems thinner than the others, and his fur is dry and sickly-looking."

"He doesn't look very happy," Haller agreed.

First she tried to make the kitten stand up, and then she took the others away and left the sick kitten with the mother cat. He soon lost interest, and Abbie tried to make him suck and found that it couldn't be done. She felt the kitten's vertebrae thoughtfully, and announced that its back was broken; there was a ridge that was definitely out of place. She made Haller feel it. When he said that if the kitten's back was broken oughtn't they to chloroform it, she decided that its back wasn't broken after all—though it was just possible that somebody had stepped on it. And moved by a sudden inspiration she gave the kitten cod-liver oil out of an eyedropper.

The boys came back with a new tube. When that didn't help, Leo sat down on the floor and began taking the radio apart with a screwdriver. Haller, with an unlit cigarette in his mouth, discovered that he had no matches.

"Leo, do you remember the time you soldered my glasses when they broke?" he asked fondly, going from table to table and not finding what he was looking for.

"Yes, I remember," Leo said.

"And do you remember how much it cost me afterward to have them fixed?" Haller said as he left the room and went down the hall. If he hadn't gone to the kitchen for matches he wouldn't have known about the plate that Renée was keeping warm in the oven. It was eight-thirty by the kitchen clock. Renée was sitting at the kitchen table. Her normally kinky hair was shining with pomade and hanging in straight bangs about her face. He saw the plate in the oven and said, "Who's *that* for?" She giggled mysteriously, and he opened his eyes wide in astonishment. "Tonight?" he exclaimed, and at that moment the doorbell rang.

By the time Haller got to the front hall, Francis Whitehead was inside, and Abbie and Nathan and Leo each had a piece of him, and were trying to go off somewhere with it. He put his little zipper bag down and then grinned at them. "A soldier," he said. And what a soldier. "Everything I've got on is several sizes too large for me," he said. "And I've lost ten pounds." With his hair clipped close to his skull he looked mistreated and ill. Haller was shocked.

"I've got till Tuesday," Francis said, rocking happily on his heels. "I've got thirty-six and a half more hours to do with exactly as I like. What do you think of my World War One pants?"

"They're lovely," Abbie said.

"Did you know he was coming?" Nathan and Leo were asking each other. "Did *you* know, Haller?"

"No," Haller said. "Renée is the only one who knew about it. All I was hoping for was that he'd call up."

"I called yesterday morning," Francis explained. "I picked a time when I was sure you'd all be out."

"That Renée," Abbie said, and began pulling him away from the others. "Have you eaten?"

Francis shook his head.

"Renée's got the whole dinner saved for you," Haller said.

Pushing and bumping into each other, they followed Francis Whitehead through the hall and the serving pantry into the kitchen. At the sight of them, the black woman turned her head away and laughed.

"Renée, you're wonderful!" Francis said, and threw his arms around her and hugged her. Then he sat down at the place she had just now set for him at the kitchen table. Abbie and Nathan drew up a stool and both of them perched on it, unsteadily. Leo sat on the kitchen stepladder. Haller paced back and forth, unable to settle anywhere, and asked questions that nobody paid any attention to. Francis looked at his plate heaped with chicken and creamed potatoes and asparagus and said, "I haven't seen food like this in so long. In the Army you never get a whole anything—just pieces of something. I dream about having a whole lamb chop." They were waiting to see him raise his fork to his mouth and he did, but then he put it down, with the food still on it. "I must go speak to your mother," he said, and got up and left the kitchen.

"How like him," Haller said, "to leave us all sitting here admiring his empty chair!"

When they couldn't get Francis to eat any more they tried to put him to bed but he curled up on the sofa in Abbie's room, with the other boys sitting on the floor as close to him as they could get, and he talked till one o'clock in the morning. He began with the group that had left Grand Central Station together. He described their clothes, and what they said, and how they acted. How the boy from Brooklyn who sat opposite him on the train nearly drove him crazy by reading a furniture ad in the *Daily News* over and over. He told them about the induction center: about the psychological examination, which consisted of hitting you on the kneecap and asking, "Any nervous disorders in your family, buddy?"; about the medical examination, which was perfunctory but nevertheless took hours, in a place so jammed with naked inductees that there was nowhere to stand without touching somebody. And how, one by one and still naked, they were started down the length of a long room while voices called out the sizes of shoes, socks, shorts, shirts, trousers, and they found themselves at the other end, fully clothed and outfitted in four minutes.

He didn't really mind being continually pushed and shoved,

herded from place to place, and sworn at. After all, it was the Army. It was not a school picnic. What he couldn't stand, as the day wore on, was the misery that he saw everywhere he looked. A great many of the men were younger than he was, and they became so worn out finally that they lost all hope and leaned against the wall in twos and threes, with the tears streaming down their faces. Eventually, he worked himself into such a fury that he began to shake all over, and a tough Irish sergeant came up to him and put both arms around him and said, "Wait a minute, buddy. You're all right. Take it easy, why don't you?" in the kindest voice Francis had ever heard in his life.

But the strangest thing was the continual pairing off, all day long—on the train, at the induction center, at the camp, where, long after midnight, you found yourself still instinctively looking around for somebody to cling to, and look after. Somebody you'd never laid eyes on before that day became, for two hours, closer than any friend you'd ever had. When you were separated, your whole concern was for him—for what might be happening to him. While you had one person to look after, among the crowd, you were not totally lost yourself. When the two of you were separated for good, you looked around and there was someone in obvious desperation, and so the whole thing happened all over again.

When they arrived in camp, somebody talked back to a sergeant who was not Irish, and he said, "All right, you sons of bitches, you can just wait." And they did, from midnight until one-thirty, when they were marched two miles in what proved to be the wrong direction and three miles back, before they sat down, at 2:15 A.M., in a mess hall, before a plate of food they couldn't look at, let alone eat. All through the next day it continued—the feeling that each thing was a little more than you could stand. And the pairing off. But the next day was better. And the third day they began to relax and settle into their ordinary selves. . . .

Of the three boys sitting on the floor in front of Francis Whitehead, listening to him gravely, Leo was still too young for military service, Nathan had drawn a high number and didn't expect to be called before September or October, and Haller was 4-F because of his bad eyes. Most of the things Francis told them they knew already, from what they had read in newspapers and magazines. It was his voice that made the experience real to them. The voice of the survivor. And here and there a detail that they couldn't have imagined. And because it happened to Francis, whom all three of them loved.

When Haller went home, Nathan and Leo put up the overflow cot in their room, and Abbie brought sheets from the linen closet, and a blanket and pillow from the other bed in her room. The boys knocked on the wall when they were in bed, and she came back to say good night. Nathan was sleeping on the cot, Francis was in Nathan's bed, and Leo in his own. After she had turned out the light and gone back to her own room she could hear them talking together, through the wall. The talking stopped while she was brushing her hair, and then there was no sound but Francis's coughing.

She was almost asleep when the kitten commenced complaining from the box on the floor. She had entirely forgotten about it in the excitement of Francis's homecoming. "A little chloroform for you, my pet," she said, "first thing in the morning," and rolled over on her back. I'm twenty-five, she thought. Finally. Thanks to one thing and another, including Haller and his "Oceanides."

Then she thought about Haller—about her grievance against him, which was that he went on courting her year after year, as if faithfulness, the *idea* of love, was the answer to everything, and had no instinct that told him when she was willing and when she couldn't bear to have him touch her. Why, when he was so intelligent, was he also so stupid—for she did like him, and sometimes even felt that she could love him.

As for Francis, it was as Haller had said. Nothing that

happens over and over is pure accident, and what they (and God knows how many other people) were faced with, at the critical moment, was his empty chair.

Out of habit, her mother referred to them as "the children," and it was only too true. She and Nathan and Leo. And Haller. *And* Francis. They were all five aiming the croquet ball anywhere but at the wicket, and playing the darling game of being not quite old enough to button their overcoats and find their mittens. But for how long? *For ever*, the curtain said, blowing in from the open window. But what did the curtain know about it?

The kitten was quiet, but the coughing continued on the other side of the wall. Listening in the dark, she decided that Francis didn't have enough covers on. If he had another blanket, he'd stop coughing and go to sleep. She could not get to the extra covers without disturbing her mother and father, and so she took the blanket from her own bed, slipped a wrapper on, and went into the boys' room. All three of them were asleep, but Francis woke up when she put the blanket over him. He didn't seem to know where he was at first, and then she gathered from his sleepy mumbling that he didn't want her to go away. When she sat down, he wormed around in the bed until his thighs were against her back and his forehead touched her knee. There he stayed, without moving, without any pressure coming from his body at all. This time it was not the empty chair but a drowned man washed up against a rock in the sea.

The Gardens of
Mont-Saint-Michel

The elephantine Volkswagen bus didn't belong to the French landscape. Compared to the Peugeots and Renaults and Citroëns that overtook it so casually, it seemed an oddity. So was the family riding in it. When they went through towns people turned and stared, but nothing smaller would have held the five of them and their luggage, and the middle-aged American who was driving was not happy at the wheel of any automobile. This particular automobile he loathed. There was no room beyond the clutch pedal. To push it down to the floor he had to turn his foot sidewise, and his knee ached all day long from this unnatural position. "Have I got enough room on my right?" he asked continually, though he had been driving the Volkswagen for two weeks now. "Oh God!" he would exclaim. "There's a man on a bicycle." For he was suffering from a recurring premonition: *In the narrow street of some village, though he was taking every human precaution, suddenly he heard a hideous crunch under the right rear wheel. He stopped the car and with a sinking heart got out and made himself look at the twisted bicycle frame and the body lying on the cobblestones. . . .* A dozen times a day John Reynolds could feel his face responding to the emotions of this disaster, which he was convinced was actually going to happen. It was only a matter of when. And where. Sometimes the gendarmes came and took him

away, and at other times he managed to extricate himself by
thinking of something else. At odds with all this, making his
life bearable, was another scene—the moment in the airport at
Dinard when he would turn the keys over to the man from the
car-rental agency and be free of this particular nightmare forever.

Dorothy Reynolds, sitting on the front seat beside her husband, loved the car because she could see out of it in all directions. Right this minute she asked for nothing more than to be
driving through the French countryside. Her worries, which
were real and not, like his, imaginary, had been left behind, on
the other side of the Atlantic Ocean. She could only vaguely
remember what they were.

"In France," she said, "nothing is really ugly, because everything is so bare."

"In some ways I like England better," he said.

"It's more picturesque, but it isn't as beautiful. Look at that
grey hill town with those dark clouds towering above it," she
said, turning around to the two older girls in the seat directly
behind her. And then silently scolded herself, because she was
resolved not to say "Look!" all the time but to let the children
use their own eyes to find what pleased them. The trouble was,
their eyes did not see what hers did, or, it often seemed, anything at all.

This was not, strictly speaking, true. Reynolds' niece, Linda
Porter, had 20/20 vision, but instead of scattering her attention
on the landscape she saved it for what she had heard about—
the Eiffel Tower, for example—and for the mirror when she
was dressing. She was not vain, and neither was she interested
in arousing the interest of any actual boy, though boys and
men looked at her wherever she went. Her ash-blond hair had
been washed and set the night before, her cuticles were flawless, her rose-pink nail polish was without a scratch, her skirt
was arranged under her delightful young bottom in such a way
that it would not wrinkle, her hand satchel was crammed with

indispensable cosmetics, her charm bracelet was the equal of that of any of her contemporaries, but she was feeling forlorn. She had not wanted to leave the hotel in Concarneau, which was right on the water, and she could swim and then lie in the sun, when there was any, and she had considered the possibility of getting a job as a waitress so she could spend the rest of her life there, only her father would never let her do it. She had also considered whether or not she was in love with the waiter in charge of their table in the dining room, who was young and good-looking and from Marseille; when a leaf of lettuce leaped out of the salad bowl, he said "*Zut!*" and kicked it under the table. He asked her to play tennis with him, but unfortunately she hadn't brought her own racquet and he didn't have an extra one. Also, it turned out he was married.

How strange that she should be sitting side by side with someone for whom mirrors did not reflect anything whatever. Alison Reynolds, who was eleven and a half, considered the hours when she was not reading largely wasted. "If Dantès has had lunch," she once confided to her father, "then I have had lunch. Otherwise I don't know whether I've eaten or not." With a note of sadness in her voice, because no matter how vivid and all-consuming the book was, or how long, sooner or later she finished it, and was stranded once more in ordinariness until she had started another. She couldn't read in the car because it made her feel queer. She was very nearsighted, and by the time she had found her glasses and put them on, the blur her mother and father wanted her to look at had been left behind. All châteaux interested her, and anything that had anything to do with Jeanne d'Arc, or with Marie Antoinette. Or Marguerite de Valois. Or Louise de La Vallière.

Because her mind and her cousin's were so differently occupied, they were able to let one another alone, except for some mild offensive and defensive belittling now and then, but Alison and her younger sister had to ride in separate seats or they quarrelled. Trip was lying stretched out, unable to see anything but the car roof and hating every minute of the drive from Fougères, where they had spent the night. It didn't take much to make her happy—a stray dog or a cat, or a monkey chained to a post in a farmyard, or an old white horse in a pasture—but while they were driving she existed in a vacuum and exerted a monumental patience. At any moment she might have to sit up and put her head out of the car window and be sick.

They passed through Antrain without running over anybody on a bicycle, and shortly afterward something happened that made them all more cheerful. Another salmon-and-cream-colored Volkswagen bus, the first they had seen, drew up behind them and started to pass. In it were a man and a woman and two children and a great deal of luggage. The children waved to them from the rear window as the other Volkswagen sped on.

"Americans," Dorothy Reynolds said.

"And probably on their way to Mont-Saint-Michel," Reynolds said. "Wouldn't you know." They were no longer unique.

He saw a sign on their side of the road. She also noticed it, and they smiled at each other with their eyes, in the rearview mirror.

Eighteen years ago, they had arrived in Pontorson from Cherbourg, by train, by a series of trains, at five o'clock in the afternoon. They had a reservation at a hotel in Mont-Saint-Michel, but they had got up at daybreak and were too tired to go on, so they spent the night here in what the "Michelin" described as an *"hôtel simple, mais confortable,"* with *"une bonne table dans la localité."* It was simple and bare and rather dark inside, and it smelled of roasting coffee beans. It was also very old; their guidebook said it had been the manor of the counts of Montgomery, though there was nothing about it now to indicate this. Their room was on the second floor and it was enormous. So was the bathroom. There was hot water. They had a bath, and then they came downstairs and had an apéritif sitting under a striped umbrella in front of the hotel. He remembered that there was a freshly painted wooden fence with flower boxes on it that separated the table from the street. What was in the flower boxes? Striped petunias? Geraniums? He did not remember, but there were heavenly blue morning-glories climbing on strings beside the front door. Their dinner was too good to be true, and they drank a bottle of wine with it, and stumbled up the stairs to their room, and in the profound quiet got into the big double bed and slept like children. So long ago. And so uncritical they were. All open to delight.

In the morning they both woke at the same instant and sat up and looked out of the window. It was market day and the street in front of the hotel was full of people. The women wore long shapeless black cotton dresses and no makeup on their plain country faces. The men wore blue smocks, like the illustrations of Boutet de Monvel. And everybody was carrying long thin loaves of fresh bread. A man with a vegetable stand was yelling at the top of his lungs about his green beans. They saw an old woman leading a cow. And chickens and geese, and little black-and-white goats, and lots of bicycles, but no cars. It was right after the war, and gasoline was rationed, but it seemed more as if the automobile hadn't yet been heard of in this part of France.

They were the only guests at the hotel, the only tourists as far as the eye could see. It was the earthly paradise, and they had it all to themselves. When they came in from cashing a traveller's check or reading the inscriptions on the tombstones in the cemetery, a sliding panel opened in the wall at the foot of the stairs and the cook asked how they enjoyed their walk. The waitress helped them make up their minds what they wanted to eat, and if they had any other problems they went to the concierge with them. The happier they became the happier he was for them, so how could they not love him, or he them? The same with the waitress and the chambermaid and the cook. They went right on drinking too much wine and eating seven-course meals for two more days, and if it hadn't been that they had not seen anything whatever of the rest of France, they might have stayed there, deep in the nineteenth century, forever.

Reynolds thought he remembered Pontorson perfectly, but something peculiar goes on in the memory. This experience is lovingly remembered and that one is, to one's everlasting shame, forgotten. Of the remembered experience a very great deal drops out, drops away, leaving only what is convenient, or what is emotionally useful, and this simplified version takes up much more room than it has any right to. The village of Pontorson in 1948 was larger than John Reynolds remembered it as being, but after eighteen years it was not even a village any longer; it was now a small town, thriving and prosperous, and one street looked so much like another that he had to stop in the middle of a busy intersection and ask a traffic policeman the way to the hotel they had been so happy in.

It was still there, but he wouldn't have recognized it without the sign. The fence was gone, and so were the morning-glories twisting around their white strings, and the striped umbrellas. The sidewalk came right up to the door of the hotel, and it would not have been safe to drive a cow down the street it was situated on.

"It's all so changed," he said. "But flourishing, wouldn't you say? Would you like to go in and have a look around?"

"No," Dorothy said.

"They might remember us."

"It isn't likely the staff would be the same after all this time."

Somewhere deep inside he was surprised. He had expected everybody in France to stand right where they were (one, two, three, four, five, six, seven, eight, nine, *stillpost*) until he got back.

"I never thought about it before," he said, "but except for the cook there was nobody who was much older than we were. . . . So kind they all were. But there was also something sad about them. The war, I guess. Also, there's no place to park. Too bad." He drove on slowly, still looking.

"What's too bad?" Alison asked.

"Nothing," Dorothy said. "Your father doesn't like change."

"Do you?"

"Not particularly. But if you are going to live in the modern world—"

Alison stopped listening. Her mother could live in the modern world if she wanted to, but she had no intention of joining her there.

They circled around, and found the sign that said "Mont-Saint-Michel," and headed due north. In 1948 their friend the concierge, having found an aged taxi for them, stood in the doorway waving goodbye. Nine kilometres and not another car on the road the whole ride. Ancient farmhouses such as they had seen from the train window they could observe from close up: the weathered tile roofs, the pink rose cascading from its trellis, the stone watering trough for the animals; the beautiful man-made, almost mathematical orderliness of the woodpile, the vegetable garden, and the orchard. Suddenly they saw, glimmering in the distance, the abbey on its rock, with the pointed spire indicating the precise direction of a heaven nobody believed in anymore. The taxi-driver said, "Le Mont-Saint-Michel," and they looked at each other and shook their heads. For reading about it was one thing and seeing it with their own eyes was another. The airiness, the visionary quality, the way it kept changing right in front of their eyes, as if it were some kind of heavenly vaudeville act.

After the fifth brand-new house, Reynolds said, massaging his knee, "Where are all the old farmhouses?"

"We must have come by a different road," Dorothy said.

"It has to be the same road," he said, and seeing how intently he peered ahead through the windshield she didn't argue. But surely if there were new houses there could be new roads.

Once more the abbey took them by surprise. This time the surprise was due to the fact they were already close upon it. There had been no distant view. New buildings, taller trees, something, had prevented their seeing it until now. The light was of the seacoast, dazzling and severe. Clouds funnelled the radiance upward. It seemed that flocks of angels might be released into the sky at any moment.

"There it is!" Dorothy cried. "Look, children!"

Linda added the name Mont-Saint-Michel to the list of places she could tell people she had seen when she got home. Alison put her glasses on and dutifully looked. Mont-Saint-Michel was enough like a castle to strike her as interesting, but what she remembered afterward was not the thing itself but the excitement in her father's and mother's voices. Trip sat up, looked, and sank back again without a word and without the slightest change in her expression.

The abbey was immediately obscured by a big new hotel. Boys in white jackets stood in a line on the left-hand side of the road, and indicated with a gesture of the thumb that the Volkswagen was to swing in here.

"What an insane idea," Reynolds murmured. He had made a reservation at the hotel where they had stayed before, right in the shadow of the abbey.

At the beginning of the causeway, three or four cars were stopped and their occupants had got out with their cameras. He got out too, with the children's Hawkeye, and had to wait several minutes for an unobstructed view. Then he got back in the car and drove the rest of the way.

At the last turn in the road, he exclaimed, "Oh, *no!*" In a huge parking lot to the right of the causeway there were roughly a thousand cars shining in the sunlight. "It's just like the World's Fair," he said. "We'll probably have to stand in line an hour and forty minutes to see the tide come in."

A traffic policeman indicated with a movement of his arm that they were to swing off to the right and down into the parking lot. Reynolds stopped and explained that they were spending the night here and had been told they were to leave the car next to the outer gate. The policeman's arm made exactly the same gesture it had made before.

"He's a big help," Reynolds said as he drove on, and Trip said, "There's a car just like ours."

"Why, so it is," Dorothy said. "It must be the people who passed us."

"And there's another," Trip said.

"Where?" Alison said, and put on her glasses.

They left the luggage in the locked Volkswagen and joined the stream of pilgrims. Reynolds stopped and paid for the parking ticket. Looking back over his shoulder, he saw the sand flats extending out into the bay as far as the eye could see, wet, shining, and with long, thin, bright ribbons of water running through them, just as he remembered. The time before, there were nine sightseeing buses lined up on the causeway, from which he knew before he ever set foot in it, that Mont-Saint-Michel was not going to be the earthly paradise. This time he didn't even bother to count them. Thirty, forty, fifty, what difference did it make. But the little stream that flowed right past the outer gate? *Gone.* . . . Was it perhaps not a stream at all but a ditch with tidal water in it? Anyway, it had been just too wide to jump over, and a big man in a porter's uniform had picked Dorothy up in his arms and, wading through the water, set her down on the other side. Then he came back for Reynolds. There was no indication now that there had ever been a stream here that you had to be carried across as if you were living in the time of Chaucer.

The hotels, restaurants, cafés, Quimper shops, and souvenir shops (the abbey on glass ashtrays, on cheap china, on armbands, on felt pennants; the abbey in the form of lead paperweights three or four inches high) had survived. The winding street of stairs was noisier, perhaps, and more crowded, but not really any different. The hotel was expecting them. Reynolds left Dorothy and the children in the lobby and went back to the car with a porter, who was five foot three or four at the most and probably not old enough to vote. Sitting on the front seat of the Volkswagen, he indicated the road they were to take out of the big parking lot, up over the causeway and down into the smaller parking lot by the outer gate, where Reynolds had tried to go in the first place. The same policeman waved them on, consistency being not one of the things the French are nervous about. With the help of leather straps the porter draped the big suitcases and then the smaller ones here and there around his person, and would have added the hand luggage if Reynolds had let him. Together they staggered up the cobblestone street, and Reynolds saw to his surprise that Dorothy and the children were sitting at a café table across from the entrance to the hotel.

"It was too hot in there," she said, "and there was no place to sit down. I ordered an apéritif. Do you want one?"

And the luggage? What do I do with that? his eyebrows asked, for she was descended from the girl in the fairy tale who said, "Just bring me a rose, dear Father," and he was born in the dead center of the middle class, and they did not always immediately agree about what came before what. He followed the porter inside and up a flight of stairs. The second floor was just as he remembered it, and their room was right down there —where he started to go, until he saw that the porter was continuing up the stairs. On the floor above he went out through a door, with Reynolds following, to a wing of the hotel that didn't exist eighteen years before. It was three stories high and built in the style of an American motel, and the rooms that had been reserved for them were on the third floor—making four stories in all that they climbed. The porter never paused for breath, possibly because any loss of momentum would have stopped him in his tracks. Reynolds went to a window and opened it. The view from this much higher position was of rooftops and the main parking lot and, like a line drawn with a ruler, the canal that divides Brittany and Normandy. He felt one of the twin beds (no sag in the middle) and then inspected the children's room and the bathroom. It was all very modern and comfortable. It was, in fact, a good deal more comfortable than their old room had been, though he had remembered that room with pleasure all these years. The flowered wallpaper and the flowered curtains had been simply god-awful together, and leaning out of the window they had looked straight down on the heads of the tourists coming and going in the Grande Rue —tourists from all over Europe, by their appearance, their clothes, and by the variety of languages they were speaking. There were even tourists from Brittany, in their *pardon* costumes. And they all seemed to have the same expression on their faces, as if it were an effect of the afternoon light. They looked as if they were soberly aware that they had come to a dividing place in their lives and nothing would be quite the same for them after this. And all afternoon and all evening there was the sound of the omelette whisk. In a room between the foyer of the hotel and the dining room, directly underneath them, a very tall man in a chef's cap and white apron stood beating eggs with a whisk and then cooking them in a long-handled skillet over a wood fire in an enormous open fireplace.

Reynolds listened. There was no *whisk, whisk, whisk* now. Too far away. A car came down the causeway and turned in to the parking lot. When night came, the buses would all be gone and the parking lot would be empty.

In this he was arguing from what had happened before. The tourists got back on the sightseeing buses, and the buses drove away. By the end of the afternoon he and Dorothy were the only ones left. After dinner they walked up to the abbey again, drawn there by some invisible force. It was closed for the night, but they noticed a gate and pushed it open a few inches and looked in. It was a walled garden from a fifteenth-century

Book of Hours. There was nobody around, so they went in and closed the gate carefully behind them and started down the gravel path. The garden beds were outlined with bilateral dwarf fruit trees, their branches tied to a low wire and heavy with picture-book apples and pears. There was no snobbish distinction between flowers and vegetables. The weed was unknown. At the far end of this Eden there was a gate that led to another, and after that there were still others—a whole series of exquisite walled gardens hidden away behind the street of restaurants and hotels and souvenir shops. They visited them all. Lingering in the deep twilight, they stood looking up at the cliffs of masonry and were awed by the actual living presence of Time; for it must have been just like this for the last five or six hundred years and maybe longer. The swallows were slicing the air into convex curves, the tide had receded far out into the bay, leaving everywhere behind it the channels by which it would return at three in the morning, and the air was so pure it made them light-headed.

Before Reynolds turned away from the window, three more cars came down the causeway. Here and there in the parking lot a car was starting up and leaving. Though he did not know it, it was what they should have been doing; he should have rounded up Dorothy and the children and driven on to Dinan, where there was a nice well-run hotel with a good restaurant and no memories and a castle right down the street. But his clairvoyance was limited. He foresaw the accident that would never take place but not the disorderly reception that lay in wait for them downstairs.

O n the way into the dining room, half an hour later, they stopped to show the children how the omelettes were made. The very tall man in the white apron had been replaced by two young women in uniforms, but there was still a fire in the fireplace, Reynolds was glad to see; they weren't making the omelettes on a gas stove. The fire was quite a small one, though, and not the huge yellow flames he remembered.

"*Cinq*," he said to the maître d'hôtel, who replied in English, "Will you come this way?" and led them to a table in the center of the dining room. When he had passed out enormous printed menus, he said, "I think the little lady had better put her knitting away. One of the waiters might get jabbed by a needle." This request was accompanied by the smile of a man who knows what children are like, and whom children always find irresistible. Trip ignored the smile and looked at her mother inquiringly.

"I don't see how you could jab anybody, but put it away. I want an omelette *fines herbes*," Dorothy said.

The maître d'hôtel indicated the top of the menu with his gold pencil and said, "We have the famous omelette of Mont-Saint-Michel."

"But with herbs," Dorothy said.

"There is no omelette with herbs," the maître d'hôtel said.

"Why not?" Reynolds asked. "We had it here before."

The question went unanswered.

The two younger children did not care for omelette, famous or otherwise, and took an unconscionably long time making up their minds what they did want to eat for lunch. The maître d'hôtel came back twice before Reynolds was ready to give him their order. After he had left the table, Dorothy said, "I don't see why you can't have it *fines herbes*."

"Perhaps they don't have any herbs," Reynolds said.

"In *France*?"

"Here, I mean. It's an island, practically."

"All you need is parsley and chives. Surely they have that."

"Well maybe it's too much bother, then."

"It's no more trouble than a plain omelette. I don't like him."

"Yes? What's the matter with him?"

"He looks like a Yale man."

This was not intended as a funny remark, but Reynolds laughed anyway.

"And he's not a good headwaiter," she said.

The maître d'hôtel did not, in fact, get their order straight. Things came that they hadn't ordered, and Trip's sole didn't come with the omelettes, or at all. Since she had already filled up on bread, it was not serious. The service was elaborate but very slow.

"No dessert, thank you," Reynolds said when the waiter brought the enormous menus back.

"Just coffee," Dorothy said.

Reynolds looked at his watch. "It says in the green 'Michelin' there's a tour of the abbey with an English-speaking guide at two o'clock. We just barely have time to make it. If we have coffee we'll be too late."

"Oh, let's have coffee," Dorothy said. "They won't start on time."

As they raced up the Grande Rue at five minutes after two, he noticed that it was different in one respect: The shops had been enlarged; they went back much deeper than they had before. The objects offered for sale were the same, and since he had examined them carefully eighteen years before, there was no need to do anything but avert his eyes from them now.

The English-speaking tour had already left the vaulted room it started from, and they ran up a long flight of stone steps and caught up with their party on the battlements. A young Frenchman with heavy black-rimmed glasses and a greenish complexion was lecturing to them about the part Mont-Saint-Michel played in the Hundred Years' War. There was a group just ahead of them, and another just behind. The guides manipulated their parties in and out of the same rooms and up and down the same stairs with military precision.

"There were dungeons," Alison Reynolds afterward wrote

in her diary, "where you could not sit, lie, or stand and were not allowed to move. Some prisoners were eaten by rats! There were beautiful cloisters where the monks walked and watered their gardens. There was the knights' hall, where guests stayed. The monks ate and worked in the refectory...."

"It's better managed than it used to be," Dorothy said. "I mean, when you think how many people have to be taken through."

The tour was also much shorter than Reynolds remembered it as being, but that could have been because this time they had an English-speaking guide. Or it could just be that what he suspected was true and they were being hurried through. He could not feel the same passionate interest in either the history or the architectural details of the abbey that he had the first time, but that was not the guide's fault. It was obvious that he cared very much about the evolution of the Gothic style and the various uses to which this immensely beautiful but now lifeless monument had been put, through the centuries. His accent made the children smile, but it was no farther from the mark than Reynolds' French, which the French did not smile at only because it didn't amuse them to hear their language badly spoken.

When the tour was over, the guide gathered the party around him and, standing in a doorway through which they would have to pass, informed them that he was a student in a university and that this was his only means of paying for his education. The intellectual tradition of France sat gracefully on his frail shoulders, Reynolds thought, and short or not his tour had been a model of clarity. And was ten francs enough for the five of them?

Travelling in France right after the war, when everybody was so poor, he had been struck by the way the French always tipped the guide generously and thanked him in a way that was never perfunctory. It seemed partly good manners and partly a universal respect for the details of French history. A considerable number of tourists slipped through the doorway now without putting anything in the waiting hand. Before, the guide stood out in the open, quite confident that no one would try to escape without giving him something.

At the sight of the ten-franc note, the young man's features underwent a slight change, by which Reynolds knew that it was sufficient, but money was not all the occasion called for, and there was a word he had been waiting for a chance to use. "*Votre tour est très sensible,*" he said, and the guide's face lit up with pleasure.

Only connect, Mr. E. M. Forster said, but he was not talking about John Reynolds, whose life's blood went into making incessant and vivid connections with all sorts of people he would never see again, and never forgot.

The wine at lunch had made him sleepy. He waited impatiently while Dorothy and the children bought slides and postcards in the room where the tour ended. Outside, at the foot of the staircase, his plans for taking a nap were threatened when Dorothy was attracted to a museum of horrors having to do with the period when Mont-Saint-Michel was a state prison. But by applying delicate pressures at the right moment he got her to give up the museum, and they walked on down to their hotel. When he had undressed and pulled the covers back, he went to the window in his dressing gown. Some cars were just arriving. American cars. He looked at his watch. It was after four, and the parking lot was still more than half full. On the top floor of the hotel just below, and right next to an open window, he could see a girl of nineteen or twenty with long straight straw-blond hair, sitting on the side of a bed in an attitude of despondency. During the whole time he stood at the window, she didn't raise her head or move. He got into his own bed and was just falling asleep when somebody came into the courtyard with a transistor radio playing rock and roll.

He got up and rummaged through his suitcase until he found the wax earplugs. When he woke an hour later, the courtyard was quiet. The girl was still there. He went to the window several times while he was running a bath and afterward while he was dressing. Though the girl left the bed and came back to it, there was no change in her dejection.

"That girl," he said finally.

"I've been watching her too," Dorothy said.

"She's in love. And something's gone wrong."

"They aren't married and she's having a baby," Dorothy said.

"And the man has left her."

"No, he's in the room," Dorothy said. "I saw him a minute ago, drinking out of a wine bottle."

The next time Reynolds looked he couldn't see anyone. The room looked empty, though you couldn't see all the way into it. Had the man and the girl left? Or were they down below somewhere? He looked one last time before they started down to the dining room. The shutters in the room across the court were closed. That was that.

At dinner Reynolds got into a row with their waiter. For ten days in Paris and ten more days at a little seaside resort on the south coast of Brittany they had met with nothing but politeness and the desire to please. All the familiar complaints about France and the French were refuted, until this evening, when one thing after another went wrong. They were seated at a table that had been wedged into a far corner of the room, between a grotto for trout and goldfish and the foot of a stairway leading to the upper floors of the hotel. Reynolds started to protest and Dorothy stopped him.

"Trip wants to stay here so she can watch the fish," she explained.

"I know," he said as he unfolded his napkin, "but if anybody comes down those stairs they'll have to climb over my lap to get into the dining room."

"They won't," she said. "I'm sure it isn't used." Then to the children, "You pick out the one you want to eat and they take it out with a net and carry it to the kitchen."

"I have a feeling those trout are just for decoration," Reynolds said.

"No," Dorothy said. "I've seen it done. I forget where."

Nobody came down the stairs, and the trout, also undisturbed, circled round and round among the rocks and ferns. Though the room was only half full, the service was dreadfully slow. When they had finished the first course, the waiter, rather than go all the way around the table to where he could pick up Reynolds' plate, said curtly, "Hand me your plate," and Reynolds did. It would never have occurred to him to throw the plate at the waiter's head. His first reaction was always to be obliging. Anger came more slowly, usually with prodding.

The service got worse and worse.

"I think we ought to complain to the headwaiter," Dorothy said. Reynolds looked around. The maître d'hôtel was nowhere in sight. They went on eating their dinner.

"The food is just plain bad," Dorothy announced. "And he forgot to give us any cheese. I don't see how they can give this place a star in the 'Michelin.'"

When reminded of the fact that he had forgotten to give them any cheese, the waiter, instead of putting the cheese board on the table, cut off thin slices himself at a serving table and passed them. His manner was openly contemptuous. He also created a disturbance in the vicinity of their table by scolding his assistant, who had been courteous and friendly. In mounting anger Reynolds composed a speech to be delivered when the waiter brought the check. Of this withering eloquence all he actually got out was one sentence, ending with the words *"n'est plus un restaurant sérieux."* The waiter pretended not to understand Reynolds' French. Like a fool Reynolds fell into the trap and repeated what he had said. It sounded much more feeble the second time. Smirking, the waiter asked if there was something wrong with their dinner, and Reynolds said that he was referring to the way it was served, whereupon the waiter went over to the assistant and said, in English, "They don't like the way you served them." It was his round, definitely.

Reynolds glanced at his wristwatch and then pushed his chair back and hurried Dorothy and the three children out of the dining room and through the lobby and down the street to the outer gate, and then along a path to higher ground. They were in plenty of time. The sunset colors lingered in the sky and in the ribbons of water. The children, happy to have escaped from the atmosphere of eating, climbed over the rocks, risking their lives. Dorothy sat with the sea wind blowing her hair back from her face. He saw that she had entirely forgotten the unpleasantness in the dining room. She responded to Nature the way he responded to human beings. Presently he let go of his anger, too, and responded to the evening instead.

"What if they fall?" she said. "It could be quicksand."

"If it's quicksand, I'll jump in after them. Isn't it lovely and quiet here?"

For in spite of all those cars in the parking lot they had the evening to themselves. Nobody had come down here to see the tide sweep in. At first it was silent. They saw that the channels through the sandbars were growing wider, but there was no visible movement of water. Then suddenly it began to move, everywhere, with a rushing sound that no river ever makes on its way to the sea. It was less like a force of Nature than like an emotion—like the disastrous happiness of a man who has fallen in love at the wrong season of life.

When it was over, they walked up to the abbey in the dusk, by a back way that was all stairs, and down again along the outer ramparts, looking into the rear windows of houses and restaurants, and were just in time to be startled by a blood-curdling scream. It came from a brightly lighted room in a house that was across a courtyard and one story down from where they were. It could have been a woman's scream, or a child's. There was an outbreak of angry voices.

"What *is* it, Daddy?" the children asked. "What are they saying?"

"It's just a family argument," Reynolds said, making his voice sound casual. His knees were shaking. Listening to the excited voices, he made out only one word—"*idiot.*" Either the scream had come from a mental defective or somebody was being insulted. The voices subsided. The Americans walked on until they came to a flight of steps leading down to the street in front of their hotel.

When the children were in bed, Reynolds and Dorothy sat at the window of their room, looking out at the night. "The air is so soft," she said, and he said "Ummm," not wanting to spoil her pleasure by saying what was really on his mind, which was that they should never have come here and that nothing on earth would make him come here again. In a place where things could easily have been kept as they were—where, one would have thought, it was to everybody's advantage to keep them that way—something had gone fatally wrong. Something had been allowed to happen that shouldn't have happened.

And it was not only here. The evening they arrived in Paris, the taxi-driver who took them from the boat train to their hotel on the Left Bank said, "*Paris n'est plus Paris.*" And in the morning Madame said when she gave them their mail, "Paris is changed. It's so noisy now." "New York too," he said, to comfort her. But the truth was that nowhere in New York was the traffic like the Boulevard Saint-Germain. The cars drove at twice the speed of the cars at home, and when the lights changed there was always some side street from which cars kept on coming, and pedestrians ran for their lives. Like insects. The patrons who sat at the tables on the sidewalk in front of Lipp could no longer see their counterparts at the Deux Magots because of the river of cars that flowed between them. The soft summer air reeked of gasoline. And there was something he saw that he could not get out of his mind afterward: an old woman who had tried to cross against the light and was stranded in the middle of the street, her eyes wide with terror, like a living monument.

Reynolds was quite aware that to complain because things were not as agreeable as they used to be was one of the recognizable signs of growing old. And whether you accepted change or not, there was really no preventing it. But why, without exception, did something bad drive out something good? Why was the change always for the worse?

He had once asked his father-in-law, a man in his seventies, if there was a time—he didn't say whether he meant in history or a time that his father-in-law remembered, and, actually, he meant both—when the world seemed to be becoming a better place, little by little. And life everywhere more agreeable, more the way it ought to be. And then suddenly, after that, was there a noticeable shift in the pattern of events? Some sort of dividing line that people were aware of, when everything started to go downhill? His father-in-law didn't answer, making Reynolds feel he had said something foolish or tactless. But his father-in-law didn't like to talk about his feelings, and it was just possible that he felt the same way Reynolds did.

Once in a while, some small detail represented an improvement on the past, and you could not be happy in the intellectual climate of any time but your own. But in general, so far as the way people lived, it was one loss after another, something hideous replacing something beautiful, the decay of manners, the lapse of pleasant customs, as by a blind increase in numbers the human race went about making the earth more and more unfit to live on.

In the morning, Reynolds woke ready to pay the bill and leave as soon as possible, but it was only a short drive to Dinard, and their plane didn't leave until five o'clock in the afternoon, so after breakfast they climbed the steps of the Grande Rue once more, for a last look at the outside of the abbey, and found something they had overlooked before—an exhibition marking the thousandth year of the Abbey of Mont-Saint-Michel. There were illuminated manuscripts: St. Michael appearing to Aubert, Bishop of Avranches, in a dream and telling him to build a chapel on the Mount; St. Michael weighing souls, slaying dragons, vanquishing demons, separating the blessed from the damned; St. Michael between St. Benoît and the archbishop St. William; St. Michael presenting his arms to the Virgin; St. Michael the guardian of Paradise. There was a list of the Benedictine monks living and dead at the time of the abbot Mainard II, and an inventory of the relics of the monastery at the end of the fifteenth century. There was the royal seal of William the Conqueror, of Philip the Fair, of Philip the Bold, of Louis VIII, of Philip Augustus. There was an octagonal reliquary containing a fragment of the cranium of St. Suzanne the Virgin Martyr. There was a drawing, cut by some vandal from an illuminated manuscript, of Jeanne d'Arc, Alison's friend, with her banner and sword, corresponding exactly to a description given at her trial, and a letter from Charles VII reaffirming that Mont-Saint-Michel was part of the royal domain. There were maquettes of the abbey in the year 1000, in 1100, in 1701, and as it was now. There was an aquarelle by Viollet-le-Duc of the flying buttresses. There were suits of armor, harquebuses, a pistolet, and some cannon-balls. There was far more than they could take in or do justice to. When they emerged from the exhibition rooms, dazed by all they had looked at, Reynolds remembered the little gardens. It would never do to go away without seeing them. He couldn't find the gate that opened into the first one, and he wasn't sure, after eighteen years, on which side of the Mount they were, but Dorothy had noticed a sign, down a flight of steps from the abbey, that said "The Bishop's Garden." They bought tickets from an old woman sitting at a table under a vaulted archway and passed into what was hardly more than a strip of grass with a few flowers and flowering shrubs, and could have been the terrace of a public park in some small provincial French town. Reynolds began to look for the medieval gardens in earnest, and in the end they found themselves in what must once have been the place they were looking for. It was overrun with weeds, and hardly recognizable as a garden, and there was only that one.

Later, after he had closed and locked his suitcase, he went to the window for the last time. The shutters of the room that had contained so much drama were still closed. Looking down on the courtyard between the new wing of their hotel and the hotel in front of it, he knew suddenly what had happened. The medieval gardens didn't exist any more. To accommodate an ever-increasing number of tourists, the hotels had been added on to. So that they could hold thousands of souvenirs instead of hundreds, the souvenir shops had been deepened, taking the only available land, which happened to be those enchanting walled gardens. The very building he was in at that moment, with its comfortable if anonymous rooms with adjoining bath, had obliterated some garden that had been here for perhaps five hundred years. One of the miracles of the modern world, and they did just what people everywhere else would have done—they cashed in on a good thing. And never mind about the past. The past is what filled the gigantic parking lot with cars all summer, but so long as you have the appearance you can sell that; you don't need the real thing. What's a garden that has come down intact through five hundred years compared to money in the bank? *This is something I will never get over*, he thought, feeling the anger go deeper and deeper. *I will never stop hating the people who did this. And I will never forgive them—or France for letting them do it. What's here now is no longer worth seeing or saving. If this could happen here, then there is no limit to what can happen everywhere else. It's all going down, and down. There's no stopping it. . . .*

In order to pay the bill, he had to go to the cashier's desk, which was at the far end of the dining room. As he started there, walking between the empty tables, he saw that the only maître d'hôtel in the whole of France who looked like a Yale man was avoiding his eyes—not because he felt any remorse for putting them next to the fish tank with a clown for a waiter, or because he was afraid of anything Reynolds might say or do. He didn't care if Reynolds dropped dead on the spot, so long as he didn't have to dispose of the body. He was a man without any feeling for his métier, *tout simplement*, and so the food and the service had gone to hell in a basket.

While Reynolds was at the concierge's desk in the foyer, confirming their reservations at the airport by telephone, a gentle feminine voice said behind him, in English, "Monsieur, you left your traveller's checks," and he turned and thanked the cashier profusely.

He started up the stairs to see about the luggage and the concierge called after him, "Monsieur, your airplane tickets!"

They had banded together and were looking after him.

The same boy who carried the luggage up four flights of stairs now carried it down again and out through the medieval gate to the Volkswagen. "We were here eighteen years ago," Reynolds said to him as he took out his wallet. "You have no idea how different it was."

This was quite true. Eighteen years ago, the porter was not

anywhere. Or if he was, he was only a babe in arms. But he was a Frenchman, and knew that a polite man doesn't sneer at emotions he doesn't feel or memories he cannot share. He insisted on packing the luggage for Reynolds, and tucked Dorothy and the children in, and closed the car doors, and then gave them a beautiful smile.

It's true that I overtipped him, Reynolds thought. But then, looking into the porter's alert, intelligent, doglike eyes, he knew that he was being unjust. The tip had nothing to do with it. It was because he was a harmless maniac and they all felt obliged to take care of him and see him on his way.

The Value of Money

"M y son Ned, from New York," Mr. Ferrers said.
Why, he's proud of me, Edward Ferrers thought;
he wouldn't be introducing me like this if he weren't.

He put his thin hand through the grilled window in the
waiting room of the railway station and shook hands with the
ticket agent, who said, "Glad to know you, Ned."

The ticket agent checked Edward's return ticket (the
sleeping-car reservation needed to be confirmed in Chicago)
and ignored the telegraph key's urgent, lisping *click-click . . .
click-click . . . click-click-click . . . click . . . click. . . .* The wall
calendar, compliments of Orton Grain & Feed Co., was open
to the month of June, 1952.

Edward Ferrers came home to Draperville once every three
years, for three or four days, which wasn't quite long enough
for him to get used to the way the town looked, and so he was
continually noting the things that had changed and the things
that had not changed. He also had changed, of course, and not
changed. He had acquired the tense, alert air of a city man,
and his accent was no longer that of the Middle West but a
mixture, showing traces of all the places he had lived in. On the
other hand, people who had known him as a little boy on his
way to the Presbyterian Sunday school or marching with the
Boy Scouts on the Fourth of July had no trouble recognizing
him, even though he was now forty-three years old and the
crown of his head was quite bald.

"I want to stop at the bank for a minute," he said, as they
were leaving the station.

"What for?" Mr. Ferrers demanded.

"I want to cash a check."

"How much do you need?"

"I just want to be sure I have enough for the diner and the porters and the taxi home," Edward said. "Ten dollars ought to do it, with what I have." His voice in speaking to his father was gentle but careful, as if he were piloting a riverboat upstream with due regard for submerged sandbars and dangerous snags under the smoothly flowing surface of the water.

Mr. Ferrers took out his billfold, which was as orderly as his person, and extracted two new ten-dollar bills. "Your Aunt Alice is expecting us at one," he said. "You don't want to keep her waiting."

Edward took the money and put it in his billfold, which was coming unsewed and was stuffed with he had no idea what. "I'll give you a check when we get home," he said.

"All right," Mr. Ferrers said.

Neither as a child nor as an adult had Edward ever lied to his father, but he did hold back information that he had reason to think his father would be troubled by. For example, he didn't tell his father what his salary as an associate professor was, or how much money he had. If his father knew, it would upset him, certainly. And what would upset him even more was that Edward had failed to put anything by. One of the primary rules of Mr. Ferrers' life was that a certain percentage of what he made should be saved for a rainy day.

As a sullen adolescent Edward had accused his father—often in his mind and once to his face—of caring about nothing but money. This was not true, of course. Mr. Ferrers never confused the making of money with a man's concern for his family or his own self-respect. But he took money seriously (who doesn't?) and to this day carried about with him, in his inside coat pocket, a little memorandum book containing an up-to-the-minute detailed statement of his assets. He took it out and showed it to Edward the day before, while they were admiring the roses in the back yard. What would have happened if Edward had asked to see what was written in the little book he didn't dare think. His father would probably have said that it wasn't any of his business, and in fact it wasn't.

They got in the front seat of the car and Mr. Ferrers rolled the window up on his side, though it was a warm day. He was past seventy, and the gradual refining and shrinking process of old age had begun, and with it had come a susceptibility to drafts.

"I can raise my window, too," Edward said.

Mr. Ferrers shook his head. "I'll tell you if I feel it."

The car was a Cadillac, five years old but without a scratch. It had been washed in honor of Edward's visit and looked brand-new.

"We ought to leave Alice's around three, if you want to see Dr. McBride," Mr. Ferrers said.

"I thought he was dead."

"Not at all. Old Doc goes his merry way at eighty-eight, spending his capital and thinking he can cure his ills and pains, which at his age is impossible. And Ruth hasn't had a new dress in many years. But he knows you're here, and he'll be hurt if you don't come to see him. . . . I tried to head your Aunt Alice off, but she wanted to do something for you."

"I know," Edward said.

"You'd think that by having people at the house where they could see you that that ought to satisfy them, but it doesn't. They all want to have you for cocktails or something, and the result is that I don't get any time with you—which I don't like. But there's nothing I can do about it."

"This evening we'll have some time," Edward said.

"Three days is not enough."

"I know it isn't."

Once they had left the business district there was no traffic whatever. As Edward drove, he continued to look both at the quiet empty street ahead of them and in the little oblong, bluish

rearview mirror, at his father. Mr. Ferrers was aware that he
was being studied, but what reasonable man is afraid of the
scrutiny of his own child? Before he retired and moved back
to Draperville, Illinois, Mr. Ferrers had been the vice-president
in charge of the Chicago office of a large public-utility company. He was accustomed to speak with authority, and with
confidence that his opinion, which had been arrived at
cautiously and with due regard for the opinions of others, was
the right one. He also came from a long line of positive people.
Introspection was as foreign to his nature as dishonesty. Right
was right and wrong was wrong, and to tell one from the other
you had only to examine your own conscience. In general, Mr.
Ferrers was on the side of the golden mean, or, as he would
have put it, the middle of the road. When it came to politics,
he threw moderation to the winds and was a fanatical Republican. Though he could not swallow the Book of Genesis,
he believed every word that was printed in the Chicago
Tribune. Also that Franklin D. Roosevelt had committed
suicide. Fishing and golf were his two great pleasures. At the
bridge table he deliberated, strumming his fingers, without
realizing that he was holding up the game, and drove his wife,
Edward's stepmother, to make remarks that she had meant to
keep to herself. Now that his eyesight had begun to fail, he
had trouble recognizing people at any distance, and so he spoke
courteously to everyone he met on the street. He had no
enemies. The younger men, Edward's contemporaries, looked
up to him and came to him for advice. The older men, Mr.
Ferrers' lifelong friends, considered it a privilege to be allowed
to fasten the fly on the end of his fishing line, and loved him
for his forthrightness, and saw to it that he did not lack company at five o'clock in the afternoon, when he got out the ice
trays and the glasses and a bottle of very good Scotch.

"This part of town hasn't changed at all," Edward remarked.

He meant the houses. The look of things had changed
drastically. The trees were gone. In a nightmare of three or

four years' duration, the elm blight had put an end to the shade —to all those long, graceful, leafy branches that used to hang down over roofs and porches and reach out over the brick pavement toward the branches on the other side. Now everything looked uncomfortably exposed, as if standing on the sidewalk you could tell how much people owed at the bank. Not that there had ever been much privacy in Draperville, Edward thought; but now there was not even the appearance of privacy. . . . In the dark, cold, hungry, anxious to get home to his supper, he used to ride over these very lawns on his bicycle, and when he was close enough to the front porch he would reach backward into his canvas bag, take out a folded copy of the Draperville *Evening Star*, and let fly with it. That dead self, the boy he used to be. *The one you used to have such trouble with*, he wanted to say to his father, but Mr. Ferrers did not like talking about the past. "That's all water over the dam," he said once when Edward asked him a question about his mother. On the other hand, he did sometimes like to talk about local history—what the business district was like when he was a boy, where some long defunct drygoods store or shoe store or law office or livery stable used to be, and who the old families were. And gossip said that when he went to see old Dr. McBride, he talked about Edward's mother. So perhaps it's only that he doesn't like to talk about the past with me, Edward thought. Aloud, he said, "This car drives very easily, after our 1936 Ford."

"You ought to get a new car," Mr. Ferrers said.

"The old one runs. It runs very well."

"I know, but so does a new car. And Janet might enjoy having a car that isn't sixteen years old, did you ever stop to think of that?"

Edward smiled, without taking his eyes from the street, and did not commit himself. This was not the first time that his father had brought up the subject of their car, which had stopped being a joke and was now an affront to the whole family. Except possibly his Aunt Alice, who didn't have a car, because she had very little money—barely enough to live on. What she did have slipped through her fingers. This was equally true of Edward. When he was a little boy, his father made him lie stretched out on his hand in shallow water. "Don't be afraid, I won't take my hand away," he said, and when Edward stopped thrashing and looked back, his father was ten feet away from him and he had learned to swim. But learning the value of money was something else again.

On Edward's sixth birthday, Mr. Ferrers started his son off with a weekly allowance of ten cents—a sum so large in Edward's eyes that when Mrs. McBride gave him another dime for ice-cream cones, he wasn't sure whether it was morally right for him to take it. With advancing age, the ten cents became a quarter, all his own, to spend when and on what he pleased, and of course once it was spent there was no possibility of more until another week rolled around. In first-year high school, the quarter became fifty cents, and then, in Chicago, where he had lunch at school and carfare to consider, it jumped suddenly to three dollars. By walking to school, and a good deal of the time not eating any lunch, he could buy books, and did. Sometimes quite expensive ones. And in college he had sixty, then seventy-five, and then ninety dollars a month, with no questions asked, out of which he fed himself and paid for the roof over his head and bought still more books. If he ran short toward the end of the month, he lived on milk and graham crackers—which was not what his father had intended. And once when he ran out of money early in the month because he had shared what he had with a roommate whose check from home didn't come, he got a job waiting tables at a sorority house. What it amounted to was that he had learned when the money ran out not to ask for more.

When he finished college, he thought he wanted to teach English, but after three years of graduate work he threw up his part-time appointment with the university where he had been an undergraduate, took the hundred dollars that he had in a savings account, borrowed another hundred from his father, and went to New York on a Greyhound bus and got a job. After working three weeks, he paid his father back. A great load fell from Mr. Ferrers' shoulders with this act. He sat with Edward's letter and the check for a hundred dollars in his hand and wept. The only one of his three children who had ever given him cause for worry had demonstrated that he was responsible where money was concerned, and Mr. Ferrers felt that his work had been accomplished. It appeared to be so well accomplished that Edward, receiving raise after raise, in four years reached a point at which he must be making about as much income as his father. Since his father never revealed how much money he earned, this had to be concluded by inference, from his scale of living and his remarks about other people. Edward decided on ten thousand dollars a year as his mark, and when he reached it he rested there a few months, during the summer of 1939. His father and stepmother came East for the World's Fair in Flushing Meadow. Sitting in the Belgian Pavilion, with a clear view of the French Pavilion, where the food was better but notoriously expensive, Edward announced that he had resigned from his job in order to get a Ph.D. and go back to teaching. Mr. Ferrers took this decision calmly. Edward was a grown man now, he said, and he would not presume to tell him how to lead his life.

As Edward drove up in front of the place where his aunt lived, Mr. Ferrers said, "Don't get too close to the curbing—you'll scrape the whitewalls."

"How is that?" Edward asked.

Mr. Ferrers opened the door on his side and looked. "You're all right," he said.

Though now and then some old house would be divided into apartments, this was the only building in Draperville that had been originally designed for that purpose. It was two stories high, frame, with small porches both upstairs and down. It was painted a dreary shade of brown, and it backed on the railroad tracks. Mr. Ferrers' sister lived on the second floor, at the top of a rather steep flight of stairs.

"You go ahead, son," he said. "I have to take my time."

There were two doors at the top of the stairs. The one on the right opened and Edward's Aunt Alice said, "I've been watching for you. Come in, come in," and put her arms around him and gave him a hearty smack. Looking past her into the apartment, he saw that his stepmother had already come.

"What a pretty dress," he said.

"I put it on for you," his Aunt Alice said, and her face lit up with pleasure.

Edward loved her because his mother had loved her, and because she had been very good to him after his mother died— the one person who brought cheerfulness and jokes into a house where life had come to a standstill and people sat down to meals and went upstairs to bed and practiced the piano and read the evening paper and answered the telephone only because they didn't know what else to do. He always thought of her as she was then, and so it was a shock to find her with white hair, false teeth, wrinkles, rimless bifocals, and hands twisted out of shape by arthritis. And living alone for so many years had made her melancholy. Only her voice was not changed. Unlike most people of her generation, she could speak about her feelings. The night before, sitting off in a corner with him where nobody could hear what they were saying, she said, "I know I'm old, but my heart is young." During a long life, very little happiness had come her way and she had taken every bit of it, without a moment's fear or hesitation. And would again.

"Well, Alice," Mr. Ferrers said as he kissed her, "how are all your aches and pains today?"

"They're not imaginary, as you seem to think."

"Don't listen to him," Edward said.

"I know he just likes to get my goat," she said. "But even so."

"If you can't stand a little teasing," Mr. Ferrers said.

"I don't mind teasing, but sometimes your teasing hurts."

When they were children and he got into a fight on the way home from school, she dropped her books and sailed in and pulled his tormentors off him. Mr. Ferrers had had asthma as a boy and was not strong; but he outgrew it; the time came when he didn't need anybody to protect him. From the way she spoke his name, it was perfectly clear to Edward how much his aunt loved his father still.

The living room of the apartment was robbed of light by the porch. The deep shade that was lacking everywhere outside was here, softening the colors of Oriental rugs that were familiar to him from his childhood; like books that he had read over and over. His childhood was separated sharply from his adolescence by his mother's death, which occurred when he was ten. He was thirteen when his father remarried, and when he was fifteen they moved from Draperville to Chicago. He had known his stepmother since he was four years old. She had been his kindergarten teacher, and so it was not as if his father had married a stranger.

When Mr. and Mrs. Ferrers came East for a visit with Edward and his wife, the two couples played gin rummy with a good deal of gaiety and went for long drives. Edward's wife and his stepmother were comfortable together. If there was ever any strain, it was between father and son—because Edward had miscalculated the length of time it took to drive from the handsome street of old houses in Litchfield, Connecticut, to the inn where Mr. Ferrers could sit down to his evening drink; or because Mr. Ferrers could not keep off the subject of politics even though he knew what Edward thought of Senator

McCarthy. But when Edward was going to high school in Chicago, it was different. He did not like to think of all that his stepmother had put up with—the sullenness; the refusal to admit her completely into his affections lest he be disloyal to his mother; the harsh judgments of adolescence; sand in the bathroom, tears at the dinner table, and implacable hostility toward his father. As if to make belated amends, he sat now holding her hand in his and reminding her of things that had happened when they were living in Chicago.

"Do you remember what a time you had teaching me to drive?" he said, and they both laughed. Streetcars had exerted a fatal attraction for him. He killed the engine on Sheridan Road. Returning to the garage where the car was kept, he couldn't decide between the entrance and the exit and almost drove up on a concrete post.

"I used to hear you coming home," Helen Ferrers said, "when we lived on Greenleaf Avenue, and your walk sounded so like your dad's that I couldn't tell which of you it was."

Edward also had put up with something. For the first few years, she suffered from homesickness and she and his father went home to Draperville as often as they could, and they had a good deal of company—mostly Helen's friends, who came up to Chicago for a few days to do some shopping. There was no guest room in the apartment, and when they had company Edward slept in the dining room, on a daybed that opened out. In his room there were twin beds with satin spreads on them, and before he got into bed at night he folded the one on his bed carefully and put it on the other, but sometimes forgot to pin back the glass curtains so they wouldn't be rained on during the night. He studied at a card table, and in his closet, in a muslin bag, were Helen's evening dresses. The two pictures on the wall were colored French prints, from a series entitled "Les Confiances d'Amour." By the light switch there was a small framed motto:

Hello, guest, and Howdy-do.
    This small room belongs to you.
And our house and all that's in it.
    Make yourself at home each minute.

Helen let go of his hand in order to go out to the kitchen and help put lunch on the table. Edward heard his Aunt Alice say, "I'm all ready. As soon as the iced tea is poured, we can sit down. I know Ed likes to have his meals on time."

"You shouldn't have gone to so much trouble," Helen said —meaning sweet corn and garden tomatoes and fried chicken and a huge strawberry shortcake.

"It wasn't any trouble," his aunt said, which was of course untrue; at her age everything was hard for her, and usually she was perfectly willing to admit it. When they pushed their chairs back from the table, an hour later, she said, "No, you can't help me, any of you. I won't hear of it. I don't have Ned with me very often, and we're going to talk, we're not going to stand around in the kitchen doing dishes. I don't mind doing them if I can take my time."

What they talked about, sitting in a circle in her small, dark living room, was her health. The doctor was trying cortisone, and she thought it had helped her. She had more movement in her fingers, and could put her hair up without feeling so much pain in her shoulder.

They were late getting away—it was after three-thirty when they said goodbye and got in the car and drove off to call on Dr. McBride, whom they found sitting up in bed in the downstairs room that used to be his den. "Sit right here on the bed where I can see you," he said.

"He won't be comfortable," Mrs. McBride objected.

"How do you know?" Dr. McBride said. He was born in Scotland and spoke with a noticeable burr. "Sit down, my boy. Don't pay any attention to your auntie. I've been expecting you. You have your mother's eyes. You remember her?"

Edward nodded.

"And you like living in New York?"

"Yes."

"And you're teaching. That's a fine profession for a man to be in. Very fine. You'll never have to worry for fear your life is being wasted. And how old are you now?"

Edward told him.

"I can recall very well the day you were born. Would you like to hear about it?"

"Yes, I would," Edward said.

"It was an extremely hot day, in the middle of August. . . ."

Looking into the old man's faded blue eyes, Edward thought, This is the first real conversation that we have ever had.

While Mrs. McBride and his father talked about the new road to Peoria and what a difference it would make, Dr. Mc-Bride held Edward's hand and told him things he had done and said when he was a little boy, and then he began to tell Edward about his own boyhood in Scotland. "My father was very strict," he said, "and by the time I was eleven years old I'd had enough of his heavy hand and I made up my mind to run away to America. I told my mother, because I couldn't bear not to, and because I knew she'd feel worse if I'd kept it from her. She gave me all the money there was in the teapot, and told me I mustn't leave without saying goodbye to my father. So I did. I edged my way all around the room until I arrived at the door, and then I said, 'Goodbye, Father, I'm leaving home,' and started running as fast as my legs would carry me. . . ."

He got a job on a tramp schooner that landed him eventually on the coast of California. He was homesick and couldn't find work, slept in doorways, and was half starved when he met up with a man whose name was also McBride, a well-to-do rancher who had recently lost his only son.

Somewhere, possibly during that far-off boyhood in Scotland, Dr. McBride had been exposed to the storyteller's art. He understood the use of the surprising juxtaposition, the impact of things left unsaid. Again and again there was a detail that couldn't not be true. He never relapsed into the pointless, never said "to make a long story short," and seemed not even to be aware that he was telling stories, and yet there was not one unnecessary word.

"Oh, but did that really happen?" Edward exclaimed. "How marvellous."

"It *was* marvellous," Dr. McBride agreed.

And a minute later Edward said, "But weren't you afraid of him?" He said, "He was still waiting, after all that time?" And "It's so beautiful—that it worked out that way." Looking altogether a different person—as if the essential part of him, his true self that could never show its face in Draperville because no child after he grows up can ever be wholly natural with his parents, had come and joined them on the bed—he asked, "And then what happened?" The old man's eyes lit up. He had found the perfect audience.

Mr. Ferrers consulted his wristwatch and then said, "Much as I hate to do this, Ruth, we've got to be moving on. We're due at the Franklins' at five."

Dr. McBride winked at Edward and said, "Your father is the slave of time," and went on telling the story of his life.

Edward got up from the bed only because it was the third time his father had spoken to him about leaving, and even then it was very hard to do. The stories he did not hear now he never would, and he had the feeling that he was depriving himself of his birthright.

"I thought you'd decided to spend the rest of your life there," Mr. Ferrers said crossly when they were in the car. "Do you have any idea what time it is?"

"I know, Dad," Edward said, "but I couldn't bear to leave.

He's the most wonderful storyteller I ever heard, and I didn't even know it."

"I've heard Doc's stories," Mr. Ferrers said dryly. "He's always the hero."

What made Mr. Ferrers' anger so impressive was that it was never unleashed. The change in him now was less than it was in Edward, whose voice rose in pitch, in spite of his efforts to control it. He stammered as he defended himself from his father's remarks. The effect of this skirmish was to move them both back in time, to Edward's fifteenth year and Mr. Ferrers' forty-fifth—the difference being that Edward regarded it as a personal failure in steering the riverboat upstream, whereas Mr. Ferrers five minutes later had dismissed the incident from his mind.

At the Franklins', Edward threw himself into one conversation after another, enjoying himself thoroughly, and trying, as always, to make sure that no one was skimped —as if the amount of attention he paid to each person who had known him since he came into the world was something that he must try to apportion justly and fairly. Why this should be, he had never asked himself.

From the Franklins' they drove downtown again, to join Helen's family in the cafeteria of the New Draperville Hotel. With several drinks under his belt, Edward looked around the noisy dining room. The faces he saw were full of character, as small-town faces tend to be, he thought, and lined with humor, and time had dealt gently with them. By virtue of having been born in this totally unremarkable place and of having lived out their lives here, they had something people elsewhere did not have. . . . This opinion every person in the room agreed with, he knew, and no doubt it had been put into his mind when he was a child. For it was something that he never failed to be struck by—those sweeping statements in praise of Draperville that were almost an article of religious faith. They spoke about each other in much the same way. "There isn't a finer man anywhere on this earth," they would say, in a tone of absolute conviction, sometimes about somebody who was indeed admirable, but just as often it would be some local skinflint, some banker or lawyer who made a specialty of robbing widows and orphans and was just barely a member of the human race. A moment later, opposed to this falsehood and in fact utterly contradicting it, there was a more realistic appraisal, which to his surprise they did not hesitate to express. But it would be wrong to say that the second statement represented their true opinion; it was just their other one.

He saw that somebody was smiling at him from a nearby table, a soft-faced woman with blond hair, and he put his napkin down and crossed the room to speak to her. He even knew her name. She lived down the street from him, and when he was six years old he was hopelessly in love with her and she liked Johnny Miller instead.

When they walked into the house at ten o'clock, he was talked out, dead-tired, and sleepy, and aware that the one person who had been skimped was the person he had come to see in the first place, his father, and that he couldn't leave without a little time with his father, and that his father had no intention of permitting him to.

As they put their coats away in the hall closet, Helen said, "Ned, dear, you must be dead. I know I am. What time do you want breakfast?"

"Eight-thirty or nine o'clock will be all right," Mr. Ferrers said. "His train doesn't leave till eleven. You go on up. Ned and I want to have a little visit."

"I think I will," Mrs. Ferrers said. But first she went around the room emptying ashtrays and puffing up satin pillows, until the room looked as if there had never been anybody in it. The two men walked through the sun parlor and out onto the screened porch. Mr. Ferrers sat down in the chair that was always referred to as his, and lit a cigar. Edward sat on a bamboo sofa. They did not turn the light on but sat in the dim light that came from the living room. Mr. Ferrers began by remarking upon the many changes he had seen in his lifetime—the telephone, electric light, the automobile, the airplane—and how these changes had totally changed the way people lived. "It's been a marvellous privilege," he said, drawing on his cigar, "to have lived in a time when all this was happening."

Edward managed not to say that he would gladly have dispensed with all of these inventions. He listened to his father's denunciation of the New Deal as he would have to some over-familiar piece of music—"Fingal's Cave" or the overture to "Rosamunde"—aware that it was a necessary prelude to the more substantial part of the conversation, something uppermost in his father's mind that had to be said in order to get around to things that were deeper and more personal.

So long as Edward did not argue with his father or attempt to present the other side of the political picture, Mr. Ferrers did not investigate his son's opinions. As for converting Mr. Ferrers to the liberal point of view, history—the depression, in particular—had done more than Edward could possibly have hoped to accomplish with rational arguments. Mr. Ferrers was aware that there is such a thing as social responsibility, and he merely complained that it had now gone far enough and any further effort in that direction would weaken the financial structure of the country. So far as Edward could make out, his father's financial structure had weathered the storm very well.

When Edward put his feet up and arranged the pillows comfortably behind his head, Mr. Ferrers said, "If you're too tired, son, go to bed." But kindly. There was no impatience in his voice.

"Oh, no," Edward said. "I just felt like stretching out."

"It's too bad it has to be this way. When we lived in Chicago, there was no one to consider but ourselves, and we could talk to our hearts' content."

Actually, in those days it was Mr. Ferrers who talked. Edward was full of secrets and couldn't have opened his mouth without putting his foot in it.

"Very nice," he said, when his father asked what he thought of his Aunt Alice's apartment. "She seemed very comfortable."

"She keeps very peculiar hours. She likes to read till two in the morning. But you can't tell other people how to lead their lives, and I guess she's happy doing that. And she's got all her things around her—all those old drop-leaf tables and china doodads she sets such store by and that no secondhand dealer would give you more than two dollars for, if that."

"Aunt Alice's things are better than you think," Edward said.

"If you like antiques," Mr. Ferrers said. "I used to argue with her, but I don't anymore. I've given up. There's a first-floor apartment coming vacant in the same building that she wants to move into. It's more expensive, but she complains about the stairs, and at her age they are a consideration. I'll probably have to help her with the rent. . . . She could have been in a very different situation today. I know of three very fine men who were crazy to marry her. She wouldn't have them. They've all done well for themselves."

They probably bored her, Edward said to himself in the dark.

"Father begged her with tears in his eyes not to marry Gene Hamilton," Mr. Ferrers said. "But she wouldn't listen to him."

"She's had lots of pleasure from her life, even so," Edward remarked.

"Now she wants to sell all her securities—she hasn't got very much: some Quaker Oats and some U.S. Gypsum and a few shares of General Motors—and buy an annuity, which at her age is the silliest thing you ever heard of."

Silly or not, she had his father to fall back on, Edward reflected philosophically. And then, less philosophically, he wondered what would happen if his Aunt Alice outlived his father. Who would look after her? Her only son was dead and she had no grandchildren. The question contained its own answer: Edward and his brothers would take on the responsibility that until now his father had shouldered alone.

"What was he like?"

"What was who like?"

"Grandfather Ferrers."

"He was as fine a man as you would ever want to know," Mr. Ferrers said soberly, and then he added to a long finished picture a new detail that changed everything. He said, "Father never saw me until my brother Will died."

Edward opened his eyes. His father very seldom ever said anything as revealing as this, and also it was in flat contradiction to the usual version, which was that his father and his grandfather had been extremely close.

The earliest surviving photographs of his father showed him playing the mandolin, with his cap on the back of his head and a big chrysanthemum in his buttonhole. His brother Will died at the age of twenty-five, leaving a wife and child, and Grandfather Ferrers' health was poor, and so Edward's father, who had wanted to study medicine, dropped out of school instead and began to help support the family.

From where he lay stretched out on the sofa, Edward could see into the lighted living room of the house next door. The son-in-law sat reading a copy of *Life* under a bridge lamp. The two Scotties, whose barking Mr. Ferrers complained of, were quiet. There had been a divorce that had rocked the house next door to the foundations, but that, too, had quieted down. The whole neighborhood was still. Not even a television set. Just the insects of the summer night. His father would have been a good doctor, Edward thought, staring at the outlines of the house next door and the trees in the back yard, silhouetted against the night sky. He felt his eyelids growing heavier and heavier.

"But all that changed," Mr. Ferrers said. "Toward the end of his life we got to know each other."

Edward heard his stepmother moving about upstairs, and then without warning his mind darkened. When he came to, after he had no idea how long, Mr. Ferrers was discussing his will. Though Edward could hardly believe that this conversation was taking place at all, what made it seem even stranger was the fact that his father spoke without excitement of any kind, as if all his life he had been in the habit of discussing his financial arrangements with his children. The will was what Edward had assumed it would be. There was nothing that he could object to, nothing that was not usual. Everything was to go to his stepmother during her lifetime, and then the estate would be divided among Mr. Ferrers' three sons.

"I wanted very much to be able to leave you boys something at the time of my death," Mr. Ferrers said. "About fifteen thousand dollars is what I had planned. I wanted you to have a little present to remember me by. But with the state and federal inheritance tax, I don't see how this can be managed."

"It doesn't matter," Edward said.

"It matters to me," Mr. Ferrers said, and there they were, right back where they started.

Mr. Ferrers drew on his cigar and the porch was illuminated by a soft red glow. "When I was a young man," he said, "and just trying to get my feet on the ground, my father said to me, 'If you can just manage to save a thousand dollars, you'll never be in want, the whole rest of your life. . . .' " Though Edward had never heard Dr. McBride's stories, this story he knew by heart. His father had done it, had managed to save a thousand dollars, and his grandfather's words had proved true. As a young man, having been told the same thing by his father, Edward had put this theory to the test; he also had saved a thousand dollars, and then, gradually, unlike his father and his grandfather, he had spent it. Little by little, it went. But strangely enough, so far at least, the theory still held. He had never been in actual want, though the balance in their—his and Janet's—joint checking account at this moment his father would not have considered cause for congratulations.

It was an amusing thought that the same reticence that prevented his father from telling him just how much money he had would prevent him also from inquiring into Edward's financial circumstances. But it would not prevent him from asking if Edward was saving money. The conversation was clearly heading for this point, and so Edward braced himself and was ready when it arrived.

Mr. Ferrers said, "I assume you have managed to put something aside?"

Edward neither confirmed nor denied this.

"If you haven't, you should have," Mr. Ferrers said sternly. Then a long circuitous return to the same subject, this time in the guise of whether or not Edward had enough insurance, so that if anything happened to him Janet was taken care of.

Janet was taken care of. But not through Edward's foresight. She had money of her own, left to her by her grandmother. They did not touch the principal but used the income.

"If anything happens to me, Janet is taken care of," Edward said. And it was all he said.

"That's fine," Mr. Ferrers said. "I'm very glad to hear it."

He passed on to the subject of Edward's two brothers, who were in business together, and, though very different, were adjusting to each other's personalities. His older brother had already done extremely well; his younger brother, just starting out after a two-year period in the Army, when his schooling was interrupted, had, of course, a long way to go, but he was showing such a determination to succeed that Mr. Ferrers could find nothing but satisfaction in contemplating his son's efforts.

"I know," Edward said, and "That's true," and "He certainly does," and his answers sounded so drowsy that at last Mr. Ferrers said with exasperation, "If you're so sleepy, why don't you go to bed?"

"Because I don't feel like it," Edward said. "I'm fine here on the sofa." Leaving the riverboat with nobody at the wheel, he began to talk about himself—a thing he did easily with other people but not with his father. He talked about his teaching—what he tried to put into it, and what he got from it. And about a very talented pupil, who showed signs of becoming a writer. And then about the book that he himself had been occupied with for the past five years—a study of changing social life in nineteenth-century England as reflected in the diaries of the Reverend John Skinner.

His older brother, it appeared, considered that Edward was a failure—not only financially but as a teacher. If he were a successful teacher he would be called to Harvard or Princeton or Yale.

"I don't know that I'd be happy teaching at Harvard or Princeton or Yale," Edward said. "And I am happy where I am. And valued."

"He doesn't understand," Mr. Ferrers said. "He lives very extravagantly—too much so, I think. They're flying very high these days. But he judges people by how much money they make. I explained to him when he was here that you care about money, too, but that you also care about other things, and that you are content to have a little less money and do the kind of work that interests you. . . . But, of course, you two boys have always been very different. And I don't interfere in your lives. I've given each of you a good education, the best I could manage, and from that time on you have been on your own. And you all made good. I'm proud of each of you. I have three fine boys."

Edward, floating, suspended, not quite anywhere, felt the safety in his father's voice, and a freedom in talking to him that he had never had before, not merely with his father but perhaps not even with anybody. In an unsafe world, he was safe only with one person. Which was so strange a thought—that his father, whom he had consistently opposed and resisted his whole life, and at one time even hated, should turn out to be the one person he felt utterly safe with—that he sat up and rearranged the pillows.

He would have gone on talking, half awake, drowsy but happy, for hours, and when Mr. Ferrers said, "Well, son, it's almost midnight, you'd better get some sleep," he got up from the sofa reluctantly. They went back through the sun parlor into the living room, and Edward blinked his eyes at the light, having been accustomed to darkness. He sat down at his stepmother's desk, took her pen, and wrote out a check for twenty dollars, and handed it to his father, who, smiling, tore the check up and dropped it in the wastebasket and went on talking about how much it meant to him to have Edward home.

The Thistles in Sweden

The brownstone is on Murray Hill, facing south. The year is 1950. We have the top floor-through, and our windows are not as tall as the windows on the lower floors. They are deeply recessed, and almost square, and have divided panes. I know that beauty is in the eye of the beholder and all that, but even so, these windows are romantic. The apartment could be in Leningrad or Innsbruck or Dresden (before the bombs fell on it) or Parma or any place we have never been to. When I come home at night, I look forward to the moment when I turn the corner and raise my eyes to those three lighted windows. Since I was a child, no place has been quite so much home to me. The front windows look out on Thirty-sixth Street, the back windows on an unpainted brick wall (the side of a house on Lexington Avenue) with no break in it on our floor, but on the floor below there is a single window with a potted plant, and when we raise our eyes we see the sky, so the room is neither dark nor prisonlike.

Since we are bothered by street noises, the sensible thing would be to use this room to sleep in, but it seems to want to be our living room, and offers two irresistible arguments: (1) a Victorian white marble fireplace and (2) a stairway. If we have a fireplace it should be in the living room, even though the chimney is blocked up, so we can't have a fire in it. (I spend a good deal of time unblocking it, in my mind.) The stairs are the only access to the roof for the whole building. There is, of course, nothing up there, but it looks as if we are in a house and you can go upstairs to bed, and this is very cozy: a house on the top floor of a brownstone walkup. I draw the bolt and push the trapdoor up with my shoulder, and Margaret and I stand together, holding the cat, Floribunda, in our arms so she will not escape, and see the stars (when there are any) or the winking lights of an airplane, or sometimes a hallucinatory effect brought about by fog or very fine rain and mist—the lighted windows of midtown skyscrapers set in space, without any surrounding masonry. The living room and the bedroom both have a door opening onto the outer hall, which, since we are on the top floor and nobody else in the building uses it, we regard as part of the apartment. We leave these doors open when we are at home, and the stair railing and the head of the stairs are blocked off with huge pieces of cardboard. The landlord says that this is a violation of the fire laws, but we cannot think of any other way to keep Floribunda from escaping down the stairs, and neither can he.

The living-room curtains are of heavy Swedish linen: life-sized thistles, printed in light blue and charcoal grey, on a white background. They are very beautiful (and so must the thistles in Sweden be) and they also have an emotional context; Margaret made them, and, when they did not hang properly, wept, and ripped them apart and remade them, and now they do hang properly. The bedroom curtains are of a soft ivory material, with seashells—cowries, scallops, sea urchins and sand dollars, turbinates, auriculae—drawn on them in brown indelible ink, with a flowpen. The bedroom floor is black, the walls are sandalwood, the woodwork is white. On the wall above the double bed is a mural in two sections—a hexagonal tower in an imaginary kingdom that resembles Persia. Children are flying kites from the roof. Inside the tower, another child is playing on a musical instrument that is cousin to the lute. The paperhanger hung the panels the wrong way, so the tower is even stranger architecturally than the artist intended. The parapet encloses outer instead of inner space—like a man talking to somebody who is standing behind him, facing the other way. And the fish-shaped kite, where is that being flown from? And by whom? Some other children are flying kites from the roof of the tower next to this one, perhaps, only there wasn't room to show it. (Lying in bed I often, in my mind, correct the paperhanger's mistake.) Next to the mural there is a projection made by a chimney that conducts sounds from the house next door. Or rather, a single sound: a baby crying in the night. The brownstone next door is not divided into apartments, and so much money has been spent on the outside (blue shutters, fresh paint, stucco, polished brass, etc.) that, for this neighborhood, the effect of chic is overdone. We assume there is a nurse, but nobody ever does anything when the baby cries, and the sound that comes through the wall is unbearably sad. (Unable to stand it any longer, Margaret gets up and goes through the brick chimney and picks the baby up and brings it back into our bedroom and rocks it.)

The double chest of drawers came from Macy's unfinished-furniture department, and Margaret gave it nine coats of enamel before she was satisfied with the way it looked. The black lacquered dining table (we have two dining tables and no dining room) is used as a desk. Over it hangs a large engraving of the Spanish Steps, which, two years ago, in the summer of 1948, for a brief time belonged to us—flower stands, big umbrellas, Bernini fountain, English Tea Room, Keats museum, children with no conception of bedtime, everything. At night we drape our clothes over two cheap rush-bottom chairs, from Italy. The mahogany dressing table, with an oval mirror in a lyre-shaped frame and turned legs such as one sees in English furniture of the late seventeenth century, came by express from the West Coast. The express company delivered it to the sidewalk in front of the building, and, notified by telephone that this was about to happen, I rushed home from the office to supervise the uncrating. As I stepped from the taxi, I saw the expressman with the mirror and half the lyre in his huge hands. He was looking at it thoughtfully. The rest of the dressing table was ten feet away, by the entrance to the building. The break does not show unless you look closely. And most old furniture has been mended at one time or another.

When we were shown the apartment for the first time, the outgoing tenant let us in and stood by pleasantly while we tried to imagine what the place would look like if it were not so crowded with his furniture. It was hardly possible to take a step for oak tables and chests and sofas and armoires and arm-chairs. Those ancestral portraits and Italian landscapes in heavy gilt frames that there was no room for on the walls were lean-ing against the furniture. To get from one room to the next we had to step over pyramids of books and scientific journals. An inventory of the miscellaneous objects and musical instru-ments in the living room would have taken days and been full of surprises. (Why did he keep that large soup tureen on the floor?) We thought at first he was packing, but he was not; this was the way he lived. If we had asked him to make a place in his life for us too, he would have. He was a very nice man. The disorder was dignified and somehow enviable, and the overfurnished apartment so remote from what went on down below in the street that it was like a cave deep in the forest.

Now it is underfurnished (we have just barely enough money to manage a small one-story house in the country and this apartment in town), instead, and all light and air. The living-room walls are a pale blue that changes according to the light and the time of day and the season of the year and the color of the sky. The walls are hardly there. The furniture is half old and half new, and there isn't much of it, considering the size of the room: a box couch, a cabinet with sliding doors, a small painted bookcase, an easy chair with its ottoman, a round fruitwood side table with long, thin, spidery legs and a glass tray that fits over the top, the table and chairs we eat on, a lowboy that serves as a sideboard, another chair, a wobbly tea cart, and a canvas stool. The couch has a high wooden back, L-shaped, painted black, with a thin gold line. It was made for an old house in Dover, New Hampshire, and after I don't know how many generations found itself in Minneapolis. I first saw it in Margaret's mother's bedroom in Seattle, and now it is here. It took two big men and a lot of patient maneuvering to get it four times past the turning of the stairs. The shawl that is draped over the back and the large tin tray that serves as a coffee table both came from Mexico—a country I do not regard as romantic, even though we have never been there. The lowboy made the trip from the West Coast with the dressing table, and one of its Chippendale legs got broken in transit, or by that same impetuous expressman. I suppose it is a hundred and fifty or two hundred years old. The man in the furniture-repair shop, after considering the broken leg, asked if we wanted the lowboy refinished. I asked why, and he said, "Because it's been painted." We looked, and sure enough it had. "They did that sometimes," he said. "It's painted to simulate mahogany." I asked what was under the paint, and he picked up a chisel and took a delicate gouge out of the underside. This time it was his turn to be surprised. "It's mahogany," he announced. The lowboy was painted to simulate what it actually was, it looks like what it is, so we let it be.

The gateleg table we eat on has four legs instead of the usual six. When the sides are extended, it looks as if the cabinetmaker had been studying Euclid's geometry. Margaret found it in an antique shop in Putnam Valley, and asked me to come look at it. I got out of the car and went in and saw the table and knew I could not live without it. The antique dealer said the table had an interesting history that she wasn't free to tell us. (Was it a real Hepplewhite and not just in the style of? Was it stolen?) She was a very old woman and lived alone. The shop was lined with bookshelves, and the books on the shelves and lying around on the tables were so uncommon I had trouble keeping my hands off them. They were not for sale, the old woman said. They had belonged to her husband,

and she was keeping them for her grandchildren; she herself read nothing but murder mysteries.

Margaret wanted the table, but she wanted also to talk about whether or not we could afford it. I can always afford what I dearly want—or rather, when I want something very much I would rather not think about whether or not we can afford it. As we drove away without the table, I said coldly, "We won't talk about it." As if she were the kind of wife she isn't. And we did talk about it, all the way home. The next day we were back, nobody had bought the table in the meantime, I wrote out a check for two hundred dollars, and the old woman gave us a big rag rug to wrap around the marvel so it wouldn't be damaged on the drive home. Also heavy twine to tie it with. But then I asked for a knife, and this upset her, to my astonishment. I looked carefully and saw that the expression in her faded blue eyes was terror: She thought I wanted a knife so I could murder her and make off with the table *and* the check. It is disquieting to have one's intentions so misjudged. (Am I a murderer? And is it usual for the murderer to ask for his weapon?) "A pair of scissors will do just as well," I said, and the color came back into her face.

The rug the table now stands on is only slightly larger than the tabletop. It is threadbare, but we cannot find another like it. For some reason, it is the last yellowish-beige rug ever made. People with no children have perfectionism to fall back on.

The space between the fireplace and the door to the kitchen is filled by shelves and a shallow cupboard. The tea cart is kept under the stairs. Then comes the door to the coat closet, the inside of which is painted a particularly beautiful shade of Chinese red, and the door to the hall. On the sliding-door cabinet (we have turned the corner now and are moving toward the windows) there is a pottery lamp with a wide perforated grey paper shade and such a long thin neck that it seems to be trying to turn into a crane. Also a record-player that plays only 78s and has to be wound after every record.

The oil painting over the couch is of a rock quarry in Maine, and we have discovered that it changes according to the time of day and the color of the sky. It is particularly alive after a snowfall.

Here we live, in our modest perfectionism, with two black cats. The one on the mantelpiece is Bastet, the Egyptian goddess of love and joy. The other is under the impression that she is our child. This is our fault, of course, not hers. Around her neck she wears a scarlet ribbon, or sometimes a turquoise ribbon, or a collar with little bells. Her toys dangle from the tea cart, her kitty litter is in a pan beside the bathtub, and she sleeps on the foot of our bed or curled against the back of Margaret's knees. When she is bored she asks us to remove a piece of the cardboard barricade so she can go tippeting down the stairs and pay a call on the landlord and his wife, Mr. and Mrs. Holmes, who live in the garden apartment and have the rear half of the second floor, with an inside stairs, so they really do go upstairs to bed. The front part of the second floor is the pied-à-terre of the artist who designed the wallpaper mural of the children flying kites from a hexagonal tower in an imaginary kingdom that resembles Persia. It is through the artist's influence (Mr. Holmes is intimidated by her) that we managed to get our rent-controlled apartment, for which we pay a hundred and thirteen dollars and some odd cents. The landlord wishes we paid more, and Mr. and Mrs. Venable, who live under us, wish we'd get a larger rug for the living room. Their bedroom is on the back, and Margaret's heels crossing the ceiling at night keep them awake. Also, in the early morning the Egyptian goddess leaves our bed and chases wooden spools and glass marbles from one end of the living room to the other. The Venables have mentioned this subject of the larger rug to the landlord and he has mentioned it to us. We do nothing about it, except that Margaret puts the spools and marbles out of Floribunda's reach when we go to bed at night, and walks around in her stocking feet after ten o'clock. Some day, when we are kept awake by footsteps crossing our bedroom ceiling, hammering, furniture being moved, and other idiot noises, we will remember the Venables and wish we had been more considerate.

The Venables leave their door open too, and on our way up the stairs I look back over my shoulder and see chintz-covered chairs and Oriental rugs and the lamplight falling discreetly on an Early American this and an Old English that. (No children here, either; Mrs. Venable works in a decorator's shop.) Mrs. Pickering, third floor, keeps her door closed. She is a sweet-faced woman who smiles when we meet her on the stairs. She has a grown son and daughter who come to see her regularly, but her life isn't the same as when they were growing up and Mr. Pickering was alive. (Did she tell us this or have I invented it?) If we met her anywhere but on the stairs we would have racked our brains to find something to say to her. The Holmeses' furniture is nondescript but comfortable. Mrs. Holmes has lovely brown eyes and the voice that goes with them, and it is no wonder that Floribunda likes to sit on her lap. *He* wants everybody to be happy, which is not exactly the way to be happy yourself, and he isn't. If we all paid a little more rent, it would make him happier, but we don't feel like it, any of us.

I am happy because we are in town: I don't have to commute in bad weather. I can walk to the office. And after the theatre we jump in a cab and are home in five minutes. I stand at the front window listening to the weather report. It is snowing in Westchester, and the driving conditions are very bad. In Thirty-sixth Street it is raining. The middle-aged man who lives on the top floor of the brownstone directly across from us is in the habit of posing at the window with a curtain partly wrapped around his naked body. He keeps guppies or goldfish in a lighted tank, spends the whole day in a kimono ironing, and at odd moments goes to the front window and acts out somebody's sexual dream. If I could only marry him off to the old woman who goes through the trash baskets on Lexington Avenue, talking to herself. What pleasure she would have in showing him the things she has brought home in her string bag —treasures whose value nobody else realizes. And what satisfaction to him it would be to wrap himself in a curtain just for her.

The view to the south is cut off by a big apartment building on Thirty-fifth Street. The only one. If it were not there (I spend a good deal of time demolishing it, with my bare hands) we would have the whole of the sky to look at. Because I have not looked carefully enough at the expression in Margaret's eyes, I go on thinking that she is happy too. When I met her she was working in a publishing house. Shortly after we decided to get married she was offered a job with the *Partisan Review*. If she had taken it, it would have meant commuting with me or even commuting at different hours from when I did. When I was a little boy and came home from school and called out, "Is anybody home?" somebody nearly always was. I took it for granted that the same thing would be true when I married. We didn't talk about it, and should have. I didn't understand that in her mind it was the chance of a fulfilling experience. Because she saw that I could not even imagine her saying yes, she said no, and turned her attention to learning how to cook and keep house. If we had had children right away it would have been different; but then if we had had children we wouldn't have been living on the top floor of a brownstone on Thirty-sixth Street.

The days in town are long and empty for her. The telephone doesn't ring anything like as often as it does when we are in the country. There Hester Gale comes across the road to see how Margaret is, or because she is out of cake flour, and they have coffee together. Margaret sews with Olivia Bingham. There are conversations in the supermarket. And miles of woods to walk in. Old Mrs. Delano, whose front door on Thirty-sixth Street is ten feet west of ours, is no help whatever. Though she knows Margaret's Aunt Caroline, she doesn't know that Margaret is her niece, or even that she exists, probably, and Margaret has no intention of telling her. Any more than she has any intention of telling me that in this place where I am so happy she feels like a prisoner much of the time.

She is accustomed to space, to a part of the country where there is more room than people and buildings to occupy it. In her childhood she woke up in the morning in a big house set on a wide lawn, with towering pine trees behind it, and a copper beech as big as two brownstones, and a snow-capped mountain that mysteriously comes and goes, like an idea in the mind. Every afternoon after school she went cantering through the trees on horseback. Now she is confined to two rooms—the kitchen cannot be called a room; it is hardly bigger than a handkerchief—and these two rooms are not enough. This is a secret she manages to keep from me so I can go on being happy.

There is another secret that cannot be kept from me because, with her head in a frame made by my head, arms, and shoulder, I know when she weeps. She weeps because her period was five days late and she thought something had happened that she now knows is not going to happen. The child is there, and could just as well as not decide to come to us, and doesn't, month after month. Instead, we consult one gynecologist after another, and take embarrassing tests (only they don't really embarrass me, they just seem unreal). And what the doctors do not tell us is why, when there is nothing wrong with either of us, nothing happens. Before we can have a child we must solve a riddle, like Oedipus and the Sphinx. On my forty-second birthday I go to the Spence-Chapin adoption service and explain our situation to a woman who listens attentively. I like her and feel that she understands how terribly much we want a child, and she shocks me by reaching across the desk and taking the application blank out of my hands: Forty-two is the age past which the agency will not consider giving out a child for adoption.

Meanwhile, Margaret herself has been adopted, by the Italian market under the El at Third Avenue and Thirty-fourth Street. Four or five whistling boys with white aprons wrapped around their skinny hips run it. They also appear to own it, but what could be more unlikely? Their faces light up when Margaret walks into the store. They drop what they are doing and come to greet her as if she were their older sister. And whatever she asks for, it turns out they have. Their meat is never tough, their vegetables are not tarnished and limp, their sole is just as good as the fish market's and nothing like as expensive. Now one boy, now another arrives at our door with a carton of groceries balanced on his head, having taken the stairs two steps at a time. Four flights are nothing to them. They are in business for the pure pleasure of it. They don't think or talk about love, they just do it. Or perhaps it isn't love but joy. But over what? Over the fact that they are alive and so are we?

It occurs to the landlord that the tenants could carry their garbage down to the street and then he wouldn't have to. I prepare for a scene, compose angry speeches in the bath. Everybody knows what landlords are like—only he isn't like that. He isn't even a landlord, strictly speaking. He has a good job with an actuarial firm. The building is a hobby. It was very run down when he bought it, and he has had the pleasure of fixing it up. We meet on the front sidewalk as I am on my way to work. Looking up at him—he is a very tall man—I announce that I will not carry our garbage down. Looking down at me, he says that if we don't feel like carrying our garbage down he will go on doing it. What an unsatisfactory man to quarrel with.

I come home from the office and find that Margaret has spent
the afternoon drawing: a pewter coffeepot (Nantucket), a
Venetian-glass goblet, a white china serving dish with a handle
and a cover, two eggs, a lemon, apples, a rumpled napkin with
a blue border. Or the view from the living room all the way
into the bedroom, through three doorways, involving the kind
of foreshortened perspective Italian Renaissance artists were so
fond of. Or the view from the bedroom windows (the apartment house on Thirty-fifth Street that I have so often taken
down I now see is all right; it belongs there) in sepia wash.
Or her own head and shoulders reflected in the dressing-table
mirror. Or the goblet, the coffeepot, the lemon, a green pepper,
and a brown lustre bowl. The lustre bowl has a chip in it, and
so the old woman in the antique shop in Putnam Valley gave
it to us for a dollar, after the table was safely stowed away in
the back seat of the car. And some years later, her daughter,
sitting next to me at a formal dinner party, said, "You're mistaken. Mother was absolutely fearless." She said it again, per-
ceiving that I did not believe her. Somebody is mistaken, and
it could just as well as not be me. Even though I looked quite
carefully at the old woman's expression. In any case, there
is something I didn't see. Her husband—the man whose books
the old woman was unwilling to sell—committed suicide. "I
was their only child, and had to deal with sadness all my life
—sadness from within as well as from without." If the expression in the old woman's eyes was not terror, what was it?

Floribunda misses the country, and sits at the top of the
living-room stairs, clawing at the trapdoor. She refuses
to eat, is shedding. Her hairs are on everything. One night
we take her across Park Avenue to the Morgan Library and
push the big iron gate open like conspirators about to steal
the forty-two-line Gutenberg Bible or the three folios of

Redouté's roses. Floribunda leaps from Margaret's arms and runs across the sickly grass and climbs a small tree. Ecstatically she sharpens her claws on the bark. I know that we will be arrested, but it is worth it.

Neither the landlord and his wife, nor the artist and her husband, who is Dutch, nor Mrs. Pickering, nor the Venables ever entertain in their apartments, but we have a season of being sociable. We have the Fitzgeralds and Eileen Fitzgerald's father from Dublin for dinner. We celebrate Bastille Day with the Potters. We have Elinor Hinkley's mother to tea. She arrives at the head of the stairs, where she can see into the living room, and exclaims—before she has even caught her breath—"What beautiful horizontal surfaces!" She is incapable of small talk. Instead, she describes the spiritual emanations of a row of huge granite boulders lining the driveway of her house on Martha's Vineyard. And other phenomena that cannot be described very easily, or that, when described, cannot be appreciated by someone who isn't half mad or a Theosophist.

Dean Wilson brings one intelligent, pretty girl after another to meet us. Like the woman in Isak Dinesen's story who sailed the seas looking for the perfect blue, he is looking for a flawless girl. Flawless in whose eyes is the question. And isn't flawlessness itself a serious flaw? "What a charming girl," we say afterward, and he looks in our faces and is not satisfied, and brings still another girl, including, finally, Ivy Sérurier, who is half English and half French. When she was seven years old her nurse took her every day to the Jardin du Luxembourg and there she ran after a hoop. She is attracted to all forms of occult knowledge, and things happen to her that do not happen to anyone who does not have a destiny. The light bulbs respond to her amazing stories by giving off a higher voltage. The expression on our faces is satisfactory. Dean brings her again, and again. He asks Margaret if she thinks they should get married, but he cannot quite bring himself to ask Ivy this question.

On a night when we are expecting Henry Coddington to dinner, Hester and Nick Gale come up the stairs blithely at seven o'clock, having got the invitation wrong. Or perhaps it is our fault. There is plenty of food, and it turns out to be a pleasant evening. The guests get on well, but Henry must have thought we did not want to know why Louise left him and took their little girl, whom he idolizes—that we have insulated ourselves from his catastrophe by asking this couple from the country. Anyway, he never comes or calls again. But other people come. Melissa Lovejoy, from Montgomery, Alabama, comes for Sunday lunch, and her hilarious account of her skirmishes with her mother-in-law make the tears run down my cheeks. Melissa, who loves beautiful china, looks around the living room and sees what no one else has ever seen or commented on—a Meissen plate on the other end of the mantel-piece from the Egyptian cat. It is white, with very small green grape leaves and a wide filigree border. Margaret's brother John had it in his rucksack when he made his way from Geneva to Bordeaux in May, 1940. As easily as the plate could have got broken, so he could have ended up in a detention camp and then what? But they are both safe, intact, here in New York. He has his own place, on Lexington Avenue in the Fifties. On Christmas Eve he bends down and selects a present for Margaret and another for me from the pile under the tree at the foot of the stair.

On New Year's Eve, John and Dean and Ivy and Margaret and I sit down to dinner. The champagne cork hits the ceil-ing. Between courses we take turns getting up and going into the bedroom and waiting behind a closed door until a voice calls "Ready!" If you were a school of Italian painting or a color of the spectrum or a character from fiction, what school of Italian painting or color or character would you be? John is Dostoevski's Idiot, Margaret is lavender blue. Elinor Hinkley joins us for dessert. Just before midnight a couple from the U.N., whom Dean has invited, come up the stairs and an hour later on the dot they leave for another party. It is daylight when we push our chairs back. We have not left the table (except to go into the front room while the questions are being framed) all night long. With our heads out of the window, Margaret and I wait for them to emerge from the building and then we call down to them, "Happy New Year!" But softly, so as not to wake up the neighbors.

Margaret's Uncle James, who is not her uncle but her mother's first cousin, comes to dinner, bringing long-stemmed red roses. He confesses that he has been waiting for this invitation ever since we were married—eight or nine years—and he thoroughly enjoys himself, though he is dying of cancer of the throat. Faced with extinction, you can't just stand and scream; it isn't good manners. And men and women of that generation do not discuss their feelings. Anyway he doesn't. Instead he says, "I like your curtains, Margaret," and we are filled with remorse that we didn't ask him sooner. But still, he did come to dinner. And satisfied his curiosity about the way we live. And we were surprised to discover that we were fond of him—as the rabbit is surprised to discover that he is what was concealed in the magician's hat. *I am not the person you thought I was*, Uncle James as much as says, sitting back in the easy chair but not using the ottoman lest he look ill.

I realize that the air is full of cigarette smoke, and prop the trapdoor open with a couple of books—but only a crack. At eleven-thirty Uncle James rises and puts his coat on and says good night, and tromps down the stairs, waking the Venables, and Mrs. Pickering, and the artist and her husband, and Mr. and Mrs. Holmes. And we lock the doors and say what a nice evening it was, and empty the ashtrays, and carry the liquor glasses out to the kitchen, and suddenly perceive an emptiness, an absence. "Floribunda? . . . Pussy?" She is nowhere. She has slipped through the crack that I thought was too small for her to get through. Fur is deceptive, her bone structure is not what I thought it was, and perhaps cats have something in common with cigarette smoke. I have often seen her attenuate herself alarmingly. Outside, on the roof, I call softly, but no little black cat comes. In the night we both wake and talk about her. The bottom of the bed feels strange when we put our feet out and there is nothing there, no weight. When morning comes I dress and go up to the roof again, and make my way toward Park Avenue, stepping over two-foot-high tile walls and making my way around projections and feeling giddy when I peer down into back gardens.

Margaret, meanwhile, has dressed and gone down the stairs. She rings the Delanos' bell, and the Irish maid opens the door. "A little cat came in through my bedroom window last night and the mistress said to put her on the street, so I did." *On the street* . . . when she could so easily have put her back on the roof she came from! "Here, Puss, Puss, Puss . . . here, Puss!" Up Thirty-sixth Street and down Thirty-fifth. All her life she has known nothing but love, and she is so timid. How will she survive with no home? What will the poor creature do? We meet Rose Bernstein, who has just moved into town from our country road, and just as I am saying "On the street. Did you ever hear of anything so heartless?" there is a faint miaow. Floribunda heard us calling and was too frightened to answer. I find her hiding in an areaway. Margaret gathers her up in her arms and we say goodbye to Rose Bernstein, and, unable to believe our good fortune, take her home. Our love and joy.

In Chicago there is an adoption agency whose policy with respect to age is not so rigid as Spence-Chapin's. We pull strings. (Dean Wilson has a friend whose wife's mother is on the board.) Letters pass back and forth, and finally there we

are, in Chicago, nervously waiting in the reception room. Miss
Mattie Gessner is susceptible (or so I feel) to the masculine
approach. It turns out that she voted for Truman too; and she
doesn't reach across the desk and take the application from my
hands. Instead she promises to help us. But it isn't as simple as
the old song my mother used to sing: Today is not the day they
give babies away with a half a pound of tay. The baby that is
given to us for adoption must be the child of a couple reasonably like us—that is to say, a man and woman who, in the year
1952, would have a record-player that plays only 78s and that
you wind by hand; who draw seashells on their bedroom curtains and are made happy by a blocked-up fireplace and a
stairway that leads nowhere. And this means we must wait
God knows how long.

So we do wait, sometimes in rather odd places for a couple
with no children. For example, by the carousel in Central Park.
The plunging horses slowly come to a halt with their hoofs in
midair. The children get off and more children climb up, take
a firm grip on the pole, and look around for their mother or
their nurse or their father, in the crowd standing in the open
doorway. Slowly the cavalcade begins to move again, and I
take the little boy in the plaid snowsuit, with half a pound of
English Breakfast, and Margaret takes half a pound of Lipton's
and the little girl with blue ribbons in her hair.

We start going to the country weekends. And then we go
for the summer, taking suitcases full of clothes, boxes
of unread books, drawing materials, the sewing machine, the
typewriter. And in September all this is carried up four flights
of stairs. And more: flowers, vegetables from the garden, plants
we could not bear to have the frost put an end to, even though
we know they will not live long in town. And one by one we
take up our winter habits. When Saturday night comes around
we put on our coats at ten o'clock and go out to buy the

Sunday *Times* at the newspaper stand under the El. We rattle the door of the antique shop on Third Avenue that always has something interesting in the window but has never been known to be open at any hour of any day of the week. On three successive nights we go to "Ring Round the Moon," "King Lear," and "An Enemy of the People," after which it seems strange to sit home reading a book. I am so in love with Adlai Stevenson's speeches that, though I am afraid of driving in ordinary traffic in New York City, I get the car out of the garage and we drive right down the center of 125th Street, in a torchlight parade, hemmed in by a flowing river of people, all of whom feel the way we do.

How many years did we live in that apartment on Thirty-sixth Street? From 1950 to— The mere dates are misleading, even if I could get them right, because time was not progressive or in sequence, it was one of Mrs. Hinkley's horizontal surfaces divided into squares. On one square an old woman waters a houseplant in the window of an otherwise blank wall. An another, Albertha, who is black, comes to clean. When she leaves, the apartment looks as if an angel had walked through it. She is the oldest of eleven children. And what she and Margaret say, over a cup of coffee, makes Margaret more able to deal with her solitary life. On another square, we go to the Huguenot Church on Sunday morning, expecting something new and strange, and instead the hymns are perfectly familiar to us from our Presbyterian childhoods: in French they have become more elegant and rhetorical, and it occurs to me that they may not reach all the way to the ear of Heaven. But the old man who then mounts the stairs to the pulpit addresses Seigneur Dieu in a confident voice, as if they are extremely well acquainted, the two of them. On another square we go to Berlitz, and the instructor, a White Russian named Mikhael Miloradovitch, sits by blandly while Margaret and I say things to each other in French that we have managed not to say in English. I am upset when I discover that she prefers the country to the city. The discussion becomes heated, but because it is in French nothing comes of it. We go on living in the city. Until another summer comes and we fill the car, which is now nearly twenty years old, to the canvas top with our possessions; then, locking the doors of the apartment, we drive off to our other life. At which point the shine goes out of this one. The slip-covers fade and so do the seashells and thistles that are exposed to the direct light of the summer sun. Dust gathers on the books, the lampshades, the record-player. In the middle of the night, a hand pries at the trapdoor and, finding it securely locked, tries somewhere else. The man out of Krafft-Ebing shows himself seductively to our blank windows. And the intense heat builds up to a violent thunderstorm. After which there is a spell of cooler weather. And a tragedy. For two days there has been no garbage outside Mrs. Pickering's door in the morning. She does not answer her telephone or the landlord's knocking, and she has not said she was going away. The first floor extends farther back than the rest of the house, and he is able to place a ladder on the roof of this extension. From the top of the ladder he stares into the third-floor bedroom at a terrible sight: Mrs. Pickering, sitting in a wing chair, naked. He thinks it is death he is staring at, but he is mistaken; she has had a stroke. He breaks the door down, and she is taken to the hospital in an ambulance. She does not die, but neither does she ever come back to this apartment. Passing her door on our way up the stairs, we are aware of the silence inside, and think uneasily of those two days and nights of helpless waiting. Along with the silence there is the sense of something malign, of trouble of a very serious kind that could spread all through the house. To ward it off, we draw closer to the other tenants, linger talking on the stairs, and speak to them in a more intimate tone of voice. We have the Holmeses and the Venables and the artist and her husband up for a drink. It doesn't do the trick.

There *was* something behind Mrs. Pickering's door. My sister's only son turns up and, since we are in the country, we offer him the apartment to live in until he finds a job. He leads a life there that the books and furniture do not approve of. He brings girls home and makes love to them in our bed, under the very eyes of the children flying kites. He borrows fifty bucks from me, to eat on, and to get some shirts, so he won't look like a bum when he goes job hunting. He has a check coming from his previous job, in Florida, and will pay me back next week. The check doesn't come, and he borrows some more money, and then some more, and it begins to mount up. Jobs that were as good as promised to him vanish into thin air, and meanwhile we are his sole means of support. I listen attentively to what I more and more suspect are inventions, but his footwork is fast, and what he says could be true; it just isn't what he said before, quite. My bones inform me that I am not the first person these excuses and appeals have been tried out on. He comes to my office to tell me that he has given up the idea of staying in New York and can I let him have the fare home, and I dial my sister's number in Evansville, Indiana, and hand the receiver to him and leave the room.

I give up smoking on one square, and on another I go through all the variant pages of a book I have been writing for four and a half years and reduce it to a single pile of manuscript. This I put in a blue canvas duffelbag that can absent-mindedly be left behind on the curbing when we drive off to the country at eleven o'clock of a spring night. At midnight, driving up the Taconic Parkway, I suddenly see in my mind's eye the back seat of the car: the blue duffelbag is not there. Nor, when we come to a stop in front of our house on Thirty-sixth Street at one o'clock in the morning, is it on the sidewalk where I left it. With a dry mouth I describe it to the desk sergeant in the police station, and he gets up and goes into the back room. "No, nothing," he calls. And then, as we are almost at the door, "Wait a minute."

On another square Margaret starts behaving in a way that is not at all like her. Sleepy at ten o'clock in the evening, and when I open my eyes in the morning she is already awake and looking at me. Her face is somehow different. Can it be that she is . . . that we are going to . . . that . . . I study her when she is not aware that I am looking at her, and find in her behavior the answer to that riddle: if we are so longing for a child that we are willing to bring up somebody else's child— anybody's child whatever—then we may as well be allowed to have our own. Margaret comes home from the doctor bringing the news to me that I have not dared break to her.

After boning up on the subject, in a book, she shows me, on her finger, just how long the child in her womb now is. And it is growing larger, very slowly. And so is she. The child is safe inside her, and she is safe so long as she remains a prisoner in this top-floor apartment. The doctor has forbidden her to use the stairs. Everybody comes to see her, instead—including an emanation from the silent apartment two floors below. A black man, a stranger, suddenly appears at the top of the stairs. His intention, unclear but frightening, shows in his face, in his eyes. But the goddess Bastet is at work again, and the man comes on Albertha's day, and she, with a stream of such foulmouthed cursing as Margaret has never heard in her life, sends him running down the stairs. If he had come on a day that was not Albertha's day, when Margaret was there alone— But this holds true for everything, good or bad.

Margaret's face grows rounder, and she no longer has a secret that must be kept from me. The days while I am at the office are not lonely, and time is an unbroken landscape of daydreaming. When I get home at six o'clock, I creep in under the roof of the spell she is under, and am allowed into the daydream. But what shall we tell Miss Mattie Gessner when she comes to investigate the way we live?

The apartment, feeling our inattention, begins to withdraw from us sadly. And then something else unexpected happens. The landlord, having achieved perfection, having created the Peaceable Kingdom on Thirty-sixth Street, is restless and wants to begin all over again. "You'll be sorry," his wife tells him, stroking Floribunda's ear, and he is. But by that time they are living uptown, in a much less handsome house in the Nineties—a house that needs fixing from top to bottom. But it will never have any style, and it is filled with disagreeable tenants who do not pay their rent on time. On Thirty-sixth Street we have a new landlord, and in no time his hand is on everything. He hangs a cheap print of van Gogh's "The Drawbridge" in the downstairs foyer. We are obliged to take down the cardboard barricade and keep our doors closed. Hardly a day passes without some maddening new improvement. The artist is the first to go. Then we give notice; how is Margaret to carry the baby, the stroller, the package from the drugstore, etc., up four flights of stairs? *What better place can there be to bring up a child in?* the marble fireplace asks, remembering the eighteen-eighties, when this was a one-family house and our top-floor living room was the nursery. The stairway to the roof was devoted to the previous tenant (the man who lived in the midst of a monumental clutter) and says bitterly, in the night, when we are not awake to hear, *They seem as much a part of your life as the doors and windows, and then it turns out that they are not a part of your life at all. The moving men come and cart all the furniture away, and the people go down to the street, and that's the last you see of them. . . .*

What will the fireplace and the stairway to the roof say when they discover that they are about to be shut off forever from the front room? The landlord is planning to divide our apartment into two apartments and charge the same for each that he is now getting for the floor-through. For every evil under the sun there is a remedy or there is none. I soak the mural of the children flying kites, hoping to remove it intact and put it up somewhere in the house in the country. The paper tears no matter how gently I pull it loose from the wall, and comes off in little pieces, which end up in the wastebasket.

Now when I walk past that house I look up at the windows that could be in Leningrad or Innsbruck or Dresden or Parma, and I think of the stairway that led only to the trapdoor in the roof, and of the marble fireplace, the bathroom skylight, and the tiny kitchen, and of what school of Italian painting we would have been if we had been a school of Italian painting, and poor Mrs. Pickering sitting in her bedroom chair with her eyes wide open, waiting for help, and the rainy nights on Thirty-sixth Street, and the grey-and-blue thistles, the brown seashells, the Mills Brothers singing *Shine, little glowworm, glimmer, glimmer*, and the guests who came the wrong night, the guest who was going to die and knew it, the sound of my typewriter, and of a paintbrush clinking in a glass of cloudy water, and Floribunda's adventure, and Margaret's empty days, and how it was settled that, although I wanted to put my head on her breast as I was falling asleep, she needed even more (at that point) to put her head on mine. And of our child's coming, at last, and the black cat who thought *she* was our child, and of the two friends who didn't after all get married, and the old woman who found one treasure after another in the trash baskets all up and down Lexington Avenue, and that other old woman, now dead, who was so driven by the need to describe the inner life of very large granite boulders. I think of how Miss Mattie Gessner's face fell and how she closed her notebook and became a stranger to us, who had been so deeply our friend. I think of the oversexed ironer, and the Holmeses, and the Venables, and the stranger who meant nobody good and was frightened away by Albertha's cursing, and the hissing of the air brakes of the Lexington Avenue bus, and the curtains moving at the open window, and the baby crying on the other side of the wall. I think of that happy grocery store run by boys, and the horse-drawn flower cart that sometimes waited on the corner, and the sound of footsteps in the night, and the sudden no-sound that meant it was snowing, and I think of the unknown man or woman who found the blue duffelbag with the manuscript of my novel in it and took it to the police station, and the musical instrument (not a lute, but that's what the artist must have had in mind, only she no longer bothers to look at objects and draws what she remembers them as being like) played in the dark, over our sleeping bodies, while the children flew their kites, and I think if it is true that we are all in the hand of God, what a capacious hand it must be.

William Maxwell was born in 1908, in Lincoln, Illinois. When he was fifteen his family moved to Chicago and he continued his education there and at the University of Illinois. After a year of graduate work at Harvard he went back to Urbana and taught freshman composition, and then turned to writing. He has published five novels, a collection of tales and another of short stories (with Jean Stafford, John Cheever, and Daniel Fuchs), an autobiographical memoir, and a book for children. For forty years he was an editor, first in the art and then in the fiction department, of *The New Yorker*. From 1969 to 1972 he was president of the National Institute of Arts and Letters. His novel, *So Long, See You Tomorrow*, won him the William Dean Howells Medal of the American Academy of Arts and Letters and an American Book Award. He lives with his wife in New York City.

His stories have been reprinted in the annual *O. Henry* and *Best American Short Stories* collections and in Martha Foley's *200 Years of Great American Short Stories*.

A NOTE ON THE TYPE

The text of this book was set on the Linotype in Janson,
a recutting made directly from type cast from matrices long
thought to have been made by the Dutchman Anton
Janson, who was a practicing type founder in Leipzig
during the years 1668–87. However, it has been con-
clusively demonstrated that these types are actually the
work of Nicholas Kis (1650–1702), a Hungarian, who
most probably learned his trade from the master Dutch
type founder Dirk Voskens. The type is an excellent
example of the influential and sturdy Dutch types that prevailed in England up to the time William Caslon developed his own incomparable designs from them.

*Composed by Maryland Linotype Composition Company,
Baltimore, Maryland*

*Printed and bound by The Haddon Craftsmen, Inc.,
Scranton, Pennsylvania*